"Lincoln Crisler has taken pains to choose this myriad collection of stories exploring the theme of Metahumans acting out inhumanely and there are quite a few zingers to this collection. This is a collection very much in the vein of Masked by Lou Anders; however, with a tenebrious and twisted bent to it."
—Fantasy Book Critic

"Corrupts Absolutely? is a great anthology with a concept that never gets old. Each of the stories is incredibly unique, even the ones that deal with a similar power or theme. I had a great time with this and I didn't dislike a single story. That's hard to do. Highly Recommended!"
—Only the Best Sci-Fi and Fantasy

"Lincoln Crisler's compilation is commendable for showing a range of variations on its theme. The contributors address the motif from different aspects and genres. Aficionados of horror will find several tales to whet their genre appetite."
—Hellnotes

"…the large majority of the stories establish intriguing conditions, insert equally intriguing characters, add appropriately devastating consequences to either action or inaction, and let the chips—or bodies—fall where they may. Recommended."
—Michael Collings

"Really got me to thinking about who really is a 'Hero' and a 'Villain' and where is the line drawn."
—Melsworld

"…The perfect collection for horror fans with a taste for superhero prose or lovers of hero tales who enjoy a bit of corruption with a horror flavor."
—Dreadful Tales

— A RAGNAROK PUBLICATIONS ANTHOLOGY —

CORRUPTS ABSOLUTELY?

EDITED BY
LINCOLN CRISLER

CRESTVIEW HILLS, KENTUCKY

CORRUPTS ABSOLUTELY?
Ragnarok Publications | www.ragnarokpub.com
Editor In Chief: Tim Marquitz | Creative Director: J.M. Martin
Corrupts Absolutely is copyright © 2015 by Lincoln Crisler. All rights reserved.
All stories within are copyright © of their respective authors.

The characters and events portrayed in this book are fictitious or fictitious recreations of actual historical persons. Any similarity to real persons, living or dead, is coincidental and not intended by the authors unless otherwise specified. This book or any portion thereof may not be reproduced or used in any manner whatsoever without the express written permission of the publisher except for the use of brief quotations in a book review.

Published by Ragnarok Publications
206 College Park Drive, Ste. 1
Crestview Hills, KY 41017

ISBN-10: 1941987354
ISBN-13: 978-1-941987-35-3
ISBN (ePub): 978-1-941987-36-0
Worldwide Rights
Created in the United States of America

Editor: Lincoln Crisler
Additional Copy Edits: Amanda Shore
Publicity: Melanie R. Meadors
Cover Illustration: Malcolm McClinton
Cover Design & Interior Layout: Shawn T. King

CONTENTS

RETRIBUTION – Tim Marquitz
1

HOLLYWOOD VILLAINY – Weston Ochse
11

MENTAL MAN – William Todd Rose
31

THE REAL CHURCH – Jeremy Hepler
47

OZYMANDIAS REVISITED – A.S. Fox
67

ENLIGHTENED BY SIN – Jason M. Tucker
79

BEDTIME STORY – Peter Clines
99

THE ORIGIN OF SLASHY – Jeff Strand
113

CONVICTION – Edward M. Erdelac
127

THRESHOLD – Kris Ashton
143

OILY – A.D. Spencer
155

HERO – Joe McKinney
169

PRIDE – Wayne Ligon
177

G-CHILD – Malon Edwards
189

PAST IMPERFECT – Warren Stockholm
203

ILLUSION – Karina L. Fabian
227

SABRE – Anthony Laffan
239

CROOKED – Lee Mather
251

FIXED – Trisha J. Wooldridge
273

ACQUAINTED WITH THE NIGHT – Cat Rambo
299

GONE ROGUE – Wayne Helge
307

MAX AND ROSE – Andrew Bourelle
321

INTRODUCTION

SUPERHERO STORIES ARE THE MYTHOLOGY OF OUR MODERN culture. If anything, this statement is truer now than it was in 2011 when I put together the first edition of this anthology. From their humble beginnings as the staples of an entertainment medium geared toward a very specific demographic (namely, comic books), superheroes have become a phenomenon available to—and enjoyed by—an ever-growing segment of media consumers. If that sounds like unfounded hyperbole to you, spend a couple hours in a crowded public place looking for someone who's never heard of Wolverine or the Hulk. Before 2000, it wouldn't have been a difficult proposition.

Despite the prevalence of superheroes in comics and movies, however, and as much as I've loved comic books for over two decades, there's one area in which I'll always feel prose is the ideal format for superheroes specifically or at least has the most potential to be: artistic integrity and authenticity. Comic book fans have remarked upon for decades the regularity with which heroes and villains come back from the dead or with which status quos shift and reset. Since the initial publication of *Corrupts Absolutely?*, for instance, there's been an Hispanic version of a traditionally white hero, a villain's mind housed in the body of a hero, another (white) hero retiring and his mantle being assumed by one of his (black) associates and yet another's very *godhood* being assumed by a woman.

The only one of those that's had staying power to date is the first, and even that happened to the main character of a long-running *alternate universe* series. And there are good, viable reasons for this. A lot of money, time, and creativity is invested in giving life to a Spider-Man, a Batman, or a Joker or Magneto. If they die "for reals," the company who owns those characters can't use them anymore. In time, they'd fall from their honored places in the culture. When you're talking about characters created in and enjoyed since the '40s and '60s, clearing the slate and starting fresh is a difficult proposition.

In addition, companies and creators would run the risk of not being able to make lightning strike not twice but repeatedly, consistently creating new, compelling characters to be placed in authentic, real-world scenarios with authentic, real-world consequences. And as far as I'm concerned, that's why Magneto comes back when Wolverine kills him even though if I stab you with a handful of knives, you ain't

INTRODUCTION

comin' back. That's why Batman doesn't kill the Joker though the Joker's killed hundreds if not thousands of innocent Gothamites. A good prose author can create interesting characters and tell a gripping story every time. There's no corporate bottom-line, action-figure deal, or thirty years of back history to consider.

So, on a very personal level, as a creator and consumer, the opportunity to bring you this definitive version of what I feel is a masterwork collection of superhero prose couldn't have come at a better time. Every one of the stories on these pages is a labor of love for the superhero genre from award-winners and new authors alike. This new edition features not only brand-new cover art but the text of my 2012 online editor's retrospective, the author's preferred version of "Fixed," and two new stories from Peter Clines and Warren Stockholm—pieces that, by a sheer twist of fate, were solicited for the original edition of *Corrupts Absolutely?* but weren't available at the time.

From all of us to all of you, thanks for picking up *Corrupts Absolutely?*, and we hope you enjoy the hell out of it.

Lincoln Crisler
Augusta, Georgia
August 2014

RETRIBUTION
TIM MARQUITZ

SEPTEMBER 11, 2001, 8:46 A.M. THAT'S WHEN IT ALL WENT to hell.

The date and time are seared into my mind with a heat I can only pray my wife never felt. Candace had found her dream job. Just the week before, she'd started at Channel 5, WNYW. Their offices were on the 110th floor of the North Tower, and she'd worked overnight, preparing for her first time on camera. She was just a fill-in, but she wanted to be perfect. Candace always did.

She was scheduled off at 9:00.

She was also six months pregnant with our son: Joshua Michael Drake.

We'd only settled on his name a few days earlier. I never got to meet him. They never came home. Just fourteen minutes before Candace would have been in the elevator and down past the impact point, I lost them both.

I lost everything.

No, that's not entirely true. I didn't lose *everything*. After watching all I loved disappear in a roiling cloud of gray smoke as the building went down, there was still one thing left in my life. Once all the tears had dried and the empty words of comfort had soured on sorry tongues, there was still my fury.

I'd been a good husband until that moment, 8:46: the moment they took them away. I'd been a good man.

That man died with his family.

*** *** ***

September 11, 2006, 8:40 a.m. Revenge was but six minutes away.

While the world had watched my wife and child disintegrate live on television and had seen the eagle roused in righteous anger, our soldiers sacrificed in foreign lands, it would never know the truth of what had been set in motion that day. The jihadists had brought the struggle to our shores, but five years after, our nation had been dealt a grievous blow. The war had yet to truly begin. In five minutes, it would start in earnest. With me.

My job was to repay our enemies in kind.

It was my pleasure.

The road from then to now had been difficult in far more ways than I could ever have imagined when I signed up to fight. I wanted nothing more than to kill the bastards who'd stolen my family from me. All I asked of my country was a gun

and a one-way ticket to the desert. It gave me so much more.

The morning sun of northern Waziristan beat down upon my head, the heat already sweltering as I made my way along the dusty streets of Mir Ali, heading toward an open market. My skin darkened by chemical staining and my beard grown out thick, itching at my chin and dyed black like my hair, I looked as though I belonged.

I was dressed in the traditional *shalwar kameez*, colored in a simple brown and carrying nothing. The other people on the narrow lane paid me little attention. I affected a shallow limp to feign a sense of weakness and greeted those I passed with quiet courtesy, my teeth clenched to still my tongue. After five years of learning the language, I was proficient, but it always paid to be cautious. It wouldn't do for someone to note a flaw in my inflection, the anger in my voice. Not when I was so close.

In another three minutes, it wouldn't matter.

Central Intelligence reports had placed a number of ranking al-Qaeda fighters in the area, the people of Mir Ali complicit to their presence or, at the very least, complacent. No real difference between the two in my eyes. You harbor terrorists, you are a terrorist.

Inside the market, I moved amidst the jumbled stalls and carts, my eyes drifting as I weaved my way toward the thickest concentration of shoppers. I was disappointed there were so few women around, the local culture hiding them away from the eyes of men not their husbands. My dissatisfaction was tempered somewhat by the number of children that ran laughing through the crowded aisles. They were mostly boys,

but there were a few girls as well, all too young to be coveted yet even in their society. I counted nearly thirty who scampered about: twenty-seven young boys who would one day take up arms and fight against my nation and three girls who would breed more. The numbers were hardly equal, but it would be a good start.

Two minutes.

I sidled up close to the busiest of the stalls, patrons haggling in quick tongues over the price of *chapatis*, the long loaves of bread stacked a dozen high. Flies swarmed about, their humming buzz adding to the morning's furor. It was hardly the last meal I would have chosen, but then again, none of them knew just how close to death they were.

I ignored the old man barking at me to move away if I wasn't buying and let my heart settle. He'd be quiet soon enough.

My thoughts reached down, and I felt the first stirrings of heat in my veins, my blood warming in response to the pressure of my will. The man went on, threatening violence if I didn't step aside, only affirming my cause.

I raised my finger and smiled at him, mouthing, "One minute," in his own tongue. That only set him to frothing, his tantrum drawing an audience of onlookers to the stall. I should have thanked him, but I needed to concentrate.

Blocking the ranting shopkeeper out, I closed my eyes and sent the spark of my fury to light the fuse inside. My stomach roiled with stinging acid, and I could feel the sweat pushing its way from my pores, coating me instantly in a wet sheen. The man went silent as though he could hear the boiling rush that was building, the napalm sear that rippled beneath my flesh.

I opened my eyes to see him staring at me. His face was twisted in almost comical confusion, and I wondered what he thought—not that it really mattered. The people who had gathered to watch the shopkeeper's tirade had drawn back a few steps, their voices muted by the uncertainty of what was happening. They sensed something they couldn't understand, but still, they gathered thick, sheep too dim to see the culling ahead. It was too late to run.

I turned to face the crowd, my smile breaking through the blackness of my beard. "You have taken my family from me," I told them in English. Though most of them probably didn't understand a word I'd said, there was no doubt they understood my intent. Their eyes went wide at the recognition of an enemy among them, one of the great Satan, but that thought would be their last. "Now I take you from yours."

8:46.

With one more push, my blood boiled over. A flash of white stole my vision as the gift my government had given me took hold. Pain lanced through my body, growing sharper with every instant. The agony multiplied like shattered glass, each shard breaking into a million more and yet again and again and again. All but the simplest thoughts left my head, my essence too scattered for true coherence. Split into a billion pieces, my consciousness was a tiny blip in each, my body broken down into its basest molecules. Every atom imbued with the fury to match Oppenheimer's greatest achievement, I felt myself explode.

A blur of motion filled my remaining senses and I was overwhelmed by the feeling of being hurled in every direction at once, vertigo at its most exhilarating. Though it seemed, even to me, to be impossible, I noted each and every impact as my fiery essence tore through the assembled crowd, shattered the stalls, and decimated the wares, millions of me peppering the ground where I had just stood. Dust whipped about in my wake.

For the briefest of instants, I was one with everything in the market: the earth, the air, and flesh and bone. As my being tore through theirs, it was as though I could taste them, sorting the blood from wood and dirt without a thought. I could hear the people's screams inside me, though I had no ears, and could feel their lives ending as I punctured each with a million different fragments of me. The world was alive with ruin, a crimson cloud holding court amidst the carnage.

My momentum carried my discorporate particles out to a radius of about a thousand feet. My essence slowed at last as it burst through the surrounding obstacles of shops and homes and the remnants of my energies drained away. I could feel gravity's return, its gentle tug pulling the whole of me toward the ground. The sense of separation began to ease, clarity drawing closer like a ship approaching shore. Now came the hard part.

There weren't adequate words to describe the pain that came with reintegration, but as the pieces of me slammed together, becoming one again on a genetic level, no agony could steal my satisfaction away. As they had with us, I had brought the war to our enemy in a way they had never imagined.

Flesh and feeling returned with an acid bath rage, pieces of a puzzle set upon the surface of the sun. I could feel myself knitting back together and recognized every molecule as it wove itself into the whole. Sense congealed while muscles and tendons stretched and returned to their natural shapes, growing over thickening bone. The smell of char filled my developing nose, and tears spilled from newborn eyes. I was nearly me again.

Close to two blocks from the market, I was reborn, huddled naked on a mattress of wreckage brought about by my righteous fury. My skin sizzled, gray tendrils of smoke wafting about me as the energies inside slowly cooled. I drew myself up and heard my joints creak, the pain and stiffness of my transformation ebbing.

All around me, I could hear the cries of the wounded, those too far from the epicenter of the blast to have met their end with a merciful swiftness. There was no time to revel in my satisfaction.

Men shouted, and the morning air was filled with the crackle of flames and the sounds of panic. Black smoke swirled through the streets and alleys, obscuring the world from my eyes and me from the men that swarmed nearby. It was only a taste of the ruin they'd brought.

I swallowed my smile and rubbed dirt and ashes across my skin, nicking my flesh in a number of places with a sharpened piece of debris and then slathering blood across my body. For all my success, I had yet to escape. So far behind enemy lines as to be unreachable by my allies, it was up to me to find my way out.

Deep in the throes of adrenal fatigue, I had no need to fake the appearance of the walking wounded. Every step was an anchor drawn through sand as I emerged from the sheltering alley where I'd coalesced and stumbled out on the street. Mournful wails rose up as chaos began to break, the truth of what I'd wrought coming to light. I could only imagine what they saw. Flickering images of the moment twisted and tangled inside my throbbing head.

I staggered toward the desert, hoping to remain unseen, but I'd done my job too well. All of Mir Ali was in the streets, drawn by my release of power. A man shouted, his gnarled finger pointed at me, a dozen more taking up his cry. I looked about, seeking a clear path to run, but there was none. What wasn't blocked by a cluster of onlookers was made impassable by the fires set by my conflagration. My heart sank for an instant, but I remembered my guise. All of those who'd heard me speak were gone, red stains about the market floor.

Only one outward sign remained to betray my true origins. I crumpled to the ground and curled fetal, moaning incoherent. The men rushed to my side with heavy steps, but there was no anger in their voices; only concern.

"له ام سره مرسته," I told them as they closed. Help me.

Words of comfort filled my ears. They believed I was one of them.

Rough hands pulled me into the air, the largest of the men cradling me in his arms as though I were a child. His eyes narrowed as his nostrils flared as the stench of burned flesh drifted up to assail his nose. I let my hands fall to my groin as he blinked away tears, covering my genitals from

sight. None had noticed my circumcision.

I let the man carry me, burying my face in his chest to muffle my barked laughter, turning it into a cough. He jarred me about as he ran, shouting to clear the path ahead. His footsteps slapped as they struck the packed dirt roadway. A few moments later, he slowed, his breath loud in his lungs as he called out for assistance. More hands clutched at me, pulling me from his arms. I was a set upon a makeshift gurney, a woolen blanket laid overtop, only helping to hide the truth of who they had helped.

I could hear their chattered voices as they scrambled for direction, the gurney raised unsteadily beneath me. Daring a glance ahead, I saw the doors of a medical center looming before me, the Red Crescent emblem emblazoned above in chipped and peeling paint. Men in white met us at the threshold, taking the gurney from those in the street and transferring me to a rolling cart. As they wheeled me down the hall, flickering lights flashing above my eyes, they asked in clipped voices where I was hurt.

I gave them only one answer, "My heart," then I asked for the time. They looked at me strangely, but one of the interns glanced at his watch, thinking perhaps he was granting a dying man's wish by answering.

9:02.

I smiled in thanks, meeting his dark eyes as we burst through the inner doors of the hospital, the room busy with people. With a deep breath, I mustered my will once more and drew upon the fire.

9:03.

HOLLYWOOD VILLAINY

WESTON OCHSE

NO ONE PAYS ATTENTION TO THE BODY.

Instead, they watch the antics of the paraplegic pimp and his one-legged midget hooker. He holds her by a leash attached to a spiked dog collar around her neck as she hops around his wheelchair in a crazy, cavorting dance. This is what they came to see. Not the stars on the Walk of Fame. Not the handprints in the Chinese Theater. Not the gargantuan Hollywood sign that had once announced a suburb. But theater in the raw—the misfits and characters that make Hollywood the adult Disneyland promised them by every David Lynch and Tony Scott film.

The pimp has enough studs poking from his face that he could have been a cyborg. A young girl points at them and says as much to her father. The midget hooker has had a boob job that makes her look ridiculous even if she hadn't been a half-pint, one-legged fuck machine. The detraction is sad because the death of the man had been majestic to behold. And that his body lay square atop the Hollywood Star of Orson Welles was a grace note that I'd never thought to pull off. Still, people never look to the heart of things; instead, they grasp at any shiny object that happens by no matter how shallow or meaningless it may be.

*** *** ***

Who knows what evil lurks in the hearts of men? The Shadow knows. This is my mantra. This is what has fueled me through these years of too much, too young, forever. The notion of the shadow, of someone who can manipulate the minds of men to his own ends, is something that I enjoy. I say it. "Only the Shadow knows," and follow it up with dramatic, baritone laughter. But I am far from the figure of a tall, handsome, masked, and cloaked avenger. In fact, no matter how many years pass, I'll never be tall, I'll never be old, and I'll never be handsome. Instead of portraying the Shadow like a masked and cloaked avenger, I have no choice but to present myself as I am—fifteen, Chinese-American, short, odd-shaped face covered in acne and glasses the movies referred to as RPGs, or Rape Prevention Glasses, because they were so ugly. Still, even though I was born Valiant Fang in 1922, I *AM* the Shadow, and the Shadow always knows.

"Watch it, kid," an older man growls as he tries to get by.

My 1949 Schwinn Phantom is positioned in the middle of the sidewalk. I'd parked on John Wayne's star. It is as good

a view as any. It also gives me a jumping off point. After all, in an entire world filled with people, how am I to go about selecting my targets? I let the stars guide me. Not those up in the sky but the ones set in concrete as flat monuments to pop culture greatness.

And then I see him.

And he is perfect.

Especially the pink straw cowboy hat—pink enough to make John Wayne roll over in his grave.

Especially his connection to an old memory I'd long thought forgotten.

I begin the chase.

*** *** ***

Marvel thinks the kid has the oddest look about him. For one brief moment, he is reminded of that almost-forgotten John Cusack movie from the early 1980s called *Better Off Dead*. It had its moments, especially when Booger tried to inhale a mountain of snow as if it were a mountain of cocaine. One of the better gags was the newspaper boy on the bicycle chasing Cusack in random scenes, crying, "I want my two dollars." The odd kid following him on the old-time bicycle gave him a vibe just like that except maybe to say, "I want my crack rocks."

Marvel laughs as he changes hands because the bottle of Gallo is getting heavy. Two blocks and he'll be home. But the movie reminds him of how recently he'd been addicted to the magic white vapor. If it hadn't been for a solid ass-kicking by One-legged Cherry and a forced, sixty-day stay in the grind, he might still be in its clutches. The very idea the kid

is following him is like one of the paranoid delusions he used to have while under the influence. No, the kid is probably just new to the area and lost.

But a block later, the kid is still with him.

Marvel stops to tie his shoes just like he's seen in the movies a thousand times except he doesn't have any shoes, so he feels stupid. Still, he pretends because to do otherwise would be even stupider. Maybe it really isn't a kid. After all, it could be an under-sized, undercover cop out to see if Marvel Watkins is on the straight and narrow. If that's the case, then the last thing he needs to do is drag a cop to his crib, where Jimmy Raglin has the garage filled with servers loaded with porn. Marvel's chest seizes in a moment of panic. Dear God, what if Jimmy has the kind of porn that will get them all arrested? There are some questions you never ask, and this has always been one of them.

Although Marvel is short for an African-American, fear drives his thick legs fast enough to cover the distance of a man twice his height. He passes his crib, intent on walking around the block. When he turns the corner, he sees that the kid is slowing down. By the time he turns the next corner, the kid is no longer behind him.

Marvel laughs self-consciously. It was all for nothing. *I want my two dollars.* Ha!

*** *** ***

I'm waiting for him when he comes back around the block. The look on his face is precious. I just love it when they think one thing but discover the truth of it. The fat black man wearing cut-off jeans, white cowboy boots, a Culture Club t-shirt, and a pink cowboy hat slows to half his speed. I watch as he composes his face, his lips vacillating between a smile and a frown until I can't tell what the man is feeling. Except I could. Two things had happened to me in 1937. One was that I'd somehow stopped aging. The other was even cooler.

"I want my two dollars," I say, grinning like a maniac.

Marvel drops the gallon of Gallo wine, no longer capable of holding anything. It explodes like a bottle of blood, splattering Marvel's white boots. He brings his hands to his face as his eyes shoot wide.

"I want my two dollars," I say again.

Marvel turns and sprints into the house.

The place looks sketchy, so I decide to wait outside. After all, they'll eventually have to leave.

*** *** ***

Oh my God. Oh my God. Oh my God. Oh my God. Oh my God. Oh my God.

Marvel slams the door. He locks the seven deadbolts and the chain and presses his back to the two inches of wood that separate him from the outside. His breath comes fast and furious. But after a moment, he can't stand it. He spins and presses his face to the door. His hat rises so high it almost falls, but his left eye is pressed firmly enough that he's able to see through the peep hole. And there he is, a teenage Chinese kid on an ancient bike speaking words that had been living in Marvel's head.

"Where's the wine?" Jimmy asks, coming into the room.

"Shhh." Marvel presses his finger to his lips.

"Okay," Jimmy whispers. "Where is my wine, and why am I whispering?"

Marvel points to the door. "Out there." He backs away from it, shaking his head.

Jimmy gives him a look, clearly questioning Marvel's sanity, then moves to the door and looks through the peep hole. After a few seconds, he turns.

"A kid on a bike. So what?"

"He's not just a kid on a bike."

"Oh yeah? Then who is he?" Jimmy asks, putting his hands on his hips.

"I—I don't know. But I think he can read minds."

Jimmy stares at Marvel for a long moment then breaks into laughter until he bends over and grasps his knees. Finally, "You have got to get a hold of yourself, Marvel. Whatever crack-addled fancy came to you, you've gotta be mistaken. Jesus. I thought you were off that shit."

"No. Really. Seriously."

Jimmy checks the peep hole again. "Is that stain on the concrete my wine? Did you drop my wine?"

"I couldn't help it. He—he read my mind."

"Oh, for fuck's sake." Jimmy reaches down and begins the process of opening the seven deadbolts.

Marvel grabs the side of his head and pulls his hat down as far as it will go. "What are you going to do?"

"Going to ask the kid what's going on?"

"Are you sure that's safe?"

"Safe? Did you say safe?"

Marvel nods emphatically.

Jimmy rolls his eyes. "What's the worst that can happen? I mean he's a mind reader, right? Not a serial killer. Right? Listen. Everything is going to be okay."

*** *** ***

I notice two things right away when the man opens the door. First, he's wearing a Ramones *I Wanna Be Sedated* T-shirt and second that he has a sick, sick mind. I can't help but stare at his hands and wonder how a man can touch himself so many times in a single day. Images of men, women, grandmothers, grandfathers, and farm animals all engaging in some form of sex or ritual abuse comes unwanted.

"Hey, kid," the sick man calls. "Come here."

Then I recognize him.

I pedal my bike to the cracked stoop, pull out a chain from my pack, and lock the rear wheel to the rail. Then I stand, adjusting my backpack. When I finally lock eyes with the sick man, I see the root of the man's passion steeped in a wheat field south of Sacramento, where young Jimmy Raglan lies with three young migrant boys who touch each other over and over until they are all released.

"What can I do for you?" I ask.

"What'd you say to Marvel that made him go so crazy?"

"I told him that I want my two dollars."

"Does he owe you money?"

"Nah."

"Then why'd you do it?"

I shrug. "I thought it would be funny."

Jimmy turns. "Was it funny, Marvel?"

Marvel shakes his head. "He stole those words from a movie."

"Actually," I say, cutting to the chase, "I stole those words from your head. I've never actually seen the movie."

Jimmy's eyes narrow. His half-smile curls into a frown. "What the fuck game you playing here, kid?"

"No game," I say. "This is what I do. My name is Valiant Fang, and I am The Shadow."

* * * * * * * * *

Jimmy laughs out loud for the second time in as many minutes. He searches the street for Ashton Kutcher, wondering if he is about to be punked, but then remembers that he's no celebrity.

"My name is Clark Kent, and I'm Superman," he says with a wink.

"No you're not. You are James Larue Raglin, and you're a pornographer."

Jimmy's mouth drops open as he's unable to make a sound.

"Mind if I come in?" the kid asks then comes in anyway.

Jimmy steps aside then, seeing no reason to keep the door open, closes it. He ignores the locks and turns to the kid.

"And you're Marvel Watkins, or really Jerome Laverne Watkins, although you like the name Marvel from the comic books you used to read when you were a kid."

Marvel steps back. "How did you—"

Jimmy's mind reels. Who was this kid to come into their house and call them out?

"I'm The Shadow. Remember him?"

"From the old radio show?" Marvel asks.

"Exactly. *Who knows what evil lurks in the hearts of men?*"

"The—the Shadow?"

The kid nods. "The Shadow." He goes to the couch and sits. "Now let's us talk about your evil."

*** *** ***

I've done this hundreds of times, and I never lose the joy of the first few moments of confrontation. I know they won't do anything to me, so I am never afraid. Not being afraid gives me the leverage to say and do things that are right out of a comic book.

I let them get situated. Marvel sits on the other end of the couch with a pillow held to his chest. Jimmy sits in a well-worn lounger on the other side of the coffee table. Everything is in a state of decay. The floor looks as if it's hosted a hundred orgies. The furniture is tattered and filthy. The tables are scarred and scored with cigarette burns. The walls are tan from too many cigarettes. The popcorn of the ceiling seems ready to drip like snot from the nose of a flu victim.

It's Jimmy who speaks first. "We're not evil. There's nothing illegal about what we do."

"Evil cannot be contained by man's laws, which are subject to the whims of policy and influence."

"What's that you say?" Jimmy's eyes narrow.

"Immoral and illegal are two different things."

"You can't prosecute morality, kid."

"Who said I was going to prosecute?

Marvel's eyes widen, as do Jimmy's.

"Then what are you going to do? I don't think you're big enough to take me. And don't think of pulling anything out of that bag."

"That's the thing about impressions," I say. "You look at me, and you see a kid. I could be twice your age. But then age, morality, and the law aren't the reason I'm here."

"Then what is it?"

"It's potential."

"As in if I try real hard I can be somebody some day?" Marvel asks.

"Sounds like something from school," Jimmy notes.

Marvel nods. "It was, but it was all bullshit."

But I shake my head. "More like as in you are going to do something someday that I need to stop from happening."

*** *** ***

It never used to be this simple.

In fact, back in 1937, it was a bastard.

Back then, I didn't know I was going to live forever. But I did want to be like the Shadow. He was so cool. Kids didn't have X-Men or the Fantastic Four or the Avengers yet. All we had was a fledgling Superman and a few other heroes. Batman wouldn't be born until the next year. But those were paper. They didn't feel as real as the heroes on the radio. Somehow, Orson Welles' voice of the Shadow made the character seem much more substantial, much more significant. Every kid wanted to be him. But it was me who really became him.

Mr. Armbruster ran the soda fountain on Lincoln Avenue near the Santa Monica Pier. Tourists, kids, and teens on their way to or coming back from the ocean would stop in and get a root beer or a two scooper. Mr. Armbruster was really good at making those sorts of things. He was also really good at taking pictures of people going to the bathroom although, as it turned out, I was the only one who knew about it.

At first.

I'd been going around intentionally looking for someone to save. It wasn't as easy as I thought it would be. Every day, I'd end up at Armbruster's. Every day, I'd have a root beer. This went on for four months until I suddenly realized something: I knew what Armbruster was thinking. It came as a series of whispers at first. I discovered that if I concentrated on them, I could discern actual words. Soon—too soon really because I wasn't ready for the knowledge—I discovered that the thoughts that collided behind his smile were anything but nice. He wanted to touch and feel everyone. His sexual tastes had no limit. Eventually, I learned about his secret stash of photos and the camera in the bathroom. An anonymous letter to the police and Armbruster's Soda Shop was soon closed. They locked him up. Three years later, he was killed in prison.

I should have felt happy. I should have felt thrilled at my new power and how I used it. But I felt hollow instead. No one knew it was me. How can you be a hero when no one knows? Even the asshole alien Superman got applause when he was wearing his cape, so why not me?

I soon learned that no one liked a little Chinese kid superhero.

*** *** ***

It was 1938. Floods and landslides around Los Angeles had killed 200 people. Snow White and the Seven Dwarves and Boystown were a big deal in Hollywood. Superman was born. And so was Valiant Fang, The Yellow Shadow. I had a costume fashioned for me in Chinatown. It had a cape of yellow satin with a red underside over a yellow, form-fitting suit. With this, I wore red boots, red gloves, and a red mask over my eyes. When everything was ready in July of that year, I donned my costume and began to walk the streets.

At first, all I got was laughter. I hadn't grown since the year before. I wouldn't realize that I'd reached my limit until later. Still, I was a gangly kid with glasses and acne. I wasn't white like all the other superheroes; I was yellow. And my costume was yellow. They took to calling me Yellow Kid. I could have almost accepted that, but it devolved.

Hey Piss Boy!
Look Momma; it's Piss Boy!
It's a bird, it's a plane… It's Piss Boy!

They didn't even try and rhyme it, those fuckers.

When the police picked me up, I tried to explain to them that I was old enough to be out on my own, but they wouldn't hear of it. They took me to an orphanage in Ventura, where I spent the next five years until I escaped.

If the world wanted to laugh at me, then I'd show them what funny was. I spent the following years being funny and doing funny things. Then on June 5th, 1968, everything got positively hilarious.

*** *** ***

"So you're some kind of hero, aren't you?" Jimmy says, frowning around a cigarette he just lit.

"Not hardly." I smile sadly. "At least not by your definition."

"Not my definition," Jimmy says. "It's the universe's definition. I don't make shit up, I just repeat it.

I turn to Marvel, who has calmed down substantially. "What's a hero to you?"

"You mean like Spider-Man?"

"Is he a hero to you?"

"Yeah. And the Hulk too. Oh yeah. The Thing, what's his name?"

"Ben Grimm," I say.

"Yeah. Him."

"Do you realize that all those heroes you mentioned had something done to them that made them a hero?"

Marvel stares back in incomprehension.

"There are three types of heroes. There are those who have something done to them that gives them powers. There are those who actively seek out heroism, most often, but not always, attaining their powers through technology."

"Like Iron Man?"

I nod to Marvel. "Like Iron Man. And, of course, there are those who are born that way." I gesture toward Marvel. "Like your namesake. Not the D.C. version, mind you, but the Marvel version."

"There's a difference?"

"Which one was your favorite? When did you read the comic?"

"They were my father's. He went to Vietnam and came

back in a box. All he left me were his dog tags," which Marvel rattles as he explains, "and a tub of comic books from the late 1960s."

"As I thought. You like the space-born Marvel comics Captain Marvel, not the D.C version that is a weird reimagining of Egyptian mythology and possession."

Jimmy waves his hand with the cigarette. "Alright. Whatever? So there are three types of superheroes. So what?"

Marvel turns toward me and nods. "Yeah. So what?"

"So how many types of villains are there?"

"Is this a test?" Jimmy asks. "I hate tests."

"It's not a test. You don't even have to know the answer. In fact, if you did, it wouldn't change what's about to happen."

Jimmy's eyes narrow.

"There are three types of villains," Marvel says hopefully. "Just like heroes, right?"

I shake my head. "I can see why you'd think so, but no. There's only one kind of villain." I stand up and walk over to where Marvel sits. His eyes go wide. "No matter the power, no matter the ability, no matter the technology, the single factor that decides if someone is a villain or not is their desire to do evil. The comic books are certain about that. They don't fuck around with evil. You have to want to be evil to be evil."

"But what about when an evil character does something good? That happens. I see it all the time in comics and in the movies."

"The only reason an evil person would do something good is to achieve an unjust end." I give Jimmy a momentary stare. "Trust me. I know."

I watch as a light dawns in Marvel's eyes. "What about the Punisher? He's evil, right?"

"He just wants revenge. He's an anti-hero. That's where a hero does evil things to attain a just end."

"This is just weird," Jimmy says, stabbing out his cigarette and standing.

"Sit down a moment," I say. "I got a story to tell you. A story about June 5th, 1968.

I watch as Jimmy sits down slowly. Things he hasn't thought about are beginning to surface in his mind.

"Once upon a time, there was a Chinese kid who wanted to be a hero, but he learned real quickly that the universe had something else in mind for him. And you know what? He embraced the fuck out of it."

*** *** ***

Danny New was a cop on the beat for ten years before I met him. He thought I was just a kid, and I didn't do anything to stop his belief. I knew he was scheduled to be on guard detail at the Ambassador Hotel on June 5th just like I knew that Sirhan Sirhan had been paid by anonymous courier to kill Bobby Kennedy at the same hotel on the same day. They didn't know me. To them, I was just a paperboy. After all, there's not much a person of my appearance and stature can do. Knowing both of their intentions helped me envision the future. In fact, I can honestly say that it was the first time that the future was laid out before me in such a way that there was no denying what was going to happen. And I didn't like what I saw. But trying to do something about it was hard because

Danny New was too good at his job. They said that he could spot a crime before it happened. When asked, he couldn't explain it. He just knew. Danny New… knew.

Well, there was something I knew.

I knew he had a baby boy back home.

I also knew he had a fine young wife.

Before I stole the baby, I did the wife. She'd never been with a Chinese kid before. I could read her mind between the screams and the fear. She was mystified that my pecker was yellow.

Of course, I had to kill her.

But I didn't kill the baby. I mean, one has to draw a line somewhere, right?

I arranged it so the call to Danny New went out an hour before Sirhan Sirhan planned the assassination. The policeman ran to his car with the news that his wife had been murdered and his baby was missing. Then everything went as planned. Bobby was shot in the head once, the back twice, and he died 26 hours later.

Hooray for the Piss Boy.

Fucking hilarious.

*** *** ***

"But what about the baby?" Marvel asks.

I turn to Jimmy and ask him, "What about the baby?"

Jimmy's face is ashen. He looks like he's about to have a coronary. He has trouble breathing.

"Jimmy? What's wrong?" Marvel runs to him.

Jimmy waves Marvel off as he regains his composure.

Finally, he blows out a heap of air and gives me the look of hate I knew he had in him. "Why are you fucking with me like this?"

"I'm not fucking with you. I was there. I did what I said. I fucked your mother."

Marvel gives me a classic W-T-F look. "You did that?"

I nod happily.

Jimmy launches himself across the room. Knowing his intentions, it's pathetically easy to move out of his way. Finally, I leap over the couch and pull the pistol from my backpack. I snap my arm into place just as he's about to follow me over the couch. The barrel catches him dead center of his forehead. He stops, stares fire, and breathes heavily.

"But your name is Raglin," Marvel says. "If your daddy's name was New, then why isn't yours?"

"I'm adopted, shithead. My father killed himself when I was five. Picked up his service revolver, shoved it in his mouth, and blew his brains out all over the refrigerator while I was eating Count Chocula. I moved in with a family in Sacramento. June and Spencer Raglin."

"How'd you like that?" I ask, watching as he replays the molestations of the migrant boys in his mind.

"I fucking loved it." His gaze goes from my trigger finger to the barrel. "You gonna shoot me?"

"Not if you do something for me."

"What makes you think I'd help you? I wouldn't even spit into your mouth if you were drowning."

"Because I know something you don't. I know that you're going to die in three days unless you do something."

I watch as an image of his mother appears only to be replaced by his father then himself as a child. Then the purity of it all is destroyed by a hundred thousand naked men and women doing things that are as devoid of love and concern as a lizard has for a fly. He's become numb from the constant assault on his mind. Although he wants revenge, it doesn't matter to him as much as it should. A small sliver of him knows this, but he can't do anything about it.

He licks his lips as his thoughts spin from what he knows he should do to self-preservation. "How am I going to die?"

"Marvel is going to get all cracked up in an hour, get picked up by the police, and trade information about your child porn pictures for a free pass."

His gaze flicks to Marvel. "I don't have child porn."

"Does it really matter?" I point out. "I mean, once you invoke the words *child porn*, it's guilty until proven innocent, right? It's a fucking game changer."

Marvel's eyes widen impossibly. "I will not."

"Will too," I say.

"Will not."

Jimmy looks at me.

"Who are you going to believe? A John Wayne-wanna-be-RuPaul-homo-crack-addict or a Hollywood super villain who fucked your mom, killed your dad, and screwed the country?"

Jimmy looks at Marvel.

Marvel opens his mouth to say something, thinks better of it, then hauls ass to the door. He jerks it open and runs down the walk.

"Well? Are you going to go after him? You have less than

an hour."

The images of his mother and father are washed aside in a tide of naked bodies and his imagination of how it would be in prison if he were ever caught, other prisoners doing things to him he'd only watched on the computer screen. He steps back from the couch.

"Do you want this?" I ask, holding out the pistol.

A personal YouTube video of my destruction blasts through his brain.

"There's only one bullet, so you need to make a choice."

He grabs the gun and runs down the walk. By the time he hits the street, his self-respect is entirely gone.

*** *** ***

They finally notice the body.

A white woman from Ohio screams first. She bore seven children, has twenty-one grandchildren, collects ceramic squirrels, is addicted to sitcoms, and wants to have animal sex with Eddie Murphy.

A man from Lake of the Woods, Minnesota, wearing a fishing vest and a Cabela hat, grabs his chest as his heart fibrillates erratically. The single thought that goes through his mind is that he's going to die before he catches a Lake Trout.

Then they all scream.

The kid goes unnoticed. After all, why should they notice a gangly Chinese kid on an old bicycle? What could he possibly have to do with the body? The man wearing a Ramone's T-shirt is curled up in a fetal position on a nearby bus stop bench, his shoulders shuddering from hard-won tears. He

also goes unnoticed. After all, he's probably just a wino or some homeless man without two dimes to scrape together. What could he possibly have to do with the body? Instead, all eyes turn from the body back to the paraplegic pimp and the one-legged midget hooker. The hooker reaches down and picks up the pistol. Balancing on one leg, she holds the pistol in self-defense. But the crowd sees something different, and they make up their minds.

I turn and pedal away. I'm a shadow in the noonday sun as they gather around the shiny object once known as Marvel, who, had he lived, would have saved a little girl crossing the street in front of Grauman's Chinese Theater from being hit by a Compton teacher late for a conference at the Kodak Theater.

"Who knows what evil lurks in the hearts of men? The Shadow knows."

I laugh dramatically as I pedal faster and faster.

Who better to know evil than a villain? And I, Piss Boy, am the greatest villain of them all.

MENTAL MAN

WILLIAM TODD ROSE

MY THERAPIST USES METAPHORS TAILORED FOR MY UNIQUE situation. He speaks of the Fortress of Solitude with which I surround my true feelings. The Bat Cave tunneling into my psyche, so deep and dark that the secrets I hide there never know the warmth of enlightenment. In my subconscious, he says, there's a decrepit Gotham teeming with super villains; their sole purpose in life is to tear me down, to find my emotional Kryptonite and destroy me. They have names like Chronic Depression, Acute Anxiety, and Persistent Avoidance. With their henchmen, they've banded together to form an axis of evil known as the PTSD, and the fate of my inner Metropolis hinges upon their defeat.

He prescribes me pills and sits cross-legged in his chair, scribbling occasionally on his steno pad while I levitate the frog figurines lining the bookshelves in his office. This is a nervous tic that causes Dr. Thompson to peer over the top of his glasses as he peppers me with open-ended questions. Never something I can answer with a simple yes or no, these queries are specifically designed to draw me out.

"Why do you feel, Rob, that you're not living up to your full potential?"

Why, indeed.

In comic books and movies, people like me always have their counterpart, their polar opposite. Madmen hell-bent on world domination, misguided scientists who use their creations to fulfill their own twisted desires. An archenemy, if you will. And the existence of these rivals defines the hero just as much as his powers or costume. If not more so. In the real world, however, things are quite different. Junkies sweating through withdrawal rob liquor stores, jealous wives kill their husbands in fits of passion, and drunk drivers screech away from the bent and twisted frames of bicycles. There's no ultimate nemesis whose apprehension will make the world safe for decent, law-abiding citizens. Just an endless string of beautiful losers with their own sob stories and justifications. And without someone sitting on the other side of the teeter-totter of good and evil, you end up busting your hump against the unforgiving earth time and time again. So how's that for a metaphor, Doc?

See, I never really wanted this shit to begin with. I was just this kid doing his best to grow up in a neighborhood where shards of shattered beer bottles littered the sidewalks like so many broken dreams. You grew up tough in this type

of hood or you didn't grow up at all. Since there really is safety in numbers, I fell in with a bad crowd and used my powers for the good of the gang. Door locks fractured as easily as ice with only minimal concentration, and security cameras played back static once my electromagnetic field wiped the tapes clean. I struck as quietly and efficiently as sudden death, knocking out security guards before they even realized that they'd just heard something rustle behind them. But my biggest contribution was sensing when the time was right to split. Before sirens could be heard wailing in the distance, I knew five-oh was on the way; I could see the black and white cars zipping through traffic, their lights strobing blue and red against the graffiti covered walls as radios crackled with chatter. Almost as if I'd left my body and was in a different time and place.

The problem is, I developed a taste for downers, see. I popped Seconal like they were Jujubes and rode the waves of relaxation right into my downfall. With my senses dulled and reaction times so slow that I could have passed for just another member of the gang, it wasn't long before I was picked up. Extortion, strong arm robbery, larceny, breaking and entering, conspiracy, and racketeering: the boys in blue had me by the balls. Tried as an adult, I would be looking at fifteen to twenty years in a state correctional facility with no chance of parole. But all that would just go away if I took the deal they had on the table. Come work for us, they said, and we'll make sure you keep getting pussy instead of being somebody's bitch.

Sometimes I think I would have been better off just serving my time and eventually trying to find my place in a world that had moved on without me. Maybe then, I wouldn't

find my cheeks wet with tears when I watch young couples run hand in hand through the rain. Maybe I wouldn't feel like the walls of my silent apartment are closing in and that an invisible hand grips my throat when the panic attacks set in. Maybe I could actually appreciate life.

As it is, I sleep about thirteen to fourteen hours a day. I insist that powers like mine burn a lot of energy—that I need time to recharge my batteries, so to speak. Dr. Thompson, however, says it's escapism. Wrapped in dreams, I am safe from the quiet voice in my head that whispers I'm not good enough, that I'm just a freak and will never fit in, will never know what it means to be truly loved instead of having just another booze-soaked romp with a horny groupie.

"What's wrong with horny groupies?" I want to know. He says they're a poor substitute for true affection and are only feeding my need for validation. I say I just want to get my jollies and get out. That I want at least one thing in my life simple. We'll never agree. Not on the bimbos and not on the sleep.

Regardless of why I sleep as much as I do, I always awake to the same thing: my phone ringing in the darkness as insistent as a needy lover. The muffled voice on the other end breaks up as reception fades in and out. I rub my eyes and scrawl an address on a scrap of paper. Too-strong coffee that tastes bitter and burnt at the convenience store around the corner, a couple of No-Doz washed down with the scalding liquid, my cigarette ember winking in the rearview mirror as I stifle a yawn: This is my wake up routine, what people like me have instead of a hot shower and healthy breakfast.

Here lately, the scenes are always the same as well. A suburban home with a carefully manicured lawn surrounded by the stereotypical picket fence. The mailbox by the street will look like a wide-mouth bass or a caboose or a miniature replica of the house at the other end of the sidewalk. The street will be roped off with yellow tape while neighbors dressed in bathrobes and boxers cluster on the sidewalks, whispering to one another as their faces change color in the lights of a dozen police cars. Cruisers, unmarked sedans with flashers shining through windshields, the obligatory ambulance and van stenciled with the letters *CSU*. Just another day at the office.

Last night, I walked into a living room where the walls were covered with the arc of arterial spray. Blood had pooled on the white shag carpet in glistening puddles, and books were strewn across the floor from a toppled shelf. Sprawled half-way across the couch was a pretty blonde with one boob hanging out of her ripped nightgown. Her wrists were bound with the all-too-familiar silk rope, and silver duct tape had sealed her screams. He'd slit her throat, just like the others, and paraded her around the living room, coating the walls with her ever-diminishing blood supply before tossing her onto the sofa like a toy that had lost its sparkle.

Lying face-down between the kitchen and living room was a balding man, and the back of his head looked like a dented car door that had been splattered with red paint balls. His tighty-whities were stained brown from voided bowels, and his right hand stretched across the carpet as if, even in death, he were grasping for the Louisville Slugger that was

just out of reach. The baseball bat itself was pristine. No spatter or clumps of hair stuck to the polished wood. No cracks. It wasn't one of the murder weapons but a line of defense that ultimately proved useless.

I knew without being told that the children were upstairs. Each in their own bedroom, their hands staged over their eyes as if trying to block the horrors they'd witnessed and their throats mottled and bruised. Every mirror in the house would be shattered; if there were any family pets, they would be dead as well. In the second house, we'd found an empty bottle of bleach beside a tank of tropical fish floating upside down. In the fourth, a Scottish terrier had been strangled with its own leash, and the boy's hamster lay by the baseboard, just beneath a sunburst splatter of blood on the blue bedroom wall.

There was something different about this scene however, something that told me our unsub was becoming even more brazen, more confident in his ability to kill with impunity. For scrawled across the wall like crimson finger paint was a message: *You will never catch me.*

"It's our guy, Mental Man. Same MO." Detective Wyler frowned beneath his bushy mustache and snorted air through his nostrils, attempting to clear his sinuses of the coppery tang in the air.

"Tell me something I don't know," I grumbled, purposefully ignoring the corny nickname Wyler keeps trying to stick me with.

"Captain says the feds are coming in on this one by special request. So if you're gettin' anything, now's the time to shine."

I closed my eyes and tried to picture the living room as

it had been. Before the yellow evidence markers had been propped across the floor. Before the walls were streaked and smeared with wasted life. I reached into the past with my mind the same way I'd searched for cops in my misspent youth, probing time and space as if it were a film I could manipulate at will.

Mr. Cooper awoke to a thump from downstairs. Sitting up in bed, he stared into the darkness, listening past the hum of the air conditioner for whatever it was that had pulled him out of a dream in which he was just about to bend his secretary over a desk. As he sat there, the tinkle of breaking glass awoke Mrs. Cooper as well and she sat up, clenching the sheets just below her chin. With her eyes wide with panic, she pushed her husband out of bed and hissed, "Stanley, there's someone downstairs." I could feel her heart pattering like a frightened rabbit and smell the stink fear leaking from the beads of sweat on Stan's brow as he swung his feet over the edge of the bed.

He tiptoed across the room, freezing in place as the floorboards squeaked beneath his substantial weight. With eyes clenched shut, he stood as still as the dresser and listened with his head cocked to the side. His stomach felt as if the White Russian he'd downed before bed had turned rancid, and he made a silent promise to God: *Let everyone be okay, and I'll never think about Annette like that again. I'll be a good father, a better husband—just let everyone be okay.*

When there was no response to his misplaced step, he crept to the bedroom doorway and snatched the bat that leaned against the wall with the deftness of a master thief.

Mrs. Cooper watched him disappear through the door

and plucked the phone cradle from the night stand. She didn't notice that the keypad didn't light up as she dialed 911. In fact, she had no clue until she placed the receiver to her ear and heard nothing.

The line was dead.

Her cell phone was in her purse downstairs.

Help was not coming.

Her bladder felt so full that her abdomen ached, and chills crept over her arms and scalp. Part of her insisted that she get out of bed, that she gather the children and crawl out the window if she had to. She had to go, she had to run, she had to do it now.

But she couldn't. Her muscles felt as if they'd turned to stone, and a single, reoccurring thought overrode instructions from her brain: *The realtor said this neighborhood was safe; he said it was safe, damn it, safe.*

A muffled grunt from downstairs was followed by a thud so loud that windows rattled in their panes. Then silence.

"Stanley?" Her whisper was more of a plea than a question, a desperate petition for all to be right in her little cookie cutter world. "*Stanley?*"

There was a tightness in her chest; somewhere beneath breasts that still ached from her recent mastopexy, a scream built the pressure required to shoot up through her vocal cords. Her hands trembled as the temperature in the room seemed to drop ten degrees, but wisps of hair were plastered by sweat to the back of her slender neck.

She heard footsteps on the stairs. Slow. Deliberate. Methodical.

"Stanley…you're *scaring* me."

The hallway light flicked on, and Mrs. Cooper scrunched her knees against her chest as she pressed her back against the padded headboard. She wanted to curl into a ball so tightly that her body collapsed in on itself, that she simply winked out of existence.

"Damn it, Stanley, I swear to God, if you're messing around…"

The shadow of a man stretched across the hallway carpet. She could no longer hear anything other than her own blood whooshing through her veins, and the back of her throat stung with the bitterness of bile.

"S-Stanley…" No longer whispering, her husband's name bubbled from her quivering lips as tears glistened in her eyes.

The shadow grew larger.

Closer.

Just on the other side of the wall now, separated only by a few inches of plaster and wood. Warmth spread across her crotch, but the acrid stench of urine was blocked by the snot bubbling from her nose.

She would see him. Any second now.

Her killer revealed.

Pain, guilt, remorse, agony, despair, terror. A tsunami of emotion and sensation crashed over me as the scene exploded in a brilliant burst of light like a flashbulb going off in a darkened room. I found myself pulled into the fetal position on the floor, my throat raw with Mrs. Cooper's released scream and tears warming my cheeks.

Wyler was crouched beside me, his face looming so close

that I could see the crater-like pores on the tip of his bulbous nose. He didn't offer a helping hand as I struggled to sit up but finally vocalized the question his eyes had asked all along. "Anything?"

I shook my head and gulped in lungfuls of cool air as I wiped my eyes with the back of my knuckles. Though not looking directly at my unofficial partner, I could feel the heat of his gaze as it burned into my soul.

"Damn it, Mental Man, you better be gettin' us some usable shit. I mean it, you son of a bitch. You know what the papers are callin' this guy? The Suburb Slayer. How well do you think that's going to go over with the mayor?"

The Suburb Slayer. This madman is the closest thing I have to an archenemy. He's always there, looming on the outskirts of my perception, taunting me with his proximity while remaining thoroughly cloaked in shadow. Seven families so far and, if experience holds true, we won't have to wait long for the eighth.

Seven families. Twenty-six lives. Two months.

I want this fucker so bad I can taste it. He haunts my dreams, a faceless shadow dancing on graves that bulge as if they're about to explode with the expanding gasses of the corpses below. His laughter echoes through the corridors of my mind, mocking me with haughty arrogance as I stumble about in the darkness like a blind man. Every waking hour I spend touching the possessions of corpses, revisiting their final moments again and again as I search for some little detail I may have previously overlooked. I feel their fear and pain, experience their deaths without ever so much as a glimpse

of their attacker, and cry until my eyes are in a constant state of puffiness.

Our destinies are inexplicably intertwined now, two strangers in a city of thousands engaged in the most primal of dances. Hunter and prey. Predator and quarry. He stalks his victims and I chase him, always a few steps behind, always just out of reach.

You will never catch me.

Just you watch me, asshole.

Just you fuckin' watch me.

*** *** ***

Family number eight. Lucas and Laura Wilson—their children Larry and Lana, ages eight and eleven respectively. I used to hate theme families where the names all played on a single sound or letter, thinking of them as being more like a franchise than an actual unit. But the Wilsons changed all of that. Four more lives snuffed out in the middle of the night, four more bodies waiting for me to use my powers to explore the last moments of their lives. Four more chances to catch this sadist who slaughters families as easily as I change clothes.

There was a new message on the wall at the Wilson's: *They are Mine.*

It's another jab that I take personally. When I finally catch this bastard, I'll crush his bones like I used to shatter locks when pulling a heist. The little ones first, the thin ones in his wrist and the metatarsals within the toes; his joints will pop out of socket as if smashed with a ball peen hammer, and I'll make him experience every second of agony I've suffered

through while revisiting his victims.

I no longer entertain the starry eyed vixens who twirl hair around their fingers and pop their gum as they giggle with ludicrous innuendo. There's simply no time for pleasures of the flesh. There's too much evidence to explore, too many details to comb through. Dr. Thompson says this proves his theory: With a worthy adversary to test my skills, I no longer need the authentication I used to receive from their lofty praises. He may be right. But I no longer care. His opinions mean less to me now than the drivel spewed by the profilers from the Federal Bureau of Intimidation.

Even my sleep patterns are evening out. I spend maybe one night every two to three weeks where I dream the majority of the day away; the rest of the time, I'm up and at 'em after a solid eight hours of rack, ready to take on the day.

Yesterday, I even told Dr. Thompson I didn't feel like I needed to see him anymore. His brow furrowed with concern as he leaned forward and told me how I shouldn't be hasty. The human mind is a complex thing, he said, full of twists and turns and corridors we never even knew existed.

"In someone like you, Rob," he said, "it gets even more complex. You really need to think about this."

But there's nothing to think about. The panic attacks are gone, the whispering voice in my head has fallen silent, and my tears have been replaced with resolve. I truly feel I'm finally living up to my full potential, and my unique gifts were not just some cruel trick of nature. I'm even embracing the nickname Wyler has tried to tag me with for years. Mental Man. Kind of has a nice ring to it, doesn't it?

Not to say that I don't have bad days. Everyone does. They're just not crippling anymore. Today, for example, was an experiment in frustration. I revisited each of the eight crime scenes again, walked through each house just moments before the massacres began. This time, however, I was able to focus my powers intently. Rather than experiencing the horror and suffering of the victims, I stepped into the mind of the killer himself.

I felt the flutter of nervous excitement in the stomach, like a schoolboy watching the school slut strip off her clothes and knowing that my time as a virgin was coming to an end. Surges of power and control gushed through my veins, filling me with God-like dominion over the realms of Life and Death. I knew the thrill of carting my writhing captives around their living rooms, the sweet futility of their squirming as I painted the walls with my medium of choice.

Yet I never saw the face. With all the mirrors broken, there was no reflection, nothing I could use to make a positive ID. Tomorrow, I'll do it all over again; this time, I'll try to focus on the wide, glassy eyes of the victims just before they die. When the last thing they see is my face grinning at them. Maybe there, I'll find a reflection. I have to. It's been weeks since this bastard has struck, which means there's another family out there somewhere whose time is short. Cuddled up in front of the television, laughing over a bowl of popcorn while the television flickers bluish light on smiling faces… never suspecting that within days, they'll all be dead.

There's a message on my answering machine from Dr. Thompson. He's prattling on about the results of my most

recent psychological battery, how some disturbing patterns have emerged, and he really believes I need to rethink my position on therapy. Something about fugue states. I tell myself I'll Google that term later but recognize the lie the moment it flits through my mind. Instead, I punch the delete button so hard that the plastic casing of the phone cracks beneath my touch.

I don't need his shit. He's just thinking about all the billable hours he's losing, the book that will never be finished. I've got my adversary now, the counterweight on the other end of my teeter totter. Who the fuck is this little man with his degree and collection of frogs to imply that I'm still broken, that I'm somehow damaged and weak? Just who the hell does he think he is, anyway?

I catch a reflection of myself in the bathroom mirror, and the stress of the day bursts from me like a demon from the gates of Hell. I feel the power swell and shoot out like a cosmic ejaculation, and the mirror shatters into a thousand pieces. Tiny pieces shower through the air, each flashing in the light and reflecting miniature images of the mask of rage my face has become before smashing against the sink and floor.

Son of a bitch. This is getting expensive. That's the ninth mirror I've gone through, and as always, the outburst leaves me feeling hollow and drained. It's as if that blast of energy latched onto every emotion I have and pulled it out in long, invisible strands.

I collapse onto the bed because I no longer have the energy to stand. My eyes sting with fatigue, and my muscles feel as though they've turned into overcooked spaghetti. I yawn as

I close my eyes.

Somehow, I know that this will be a thirteen-hour slumber. It's as if my body is now attuned to the Suburb Slayer and only stockpiles energy on the nights he strikes. I know my dreams will be interrupted with the jangling of the phone, and I'll jot down address number nine, somehow feeling as if I've known the location all along.

In some ways, I almost look forward to it.

As long as he's out there, my life has meaning.

My life has purpose.

I've finally become the hero I was always meant to be.

THE REAL CHURCH

JEREMY HEPLER

IT STARTED WHEN I RESURRECTED MR. FULTON'S CHIHUAHUA, Brutus.

It was a hot August afternoon, two weeks shy of my twelfth birthday, and Dad was on a rampage again. When he found Mom kneeling in the bathroom mumbling to Jesus about his drinking problem, I knew it was time to get out of the house. "Jesus Christ, Ella. Get the fuck up," was all I needed to hear. I had learned at an early age not to get involved in their fights unless I wanted to get hurt or blamed, so I grabbed my glove and baseball and quietly darted from shadow to shadow until I reached the back porch.

The fence separating our backyard from Mr. Fulton's had been there since our house was built in the late sixties. It was propped with two-by-fours and anchored to the ground with nylon rope and tent stakes to prevent the gusty Texas Panhandle wind from bringing it down. Termites had eaten a good four to five inches off of the bottom, leaving enough room for Brutus to stick his head into our yard.

Walking in slow circles, I tossed the ball into the air and caught it. The windows might as well have been open.

"Shut up, Ella!"

Brutus started to yip.

"Terry, you need to—"

Toss. Yip. Catch.

"I don't need to anything!"

Yip. Yip.

"You need to pray. You need Jesus, Terry."

Higher toss. Yip. Catch.

"You're a stupid bitch. You know that? You need your head examined if anybody around here needs anything."

Toss and catch. Louder yipping. Faster.

"Owen doesn't need to see you like this."

Yip. Toss. Yip. Catch.

"The boy. Jesus. The boy! Jesus! It's always about the boy or Jesus with you!"

I stopped walking, spun around, and faced the house when a crashing sound came from the kitchen. The window was cracked. Beer ran down the inside. I gritted my teeth and squeezed the ball as hard as I could.

Every weekend was the same. Dad got drunk. Mom prayed for the power to fix him. Dad got mad and loud. I went outside. Dad cussed and threw stuff and sometimes hit her a few times and then left. I went back inside, and Mom made

me pray with her and told me that someday, Dad would be healed. And the whole time, that damn dog never stopped yipping.

Fueled by frustration, I reared back and threw the ball at Brutus' head as hard I as possibly could. I hadn't actually played catch with anyone in years, had terrible mechanics, and normally wouldn't have been able to hit the fence if I tried, but that day, Jesus must have guided my arm because I nailed Brutus square in the face. He instantly collapsed, blood dotting the ground and ball in front of him.

Staring at Brutus' shaking body, I stayed perfectly still when a second crash rang out inside the kitchen.

"Get out. Now!"

"Fuck you!"

Brutus' little paws continued to twitch as a bottle shattered on the driveway, and Dad's truck peeled out and sped down the street. After the roar of his engine faded, a crushing silence seemed to slow time to a crawl. The reality of what I'd just done began to sink in. I dropped my glove and ran toward the fence.

How was I going to explain this to Mom? To Mr. Fulton? He was almost eighty years old and had no immediate family. In fact, I'd never seen anyone go into his house other than Mom and the skinny man who drove the Meals-on-Wheels Van. Brutus was the one and only thing in the world that I'd ever seen make him smile.

A couple of years earlier, I'd told Mom how much I hated Brutus and his yipping. "Brutus is like Mr. Fulton's child," she'd said. "Without that dog, I don't know if he'd have much of a

reason to live. That dog gives him purpose, Honey. Like you do me. You need to remember that sometimes, people have to suffer in order to help someone else."

The memory of these words forced me down to my knees next to the fence. Brutus was still shaking, his eyes rolled back. The left side of his face was caved in, his black nose and brown cheek fur were streaked with blood, and his tongue hung out. I placed my hand on his neck and whispered his name. I couldn't let Mr. Fulton see him like this. I tried to pull him under the fence into my yard (maybe he could have just run away), but his belly was too round to make it through. I don't know if it was instinct or environment, but in desperation, I closed my eyes and did what Mom did when Dad went ballistic.

"Please, Jesus, give me the power to heal." I placed my hand over the indented part of his face. "I heal you, Brutus. I heal you because you don't deserve this."

Mr. Fulton's sliding glass door flew open. "Brutus? Come here boy."

I squeezed my eyes tighter. "I heal you, Brutus. I heal you. I heal you. Now get up."

As Mr. Fulton shuffled his walker outside, it happened. I felt Brutus's face inflate into its proper form beneath my hand, like a misshapen balloon filling with air. The bones locked. The skin zipped shut. I opened my eyes and looked down. Brutus' fat, brown eyes rolled back into place and fixed on mine. Yipping and angry, he jerked away from my hand, pulling himself back onto his side of the fence.

"Brutus?" Mr. Fulton called from the edge of the porch. "Come here." He reached down and scooped up Brutus. "What

the Hell have you done to him, boy? Why does he have red paint all over his face?"

"Sorry, Mr. Fulton. It was an accident." I struggled to make the words audible, to straighten my legs to stand, as I stared at the blood on my hand.

Mr. Fulton mumbled something I didn't understand and headed inside with Brutus.

Glancing back and forth from the blood on my hand to the fence, I somehow managed to pick up my bloody baseball and glove and head inside to check on Mom. She had a small cut on her hand from picking up glass shards but was otherwise fine.

I told her about Brutus after dinner. She gave me a smile of joy I'll never forget, pulled my head to her chest, and said: "See, Honey? I told you that you were always meant for something big. Something great."

I didn't sleep that night. I sat in bed and read every story of Jesus' healings again and again. Reading Bible verses had always comforted me on nights when Dad got out of control and I felt scared. That night, they made me feel connected, special. I had always talked to Jesus about all of my problems just like Mom had told me to, and whether I was alone on the playground at school or in the backyard, He always listened. As I watched the sunrise through my window that morning, I felt amazing. He had not only listened this time, He'd given me a gift—the same special gift that He'd had while on Earth.

I didn't heal again for more than eight years.

*** *** ***

Dad never slept another night in our house after the Brutus incident, and I talked to him only a handful of times before he died. Three months after he moved out, he drove his truck into the back end of a parked diesel and was decapitated. He had never changed his will and had never legally divorced Mom, so she received a nice chunk of money from Phillips Petroleum Company after his death.

Over the years, she had become more and more disenchanted with the nondenominational church we attended. She thought Pastor Heely was starting to misinterpret the Bible, leading people straight to Hell. There was no way she'd ever let us step foot in one of the Baptist or Lutheran or Presbyterian Churches (G.C.C.s she called them: Greedy Commercial Churches) that dominated our small Bible Belt town. So now that we had enough money—and we both believed I had the power to heal, a power to be used for Jesus—we decided to buy an old warehouse on the edge of Dresden and open our own church.

The Real Church.

We started out small: anywhere from five to ten people a week. We painted the building white and stenciled the church's name in an arch over the blue doors. We didn't ask for money from the attendees, just an open ear. Mom sat on a stool in front of forty fold-out chairs and delivered her interpretations of the Scriptures and led the congregation in prayer. I lit the candles, helped serve communion, and read the Psalm of the Day.

Within a month of opening, The Real Church had become the main topic in gossip circles around Dresden. So many bad things were said. Mom was a witch, I a demon. I was her lover, her brother. We were a satanic cult, pagan orgy partiers, a colony of loonies, a group of left-footed loopies.

One time, someone painted a pentagram on the side of our church. Another time, someone tried to torch the place but only burned down a couple of Mesquite trees in the vacant lot next door. Beer cans and feces often decorated the porch on Sunday mornings. By the time I dropped out of high school at sixteen and earned a G.E.D., The Real Church had so many sinister, twisted members and terrifying truths that stories about us were beginning to rival the local Haunter of Mirrors, Blood-Eyed Stella, in sleepover scares.

Despite the negative backlash, Mom continued to work at Gerald's Cleaners, and I worked nights at Sonic so that we could afford to pay the taxes and insurance on the church. To make things easier, we sold the house on Matador Street and started sleeping in a double-wide behind the church.

I continued trying to use my healing powers every chance I got. I knew that once Jesus allowed me to figure it out, it would show everyone that *He* was with *us*, which would catapult us to that Something Great.

At first, I tried to heal any injured animal I came across. I tried to repair birds' broken wings, a cat's lacerated ear, a squirrel's broken leg, half-squashed roaches, claw marks down a dog's belly, and on and on. After each unsuccessful attempt, I prayed harder for an answer. One night, Jesus spoke to me in a dream and told me to use my powers on humans, not animals. Mom said she'd had a similar premonition and let me practice on her when she fell ill with a cold or the flu or

anytime she got a bruise or scrape. She never lost faith in me. She even helped me sneak into Mr. Fulton's house after he was diagnosed with cancer. We'd sneak into his house during the afternoon while he napped. I'd place my hand on his chest where the tumor was and repeat the same words I had over Brutus years earlier. But no healing ever took place.

My most disappointing, unsuccessful attempt was last April. Mom had a stroke while washing the double-wide. By the time I found her lying on the ground, the sponge in her hand was dry. She wasn't breathing and didn't have a pulse. I tried to heal her for hours until my head ached. I said the words over and over and over. I asked Jesus to show me how to do it again and again and again. Finally, in tears, I called an ambulance. Mom was buried three days later. I read the eulogy. The eighteen members of The Real Church and a couple of ladies from Gerald's Cleaners were the only other attendees.

I had to wash graffiti off her tombstone two days later.

*** *** ***

Mom always said that Jesus does everything, good and bad, at the perfect time. And she was right.

The Bad: I got blistering drunk and questioned my purpose the day after she was buried.

I'd had a beer when I was a fourteen. Back then, it was a rite of passage thing; you know, sneak a beer with a few friends in the alley at lunch to prove you would. But alone inside the church that first night, in the crushing silence, the cases of communion wine stacked in the corner seemed to be calling out to me.

Here we are, delivered and waiting, your own personal ready collection of feel-good healing potion. Give us a chance. Satisfaction guaranteed.

I guess the McKinney family alcoholic monster had been hiding inside me the whole time, lingering below the surface somewhere, waiting for an opportune time to jump up and bite me. Not being able to heal Mom had put me in the perfect emotional and mental state to be attacked.

I canceled that Sunday's service, and every night that week, I sat on Mom's stool in the church, bottle of healing potion in hand, and talked to Jesus.

What had I done wrong? What had she done wrong? Was I delusional about my power? I asked Him if I should close the church, put the warehouse up for sale, and take the double-wide down to Austin or something. Did He want me to leave Dresden and start a new church somewhere else? I didn't know if I could lead The Real Church without Mom anyway. I needed answers. I needed direction. And on the Friday afternoon after Mom's funeral, when no booming voice came forth to answer my slurred questions for the seventh straight day, I smashed a half-empty bottle onto the ground, hopped in my Taurus, and headed for Tom Walter's Realty.

The Good: I crashed into thirteen-year-old Melinda Brown because I leaned over into the passenger's seat to grab a piece of gum.

Fourth Street winds over a series of small hills like a slithering snake. When I rounded the third curve at thirty miles per hour and reached over for the gum, the Taurus drifted onto the shoulder and smacked into Melinda and her

bike. She flipped up onto the hood and violently rolled off when I slammed on the brakes.

I hurried over to her and knelt down. Her eyes were open but unfocused. Blood ran into her thick, black hair from a gash on her forehead. Her purple jacket and jeans were torn, and her left femur poked its splintered tip out of her thigh. Jesus only knows what kind of internal injuries she may have had. I didn't panic. Without hesitation, I placed my right hand on her forehead, my left on her shattered leg.

"Stay still," I told her as her fearful eyes met mine. "I heal you. I heal you because I can. I heal you because you don't deserve this."

She began to writhe under my hand, trying to pull away. I pressed down harder and closed my eyes. "I heal you because Jesus wants me to. I heal you. I heal you."

She let out a soft whimper that sounded a bit both like pleasure and shock as the bones in her leg drifted back into a straight line. She stopped struggling against me and settled down onto the pavement. I opened my eyes just as the gash on her forehead finished closing.

We locked eyes, both in disbelief. She didn't know what had just happened, and I had waited more than eight years for this to happen.

"Are you all right?"

She nodded. Her lips trembled. She glanced at her bike crunched under the Taurus' front tire then back at me.

I stood and reached out to her. She placed her hands in mine, and I pulled her upright. "What's your name?" I asked.

She looked down at her body then back at me. Her hands

were trembling like her lips. "M-M-Melinda. Melinda B-B-Brown."

"Right." I squeezed her hands a little firmer. "I know your mom. Doesn't she work at the Toot 'N' Totum on Third?"

She nodded.

"Nice lady," I said. "You have her skin and eyes."

She eased her hands out of mine, took a step back. "What just happened?"

I smiled for the first time since Mom had died. "I healed you."

"But…how did…you…"

I placed my hands on her shoulders "I'm sorry. I didn't see you."

Her eyes searched me for what felt like hours, days, years. "You're that guy from The Real Church, aren't you?"

I nodded, still smiling.

"And your mom just died."

I nodded again. "Yes."

"Are you really friends with the Devil?"

She'd obviously heard the stories. "No. I'm friends with Jesus."

She just stared.

"Are you sure you feel all right?"

"Yes."

I stepped forward and gave her a good hug. "I've got to go now," I said. "Do you want me to give you a ride home?"

"I was supposed to meet Mom at the store."

"I'll take you there then."

We got into the Taurus. I backed it off of her bike then got

out and put the bike in the trunk. "If you come by the church tomorrow, I'll give you money to go pick out a new one."

"Okay."

I felt her eyes on me as we drove in silence. Eventually, she asked, "Why didn't you call the cops?"

I looked at her then back at the road and sighed. "Because I knew I could heal you," I lied. "And I didn't want either of us to get into trouble."

"Do I need to keep it a secret then?"

I thought about it for a moment. "No. You do what you want."

I parked on the side of the Toot 'N' Totum and popped the trunk. I saw Melinda's mom walk up to the glass door and look at me before heading back to the register. I leaned Melinda's bike against the brick wall. "Remember," I said. "Come by tomorrow, and I'll give you money for a new bike."

"Okay."

She didn't move as I quickly got in the Taurus and left.

I drove out to Lake Meredith in case Melinda's mom turned me in and the cops came looking for me. I parked behind a copse of red oaks, walked down a worn cow path, and sat on the large, round rock in Jasper Cove that Mom and I used to sit on and fish.

Skipping rocks across the calm water, I thought about Brutus, the other animals, Mr. Fulton, Mom, Melinda. What was different? What was the same? I slung rocks for hours, rambling, struggling to understand, to solve. Then, like all good moments of realization and inspiration, like a bolt of lightning from a clear blue sky, it hit me out of nowhere. *I* had

caused Brutus' injuries. *I* had caused Melinda's injuries. And I had healed them. But I hadn't had the slightest impact in the cases where I hadn't caused the injury or illness.

This was it; but how twisted it seemed. I had to cause the injury to fix it? I sat on the edge of the water all night talking to Jesus, devising a plan to test my theory.

*** *** ***

The police never came to question me about Melinda Brown, but two days later, Sunday, she, her mom, two of her aunts and uncles, and couple of the family friends all attended The Real Church. My first day as its outright leader.

After the service (I used one of Mom's old sermons about The Good Samaritan), Ms. Brown approached me and grabbed my hand. "It's true, isn't it, Owen? I can tell just by looking at you."

I nodded. She smiled. "I knew it. Melinda and I have a close bond. And when she told me, and the way she told me, I just knew she was telling the truth. There was no doubt about it."

I smiled back at her. "Let me go get you some money. I promised Melinda a new bike."

"Don't you worry about *that*. There are things in this world way more important than that. We'll get her another bike. You just keep on healing people like the Good Lord wants you to."

"Yes, ma'am," I said. "And thanks for coming today."

"No problem, Sugar." She let go of my hand and placed hers on my chest. "If I have anything to say about it, you'll be seeing a lot more people around here when they hear what

you did for Melinda. The Lord is strong with you, young man. Strong."

That afternoon, as word of the healing spread across Dresden like wildfire, I went and emptied the prairie dog traps I'd placed in the dirt pasture behind the church. I took the animals inside, got out a knife, and started testing.

I stabbed them in the chest and healed them. Cut off their limbs and healed them. Then I took a couple out into the pasture, shot them with Mom's pistol, and healed them. I even poisoned a few with arsenic, and when they started to convulse, I healed them. I got to where I didn't even have to say anything, just lay my hands on them and will what I wanted done.

I'd figured it out.

I know it sounds morbid, heartless, callous, but I assure you that I *did* struggle with plunging the knife in initially. I hadn't harmed one animal since Brutus. What allowed me to do it that day was my devotion to The Real Church, Jesus, and especially Mom. The advice she'd given me when I'd complained about Brutus years earlier found me again as I stood there dagger in hand.

"*Sometimes, people have to suffer in order to help someone else.*"

In this case, it was prairie dogs instead of people, but the basic principle was the same. I'd been hearing and believing in it my whole life. Jesus suffered to help others. The Apostles Paul and Peter suffered to help others. Parents were always suffering to help their kids. Now, I'm not on the Jesus level. I'm not *personally* destined to suffer to help others, but Jesus obviously wanted me to do something along the lines of suffering and helping. And he had already told me that it wasn't supposed to be focused on animals.

*** *** ***

Around 11:20 on the last Wednesday in May, I snuck into Debra's Day Care through the open back kitchen door.

I know what you're thinking: *Children?*

But if I wanted people to come to The Real Church and find salvation, the easiest and quickest way to get them through the door was through their children. Everyone knows that. Besides, the children's suffering would be minimal compared to the amount of good that would come out of it in the long run. And I was certain that none of them would die.

Everyone in Dresden knew that every Wednesday, weather permitting, Debra's Day Care took their twenty-plus kids to Keeler Park for lunch. The park was right across the street from the day care, and around 11:30, Debra and her workers, carrying baggies with sandwiches, bags of chips, and two heaping jugs of Kool-Aid, would march the kids across the street.

Dressed in jogging pants, a T-shirt, and running shoes, I slipped into the kitchen and hunkered down behind a large cutting block. The yellow-shirted workers were corralling the kids, slathering them with sunblock. I assumed the Kool-Aid was already made and chilling in the fridge. I was right. I pulled a baggie of dried, powdered Hedera Helix out of my crotch and split it between the two jugs. I gave each a good swirl, until the powder vanished, then hurried out of the building.

After we moved into the double-wide, Mom and I had begun growing our own vegetables and herbs. She had many books on their healing and poisoning properties, and I learned everything I needed to know to stay healthy and safe. If consumed, the leaves of a Hedera Helix, which can be found pretty easily, will cause stomach pains, labored breathing, vomiting, and in rare cases can result in a coma.

Both excited and terrified, I rushed down the alley, crossed the street to the park a block north of the day care, and started jogging on the track. It was a mile loop. A couple of walking elderly people greeted me as I passed. About ten minutes later, Debra led the kids and other workers to the picnic tables in the shade of an oak tree in the center of the park. They began to eat right away.

I jogged and tried not to watch. A few other joggers had made their way onto the track too. I'd completed two laps when the kids were all released to go play on the swings, teeter-totters, and slides. I slowed, placed my hands behind my head, and started walking. I knew that within twenty minutes, the first symptoms would start to kick in.

When I glanced across the park during my second walking lap, I saw a couple of kids holding their stomachs walk over to Debra and the other workers. A few others by the swings were obviously having trouble breathing. My pace quickened. I needed to make it to the section of track closest to the picnic tables.

By the time I made it there, all the kids but three were huddled around the table, three lying down, two vomiting, and the rest hunching over in pain. Debra was freaking out.

Two of her workers looked like they were beginning to feel nauseous as well.

I took a few steps off the track and yelled, "Is everything all right, Debra?"

Debra didn't answer. She had whipped out her cell phone and was dialing 911. I ran toward the kids.

"What's wrong?" I asked as I slowed and placed my hand on a pig-tailed girl lying on her back on the table.

"We must've gotten food poisoning or something," one of the workers said. She was covered in sweat, panicking. "Everyone's stomach hurts. Some of them can't breathe."

"Don't worry. I can help"

"Are you a doctor?"

"No."

The worker stepped forward. Her eyes searched me hard. "You're that guy from The Real Church, aren't you?"

I nodded.

"Owen. Owen McKinney, right?"

I nodded.

"The Owen who supposedly healed Melinda Brown?"

I nodded again then focused my attention on the little girl. I healed her and moved on the next kid. And the next. And the next. Then I laid hands on Debra and all the workers. Then, just in case, the three kids who said they didn't have any stomach pain or problems breathing. Before the ambulance and police arrived, most of the kids were playing again.

I had to answer questions for almost two hours. I was never a suspect. They couldn't test the Kool-Aid since it had all been drunk, the pitchers rinsed out and filled with water

afterward. And since the kids were all fine, no blood tests were administered. That's small towns for you. The police and most others in Dresden assumed that it was accidental food poisoning.

But what they didn't find accidental was my healing abilities. The following Sunday, so many people showed up at The Real Church that we didn't have enough chairs. People stood along the back wall and sat on the cement floor to hear me talk about how Jesus raised Lazarus from the dead.

So many people hung around to talk to me about the healings after the service that I didn't get to eat lunch until three o'clock.

I know Mom watched everything from Heaven, but I wish she could've been there with me.

*** *** ***

I've healed one other man, Mr. Turner, the owner of Lenny's Liquor Store, after a masked man took a baseball bat to his seventy-year-old legs (supposedly in an attempt to rob him) as he locked up the store late one Saturday. I healed him at the hospital that night. I was there counseling a pregnant nurse who attends my church.

So far, I've had only a few random requests for healings, but I know that eventually, these requests will become more frequent. I did lay hands on those who've asked, and I hope some will heal, but I'll remind those who don't that Jesus didn't heal *everyone* either.

Though The Real Church continues its policy of not asking for donations, we are getting them left and right now. Ms.

Brown has taken over the church's financial and organizational responsibilities. She suggested we use the money to upgrade to a bigger location downtown. I agreed but only on the condition that we wouldn't make it showy or fancy like the G.C.C.s and that we would furnish it with used items, nothing new or colorful.

In two weeks, I'm driving to Dallas with Ms. Brown. She wants me to speak to a group of women from her mother's Catholic church and try to convert them to our side. I'm going even though I would normally never step foot in the place. I've been doing a lot of internet research over the last month, and I think that Dallas is a prime place for a terrorist attack.

Who knows? A horrible fire could torch the hotel we're staying at. Or maybe a homemade explosive will be tossed into a nearby church. Or maybe a car bomb will go off in a high-traffic area. As long as I'm in the proper place when whatever happens happens, I'll heal everyone I can. And think of the possibilities. A healing on that stage, in that media spotlight. The Real Church would springboard to heights unrivaled by the G.C.C.s. Maybe I could even get The Real Church on television—compete with money-hungry, rich fakes like Joyce Meyer and Joel Osteen. How many people could I lead to salvation then?

Finally, everything that Mom and I knew would happen is about to happen.

Something Big. Something Great.

OZYMANDIAS REVISITED

A.S. FOX

GRAVITY'S A FUNNY THING. YOU KNOW IT'S THERE AND you know you're supposed to understand it, but really, you can't. It *is*. Like *I* am. I am the new gravity, baby. And you know what? I'm fucking bored. Bored, bored, bored. Didn't expect that. Didn't expect a lot of things.

Does my name matter? Call me Ozymandias. You know the poem—we all know it. It's the high school bullshit they make you read because they're morally bankrupt, and trying to justify the shit they've done to your world, they offer you this frankly brilliant, ironic self-despair and claim Shelley was warning us. Like hell he was. It's about Shelley and about being brilliant, not about being the arrogant, asshole Ozymandias. Still, call me Oz.

And I quote: "I met a traveler from an antique land who

said: Fuck You." Or something like that.

I live somewhere in a city you know and revere. It's open twenty-four-seven, and you want to be as cool as the kids in the street, wearing black to look like they belong there. I'm an artist but not like any you've known. I sculpt reality. Like those guys in that book by Zelazny. Look it sheep. Only better. I'm subtler, and it takes longer, and the world simply *bends* to my vision. And you don't believe me, by the way, because I don't want you to. Dwell on that for a while.

If you did believe me, well, wouldn't life get real interesting real quick? Nuking my city might take me out—if I didn't know it was coming. Then again, maybe I'm out of town that week. Feel free to wipe out every major city on Earth looking for me. That would make things exciting for a while, and I really need a new thrill.

Ah…superpowers. Supposed to be awesome, right? C'mon; genie in the bottle, three wishes, stranded on a desert island with only ten people, bitten by a radioactive space alien—we've all played the game. Wishing for more wishes? Doesn't work by the way. You get five, and you get them by saving a magic fish in Lake Michigan. Not really, but it sounds better than what happened to me. Let's just say I did some research and found a book, which led me to a few other books. Let's for sake of argument pretend Alexandretta did burn to the crisp you were led to believe, and some of the ancient texts survived. And for argument's sake, let's assume some dick—we'll call him Ozzy—pieces together all that conspiracy crap and old legends and blah and—voila!—finds the Book. A book *stamped on these lifeless things, The hand that mocked them, and the heart*

that fed. The one that really grants wishes.

I got what I wanted. Which is not what I asked for by the way. Ever wonder what Hell looks like? It looks like a suburban Thursday night, where you can score as much coke, meth, girls, and danger as your body can endure and come away unscathed. It means crashing your car, killing six pedestrians, and having the cop thank you for sticking around to sign the accident report. It means fucking every girl you ever wanted, hated, or noticed or who put you down or screwed your best friend and then fucking their moms, sisters, daughters, and hot exchange student friends visiting from Europe. Imagine me: my cool face in the mirror *Half sunk, a shattered visage lies, whose frown, And wrinkled lip, and sneer of cold command.*

Everything and nothing, and no one and everyone matters. I simply have to will it, and sooner or later, it happens. There are no consequences, no limits, no challenges, no enemies, no obstacles. No one left to say, "no." Every woman wants me, every man wants to be me, every cat sits in my lap or pisses off or does that one trick that's soooo cute.

Yesterday, I killed a busload of Brownies on their way to camp and then made the evening news claim they were terrorist drones and publicly decry the grieving parents. Within hours, their houses were gone, they were in the hospital having been stoned (like, with real stones), and I managed to engineer two lynchings. Imagine. And no one came looking for me. I've blown planes out of the air, savaged three islands with Freak Storms of the Millennium. I made it snow in Disneyland in July for two weeks running. Nothing.

Just for fun, I killed everyone who deserved the Rapture.

Really. I mean, why not? They think God is going to take them up in a big trumpet call. Morons. If there was a God, would I be here? I'm immortal now. This shit is forever, and it's getting worse every day. I kill the PM of Russia. Nothing. I cure cancer. Nothing. I make all the elephants shed their tusks and make monkey noises. Nothing.

The Book said—I actually don't remember what it said. It wasn't in English anyway, so what does it matter? Cuneiform if you want to know. Oldest written language. The Epistle of Gilgamesh. You know, the lost manuscript where he achieves immortality after telling Inanna to go fuck herself? Complete with instructions. All you have to do is speak a few dead languages and know where to look. Hint—it's not in Egypt, asshole. It's not even near the Levant. Everyone looks there. *Of that colossal wreck, boundless and bare, The lone and level sands stretch far away.* News flash, asshole, you're looking in the wrong place.

Did I mention the Rapture? Funny part is, the bubba preachers all stayed. I only killed like, two million people worldwide: true and faithful believers. The rest of them got to stay. Suck on that, Billy Graham. I am the new light, and you'll worship me whenever I want you to. Or die or dance or shoot your neighbor or dress your dog up as Stalin. It's whatever I want, whenever I want.

Only what do you want when you can have anything? I had this kind of thing for my professor. Let's call her Natalie because, well, her name is—get this—Natalie. She was smart, gorgeous, and—I had to assume—a total freak in bed. It was the way she sucked on her pen caps when she was thinking.

She taught me cuneiform, and I think she knew what I was hunting. Anyway, here's me, skinny as hell, tall, pimply, and haven't seen the sun in years, totally hot for teacher. Know what happens after your drink the Elixir of Life and grasp the Mantel of the Stars? Anything you damn please.

Natalie happens. I was coming back from Place X. That's all you get, asshole. Go find it yourself. I came through Paris and had this kind of amazing frisson going. I sort of hoped that maybe I could work up the nerve to call her. I didn't quite understand what I had done yet. The books don't explain what it means to be a god, only how to become one. If they did, well, who'd do such a stupid thing?

She's there, in the airport, kind of hanging out in open sight, wearing this really clingy red dress. Just happens to be on vacation, her flight canceled due to a freak tornado, and she's caught between Barcelona and Singapore. She's there, and I'm thrilled to see her. Can't bring myself to admit I stole the cookie from the cookie jar. Just want to—you know—have a drink, soak up her dress, ogle her nipples, and kind of feel like a lucky kid who won the school lottery.

She's everything I dreamt. *Exactly like I dreamt.* For four days, we break the hotel bed, shatter two mirrors, light a bar on fire in the Rue du Faubourg Saint-Honoré (say that nine times fast), and have the BEST time ever. She's in love with me, always has been, and wants to be my everything, but you know, no pressure, and would you like a blowjob before or after I bring you a hot buttered croissant? She's so much the thing I wanted and needed. The weather is perfect every day, the lights twinkle just right, and it's going better than I could ever have imagined it. The world has started to yield to my hand: *Tell that its sculptor well those passions read, Which yet survive.*

Then I tell her. I expect a fight. Something. She just says, "I know," and proceeds to undress and make love to me like a storm rising over the Mediterranean. It's magical and terrifying, and my body drowns in the ecstasy. But not totally, you know. There's a piece of me, the controlling bastard who pored over thousands of pages of dead books looking for scraps of Gilgamesh. He's not having any of this, and he's the one inside me. So I almost drown in the ecstasy but have total control and don't succumb, don't fall prey to her wiles, don't break or stumble or make an ass of myself. I get it right. Every time. Do you know what it's like to never make a mistake? To not want to make a mistake and be able to mold all of time and space to ensure it?

Three weeks in, I realize she laughs at all my jokes. Even ones I make up to test her. Whatever I want, I can have. We have sex in public, and I get an ovation. We overdose on heroin and wake up healthier. We want to find this one book by Alexandre Dumas, fils, supposedly the revised Musketeer novella, the last taste of the Father and his magic. We find it just where and how I expected. The dust looked right, the bookseller was the right kind of old, ignorant, run-down, Parisian scumbag I wanted him to be. We made love reading pages from the book.

And I knew. I knew I could make it rain or snow or shine. I knew Natalie would love me forever just as I wanted her to and how I wanted. Because I wanted it. She was mine because I willed it. And the whole of the law shall be rule in

Hell rather than suck dick in Heaven. Seriously. I have it all.

So I killed her. I took the hotel's fire axe and told her I was going to murder her. She lay on the bed and let me, thanking me as I hacked her to pieces because I wanted it. The hotel gave me a new room and apologized for the hassle. I burned the book because I could.

Ever wonder what it takes to be the best at what you do? Think about the pinnacle of human achievement, those obsessive, power-mongering, demented geniuses who really did stuff. Fuck Einstein. I mean Genghis Khan and Richelieu and Picasso: men who forged a new consciousness or nation or ideal or mentality. Guys like me. I found the well of souls and drank. I had it all figured out and missed the point. The guy who finds the well of souls is by definition the *kind* of man who can find the well of souls.

You think—right, Indiana Jones. Not a bad guess, but let's examine that notion. This dick travels the world killing people and stealing stuff. He tricks his old teenage lover into helping him desecrate a scared tomb and steal the most valued and beloved artifact of the One True God. For glory and money. So yes, I am just like Indiana Jones.

How many people did I kill before I got to the place? I see what you did there, and I like it. Questions are did you do it because I wanted you to, and do I like you because I made you that way? I killed exactly two people before becoming immortal: my parents. They were old, I was broke, and the nursing home was eating into what little equity we had in the family home. So I added some pills to Mom and Pop's noon meal; made sure they had a glass of wine at dinner; and, like a good son, was on hand to grieve their natural deaths at the ripe age of seventy and sixty-five—two people who had maybe three years of shitting in their pants and drooling over Wopner and Donahue reruns. Seriously—Donahue? How is that even on?

Three years of indignity and suffering, and I helped them walk away a little early. Took the cash and went south, then east, then to my little wall, bricked in from the sands and jungle and rivers of blood. Like I'll tell you where it is. Give up already. But it nagged me. That I did it for me and not them, that I killed my own parents, that I had never really appreciated or loved them enough. That, you know, I was, deep down, an undeserving asshole. There's no one left now to tell me I still am.

That's who finds it. People who are sufficiently broken that they would have superpowers anyway. Batman and Iron Man and Zorro. Motherfuckers with a grudge and an obsession and some tragic backstory so you ignore the horrible things they do mainly because Natalie isn't sucking them dry and keeping them busy.

One time, I made a three-day Donahue marathon play on every set in Mexico. Didn't even make the news. *I met a traveler from an antique land, Who said:* Donahue for everyone.

Doesn't matter, and you can't prove it. That should bother you, but it's not going to. You are not here, these are not the droids you're looking for, move along. I change movie plots. Was bored so I went to see a Star Wars marathon, and Jar Jar Binks got wasted ten minutes into the first episode. It was glorious until I found out no one knew who he was. Wikipedia listed him as a minor character, and that amazing cartoon with Lucas firing Jar Jar—I erased it by mistake.

I fucked up the world in an Ohio movie theater. The Bible is missing three books, and I can't remember what they were to add them back. TL; DR. Stefan Keppelberg, the most famous American of all time? No one knows who the fucker is or what he did. Walked on the Moon for Apollo 19. Claimed it for the world and was arrested for un-American activities. Ended manned spaceflight for generations because he was, you know, a hippie and believed in the world. I hated him as a kid mainly because my dad was a Korean War vet and claimed Kep had cost him a platoon with "his little propaganda stunt." I erased him just to see if I could.

But I can't seem to put it all back. It makes me wonder. I can do any amount of damage I want. I erase and desecrate and destroy at will. But I can't add back what I took away. Not properly. I tried six times to get Kep back in the scene, as it were, and every time, it got worse, and the world distorted some more. Every god has his limits, and I am apparently gravity: good and bad. I warp the world, and it bows to me. But I leave it warped, and I can't make it new again.

Want to know the worst part? I really enjoyed killing Natalie. Just like it feels good to wipe out school buses and convention centers. I should hate it, should feel badly about the loss of life. But I feel good because that's what I wanted. I feel no guilt, sin, or sense of limitation or transgression. The infusion of power stripped away my humanity, which pretty much means feeling afraid, dirty, guilty, and unworthy as well as not knowing what will happen: being out of control and made to suffer the whims of fate. Who wants that? To be a loser, to be weak, to die, to know you're going to slave away, end up being some blip on the radar and die alone, shitting your shorts in some smelly home? Your kids will despise you. I know. I can read minds, and they do. They think you're a joke.

Would it have worked out with Natalie if I had not read the inscription? Or if I had brought her with me? Or took a left on Highway 6 all those years ago? I raised her from the dead, you know. Twenty-eight times. Every time a little different, a little more warped, the sex a little dirtier and the kink just a notch twistier. We talk about it. She's of the opinion that the soul being eternal, she endures. That Natalie of then would not have wanted me. Did I want her to say that? And you know what? She knows I am going to kill her, and she knows I will love every minute of it, and it doesn't bother me. It doesn't bother me. It bores me.

I killed the pope. I stabbed Lady Gaga. I fucked Hillary and car-bombed John Scalzi and raped a cheetah at the zoo. Bored. I started a TV station in Jerusalem broadcasting this new religion. I took the worst parts of every major faith. I call it New Manichaeism. I tell people I'm Mani reborn but now with messianic powers. I hurl threats at world leaders and predict deaths. Sometimes, I curse them on air. They still haven't nuked Jerusalem—not that I'm there, mind you. After I snuffed the King of Siam and the PM of Brasil, I got three million fresh hits on Google Plus and a congratulatory call from the G11. I erased Italy for the fun of it—used to be the G12. Serves 'em right for sucking at football. *I met a traveler from an antique land, Who said:* screw Italy.

*** *** ***

Call me Ozymandias. You know the poem. Or you will until I erase that shit too. Go ahead; stop me. You can't. If anything, you'll thank me. Even if I want you to hate me, some part of me, some wonderful, dark, squishy, lizard-brained instinct cries out for worship and obedience. Oh, my slaves, I own you all. Natalie has me reading the Gnostic gospels, says it will help me as I transition. Into what, I wonder? I have all the time in the world really. But then, if I burn down the whole planet, will I endure? Boil the seas, kill the grass, cut down the children with radiation and pollution and plague. Sounds almost worth doing. I am the new gravity, baby. And the new gravity is fucking bored. Bored, bored, bored. So watch this…
Look on my works, ye Mighty, and despair: Nothing beside remains.

ENLIGHTENED BY SIN

JASON M. TUCKER

"I KNOW THE BAD THINGS YOU'VE DONE. I KNOW THE horrible things you are *going* to do. Your fear betrays you. I can smell the blackness on your soul, and I see your inhumanity flash in my mind's eye. You can't hide your corruption. No one can. And *that's* why you have to die," Victor Ives said.

He'd said those words in the same order and with the same inflection a hundred times over. It was ritual. The incantation of death was a staple of the funerary rites he'd developed. The words provided him with peace when nothing else would.

Through all the years of using his dark Aberrant power to root out the worst humanity offered, he clung to those words as a form of salvation. The words didn't mean anything. They simply helped him sleep unburdened. He didn't know what his victims thought about it. He'd never asked. He doubted they were fans. Especially when the cutting began.

Victor squatted down in front of his latest catch.

Sweat slithered off the man who lay bound and gagged near the drain on the sloping, concrete floor. He strained against the far-too-tight plastic zip ties around his bloodied wrists and ankles. He was a large man, heavily muscled and thoroughly pierced with nose rings, lip rings, eyebrow rings, and every other ring known to humankind. His name was Xavier Ford, and he was rotten from the top of his bald, tattooed pate to the bottom of his fake snakeskin boots.

Ford had worked for Doctor Z, a drug dealer who also happened to be an Aberrant. Z had the ability to manipulate the minds of those around him, effectively turning them into zombies. Doctor Z also had a penchant for little kids, and Ford was the non-powered human gopher who would find them and bring them to the not-so-good doctor.

Victor had made Z disappear last month.

Now, it was Ford's turn.

Victor grabbed several skewers and a cleaver from his worktable. "I want you to know this is going to hurt."

*** *** ***

Victor didn't revel in Ford's final breath. He found no joy in the act of murder. Yet the power within him seemed to need those deaths. It was necessary.

He turned on his computer and found his favorite internet radio station. He listened while he went about the grisly task of dealing with Ford's remains. Making a body vanish was no magic trick. It involved cutting, burning, dissolving, and

a terrible amount of time spent cleaning the walls and floor of the Chamber in the sub-subbasement of his home.

Music helped. He loved oldies and the innocence so many of those songs possessed. Billie Holiday sang "Night and Day" followed by Patsy Cline's "I Fall to Pieces," which gave Victor a laugh as he continued to saw into Ford. Good working music.

Patsy's voice faded from the speakers and Miss Olivia, the late-night DJ, cut in with her voice of silk and honey. He smiled when he heard her. Unbeknownst to Miss Olivia, she'd accompanied him on his nighttime hunts via the radio in his car and spoke to him during the dismemberments in the Chamber for nearly five years now.

Only this time, her words set him on edge.

Victor stopped sawing and listened to the buttery-voiced DJ read from the newswire. Apparently, Red Dahlia had once again issued a cryptic threat. Dahlia was already responsible for the murders of at least thirty-eight men and women as well as vicious assaults on at least twice that many. All of the victims were wealthy. They were politicians, executives, celebrities. Their wealth and influence seemed to be the only connection they shared. Red Dahlia was dangerous, and she always followed through with her threats. More people were going to die.

Victor would give anything to get Red Dahlia into his Chamber.

"Not to worry, my insomniac zombies, the valorous Captain Justice has vowed to unmask Red Dahlia and put an end to her 'reign of blood,' as he calls it," Miss Olivia said to her audience. "Justice announced this at a ribbon-cutting

ceremony of his corporate sponsor, Bishop Security. It looks like we can all rest easy with one of the nation's *top heroes* on the job."

Victor detected several gallons of sarcasm dripping from Miss Olivia's words. He couldn't blame her for feeling that way. Hell, he felt the same thing toward Justice and the parade of Aberrants in their four-color tights and unwieldy capes.

Most of the "heroes" were media whores, useless puppets tap dancing for dollars, doing whatever it took to enhance their own brand and align with the company that could pay the most. Just because a man could fly or bat missiles out of the sky didn't mean that Victor wanted to buy cereal from him. Just because a woman could shoot fire from her palms or call down lighting from the sky didn't mean Victor trusted her advice on choosing a cell phone plan. Even politicians courted Aberrant heroes now, trotting them out on their campaign trails. What could go wrong there?

In Africa, entire villages could fall to a warlord's tyranny. Monks in Tibet could have their heads lopped off simply because they defied their government. Rapists, murderers, and molesters all walked free while Aberrant shills smiled and showed off for the cameras and their corporate masters. The sad part was that the underwear-on-the-outside league and their supporters actually thought they made a difference.

Fuck them. Hero was a subjective term. Victor was doing the real work, the dirty work of keeping the streets clean.

He went back to cutting with renewed vigor.

*** *** ***

"Why the sudden interest in Red Dahlia?" Margie Greer asked, tilting her head as though she were trying to understand the ravings of a toddler on a sugar high. She was the editor of *Angel City Beat*, the small newspaper where Victor worked.

"It's important," Victor said. He took a seat in the editor's cramped office. Tall columns of old magazines, yellowing issues of the paper, and other detritus threatened to topple if he breathed too hard. He hated to think what would happen to Margie in the event of an earthquake. "I think a new angle on Dahlia would help since she's back in the news."

Margie Greer was a pleasant enough woman. A bit like a graying toad with her wide lips and watery, oversized eyes that seemed even larger behind her thick glasses. She'd never done anything bad enough to warrant attention from Victor's nighttime pursuits. She'd cut people off in traffic with glee, and she lied about sneaking Metamucil into her husband's orange juice, but other than that, her bad deeds were minor. He couldn't see any major sins in her future either. She was one of the few people he trusted. He even liked her, which was more than he could say about most.

"You write local flavor," she said, adjusting her glasses. She leaned away from her ancient, wooden desk. Her chair groaned, and she matched it's timbre with her own sigh. "Dahlia is the crime desk territory."

"That's only because people go with the crime angle," Victor said. He had a feeling she would say this, so he'd prepared his counterargument when he was putting the final touches on making Ford's body disappear. "People spend time looking at the criminal aspect, focusing on Red Dahlia. I want

to learn more about her victims and their families. I want to see how they are coping now."

Margie sighed once again, a bit louder than Victor thought necessary. "You're right. I think that's a good angle. But I can't promise we'll run it. I really don't know how much you can find. Write the piece, and we'll go from there. I just don't want it to look like the paper is…"

"Profiting off the misery of others now that Dahlia made a new threat? The media would *never* do that," Victor said. When he saw the disapproving look on Margie's face, he quickly added, "I'll be very tactful. The last thing I would want to do is to cause those people more pain."

"Exactly," Margie said. "You might find something of use in the online archives, but from what I understand, most of the ones lucky enough to survive an assault by Red Dahlia went into hiding or are in protective custody under heavy security. It's going to take some digging."

"I'm a reporter. I like digging," Victor said, smiling. He didn't care about getting a story for the paper. He only wanted firsthand information on Red Dahlia.

*** *** ***

One victim didn't fit the pattern. He was neither wealthy nor famous. The good news was that he wasn't dead, and it didn't take an extraordinary amount of digging for Victor to find him. It was only a short drive to the victim's current location.

Victor stepped into the lobby of Golden Acres, an upscale, convalescent home on the outskirts of Angel City. The interior of the massive, three-story stone building was clean and antiseptic with an overpowering smell of fresh Band-Aids and more than a hint of despair. Convalescent was a misnomer. No one was recuperating here; this was where people came to wait out their deaths. It didn't matter how nice the place looked.

His shoes squeaked on the black and white tile as he made his way across to the desk, where he found a bored-looking man hunched over a computer monitor. His plastic nametag denoted him as Lonnie. His hair was tidy if a bit long, but his eyebrows had the look of untamed wildness about them. The razor had missed a few hairs on Lonnie's face, and they made Victor think of solitary cacti spread across a desert of flesh. Victor concluded that the man didn't really like grooming and the only reason he did so was to keep his job.

"What's up?" Lonnie asked.

Very professional too, Victor noted. "I called this morning. I'm here to see Tobias Clay."

"Which guy are you?" Lonnie spun slightly in his chair to face his monitor and keyboard, hands poised over the keys.

"Victor Ives from the *Angel City Beat*," he said, wondering at Lonnie's words. As far as Victor knew, Clay didn't have any living family. He pulled out his ID and showed it to Lonnie. "Someone else supposed to see Mr. Clay today?"

"Yeah," Lonnie said. He pressed a key and then grabbed a guest pass from a drawer. "Mr. Clay's got a busy schedule today."

"Any idea of who might be coming for a visit?"

"He doesn't get many people who come to see him. Only reason I remember at all is because it's so rare for anyone to

visit him," Lonnie said.

"What do you remember?" He hoped Lonnie wouldn't want a bribe. Victor was already down to eating Top Ramen for dinner. Cleaning supplies didn't pay for themselves.

"Guy called himself Arby on the phone. Said he'd be by around noon. Mean anything to you?" Lonnie asked.

"Not at all," Victor said, snatching the guest pass and smiling. Even if it did, he wouldn't share that information. And what the hell kind of name was Arby? "Thanks."

"Hey, be careful that you don't stare," Lonnie said in a conspiratorial whisper. "I don't think he likes it when people stare."

"Most people don't, Lonnie," Victor said.

*** *** ***

"I presume you are the newspaperman. I thought they got rid of newspapers now that everyone is reading everything on their phones," Tobias Clay said without a trace of humor. He was sitting in a tan recliner in the corner of his large, brightly lit room.

Clay was a small man, and he looked at least forty years older than his actual age of thirty-three. Wisps of white hair, neglected and uncombed, jutted up in random patches around his head. His blue polo shirt hung limply off his skeletal body. The surname of Clay was unfortunately apt. He looked as though a mad sculptor had tried to rework him. Angry, white scars covered his body. His blue eyes were barely visible beneath the rough tissue. One ear was missing, replaced by puckered flesh that looked strangely like a withered, peach-

colored rose. Not staring proved to be more difficult that Victor had thought.

"We have a website now," Victor offered. "Well, we have one when it's working properly."

"Good for you," Clay said. He gestured for Victor to take a seat opposite him. Victor's chair seemed newer, and the color was quite a bit darker.

Victor sat and scanned the room. Clay's quarters were large, at least three times the size of Victor's own little house. It featured all of the modern conveniences: wall-sized television, sound system, plush furnishings, and a wet bar. It was more a penthouse than a convalescent's room.

"I'm glad you agreed to meet with me. I know that you must not like talking about what happened with Red Dahlia. I can only imagine how horrible it must have been," Victor said.

"You have no idea," Clay said. His eyes, already little slits with bright blue peeking out, narrowed further.

"I'm here to learn your story and how you've been coping with—" Victor began to say. Clay cut him off.

"You are an Aberrant," Clay said.

Victor opened his mouth to protest the ridiculousness of such a statement even though it was entirely accurate. Clay raised a hand to stop him.

"I know an Aberrant when I see one. That is my gift. It is the thing that got me into this mess," Clay said. He shook his head. "No need to worry. Secrets are sacred. I know that all too well."

"I'm just here to talk about what happened with Red Dahlia," Victor said. "You don't fit the typical profile of her

other victims. You were an accountant. The others were high profile. What made her target you?"

"What makes you care?"

"I just want to know what happened," Victor said. He didn't like how Clay seemed to be looking *into* him.

"She is not the source," Clay said. "Even if you could find her, and I know that's what you want, she is deadly and quicker than most."

"How did you survive?"

"She did not want to kill me," Clay said. He turned his head to gaze out the window and onto the large lawn at the front of the property. "Dahlia is bloodthirsty. But she was just teaching me a lesson about keeping secrets."

"What was your relationship with Dahlia?"

"I suppose we will get to that soon enough," Clay said. "Tell me your true intentions first."

"I'm going to stop her," Victor said.

Clay's mouth curved into a semblance of a grin. He got up from his chair slowly, and to Victor, it looked as though Clay was in pain. He limped toward the wet bar. "Can I fix you a drink?"

"No," Victor said. "I just want to know about Dahlia." He thought about just reaching out with his power and reading Clay. It would be easy. Readings took only a few seconds. But if he weren't careful, a reading could render a person, even an Aberrant, unconscious.

"That is the reason I agreed to meet you, Newspaperman," Clay said. He grabbed a tumbler and filled it with an amber liquid. "I have decided to divulge some of the secrets I was sworn to keep, sacred or not. And I have to do it before he shows up."

"Who are you talking about?" Victor asked. He thought it must be the man called Arby and wondered if he had something to do with Dahlia.

"The man who pays for this place and who pays for my silence. An ex-accountant could not pay for this. Don't worry. It'll all become clear. And you won't even have to use any powers on me," Clay said. He winked. Or at least Victor thought he winked. Clay's scars made it difficult to tell.

"Will this lead me to Red Dahlia?"

"You focus on the wrong monster. She is just the blade. You need to take down the hand that wields it."

"The man who bought you," Victor said.

Clay nodded and downed the shot of whiskey. He licked his cracked, scarred lips. "You ready for a story?"

*** *** ***

Clay leaned against the bar with the empty glass in his hand. He stared out the window and seemed to be elsewhere.

"I worked for Bishop, but I was more than an accountant. I worked as a seeker using my ability to find others with powers. He wanted me to find him an Aberrant he could mold, someone he could buy to do some unseemly things."

"You're saying *Bishop* is the one paying for all of this? Bishop has something to do with Red Dahlia?" Victor asked, gesturing to the room. Then it hit him. Arby wasn't a name. It was R.B., the initials of one Reginald Bishop, CEO of Bishop Industries. That's who was coming to see Clay later.

"He's coming here today?"

"Do you want to hear the story, or do you want to interrupt?" Clay asked. "As I was saying, he was looking for someone to do his dirty deeds. We found her and came up with an agreeable financial arrangement. He hired Red Dahlia although that wasn't her name at the time. She is a sociopath although she masks it better than most. She strikes at high-profile targets given her by Bishop. He tells her when and where to kill. It was a good arrangement for her. He even helped her find a regular job."

"Unbelievable," Victor whispered. "People trust Bishop and his company."

"Of course they do. Dahlia targets the wealthy. People see this, and they decide to install the high-tech security bots from Bishop. Dahlia has never killed anyone who has a Bishop Security Bot. He makes countless millions on sales, upgrades, and upkeep. Every time Dahlia strikes, demand for the security bots rises, and he makes more money. Not only that, but his bots act as spies, funneling him information on his clients that he can sell."

"Why would he do that?"

"The same reason men and women do anything in this world. They want to control and dominate. They want power and money. It has always been this way, and it always will be. I'm just tired of keeping it all in. It has to stop."

"Why didn't he kill you?"

"He thought he might still need me at some point. Not many people can spot Aberrants in a crowd and know the extent of their abilities."

"So you know my power?" His stomach roiled at the thought of someone knowing what he was and what he did. His heartbeat quickened, and he felt heat rise in his face.

"I know your power, and I know how it works. You are the red right hand of God."

"I think I probably work for the guy who lives a bit further south."

Clay laughed and poured himself another drink. "I do not believe that. You cull this world of rot."

"Doesn't change the fact that I'm a murderer, does it? It doesn't change the fact that my power compels me to do these things. It needs to be let out, and this is the only way I know how."

"It is the struggle of right and wrong that everyone feels. It is a shame I did not find you instead of Dahlia back then. You might have been able to stop us a long time ago," said Clay, a wistful tone in his voice. "Are you going to kill me now for the secrets I've kept?"

"You don't seem frightened," Victor said.

Clay shrugged.

"I'm not going to kill you," Victor said. Clay was nothing more than Bishop's research tool. Reginald Bishop was the mastermind, and Dahlia was the murderer.

"Bishop monitors my calls and visitors. He knows you are here and that you are a reporter. He always travels with at least two of his security bots. You might be able to render a person unconscious when you read them, but your power is not going to be able to do much to the bots. And even then, there is the matter of the—"

"How do I get around them?" Victor asked more to himself than to Clay.

"You would not be able to."

"I have to," Victor said. His mind spun trying to come up with ruses to let him at Bishop.

"You will. I will send him after you. He may kill me. Maybe make it look like an accident. Or he will send Dahlia to finish the job," Clay said. "I deserve no better."

"You said he's always with bots."

"Bishop always has bots with him. Captain Justice does not. Justice is the one who will find you."

"What's Captain Justice got to do with anything?"

"Come on," Clay said. "How often have you seen Bishop and Captain Justice in the same place?"

"Bishop is Captain Justice? He's an Aberrant?"

Clay laughed. "He might be Captain Justice, but his powers are not of the Aberrant sort. An off-world biomechanical rig fused to his body lets him fly, gives him his strength and his other powers. It bonds with the wearer and rebuilds itself when damaged. It even repairs the wearer with some type of nanotechnology."

"Off-world," Victor whispered. "You mean alien?"

"Maybe," Clay said, shrugging. "It could be something he took from another dimension. All I know is that it is not his tech, and he has not been able to replicate it."

"Christ, this is weird," said Victor. This morning, he'd just wanted to find a serial killer. Now, he was worrying about a madman with a cape and nanotechnology.

"This is the big leagues," Clay said. "If I know Bishop,

he will come after you in the guise of Captain Justice when you are alone. He will try to take you out quickly. You have to be ready."

"I can do that," Victor said although he wondered if he really could. Clay was right when he said this was the big leagues, and Captain Justice was definitely one of the heavy hitters.

"If you succeed and people find out it was you that killed Captain Justice, they'll brand you a villain. You realize that, do you not?"

"Yeah, I understand." As much as he hated the way Captain Justice was a part of corporate and pop culture and as much as he now hated Bishop, a part of Victor felt hollow. Justice was a symbol that people loved and revered. Killing him would have unintended consequences.

But Justice was no hero.

"Before I go," Victor said as he left his seat, "tell me Red Dahlia's name."

*** *** ***

Victor nursed a bottle of cheap beer and watched the drowning sun. Silver flashes of light sparkled against the deep orange as the great orb dipped into the Pacific.

The view from the kitchen of his small, inherited house atop a hill overlooking Angel City was quite beautiful most days. He hardly noticed now. Night was on its way, and Victor waited for one of the world's most powerful heroes to come and kill him over money and power of all things. Maybe Clay was right. Maybe they were the only things that mattered.

Against the backdrop of the multihued sky, a small, silhouetted shape streaked toward the house. The shape grew larger as it came closer. It was time.

Victor opened the sliding glass door that led from the kitchen to the back patio. No reason to let Captain Justice break an expensive piece of glass.

The flying man slowed as he neared. He landed gracefully on the patio, his crimson cape billowing slightly as he did. The rest of his costume was a mixture of red, white, and blue stripes. His square jaw jutted out from the star-spangled mask. The suit was snug on his muscular frame, and Victor suddenly realized that he hadn't known just how large Captain Justice was. Justice strode through the opened door and into the kitchen.

"Hello, Mr. Bishop. I wanted to tell you that Captain Justice is a horribly clichéd name, and it isn't even accurate in your case. Also, the initials of your company are BS. Did you even think about that?" Victor asked.

The caped hero didn't seem bothered that Victor knew his identity, so Victor continued. "Are you going to start some long-winded speech now? That's what the villains in all of the old comic books would—"

Something crashed into Victor's left shoulder, and he quickly realized it was one of Justice's fists. The blow happened so quickly he didn't have time to register that Captain Justice had bridged the distance and was getting ready to kill him. He could barely move his numbed arm.

Captain Justice's other hand snatched Victor's throat.

"Do not speak," Justice said, his voice deep and

commanding. He began to squeeze. "I've laid waste to the world's most powerful Aberrants. What could you possibly do?"

Victor clawed at the vice-like fingers around his neck with his good hand. The grip was unbreakable. Trying to match strength with Justice was impossible. The world seemed to darken. If he didn't act, he would die.

Victor reached out with his power. Tendrils of inky black smoke leaped from Victor's chest and wrapped around Captain Justice's face.

The strength of the grip faded. He continued to focus on Captain Justice, whose eyes began to roll up into the back of his head. Then the visions, the worst things the man had done in his life, came rushing into Victor's mind.

As a child, Bishop pushed his twin brother off a cliff. Victor heard Bishop's brother scream as he fell. Victor saw Bishop twisting a phone cord around the neck of a man caught trying to steal information from his databases. Victor listened to the man's dying gasps. A hundred such atrocities rushed at Victor from the past and the future. They were there and gone in a flash. Then he saw Bishop and Clay standing before a woman dressed in tight, blood-dark leather. A similarly hued mask covered all but her lips, pale and delicate chin, and hazel eyes. Red Dahlia. She spoke in a silky voice, agreeing to Bishop's terms for murder.

The visions ended. He'd seen enough to feel justification in what was to come.

Victor didn't know how long Captain Justice would be unconscious. It varied from person to person. Humans could be out for as much as five or ten minutes. Invasion into the

most private and horrible thoughts was not something that the mind or the body took well. Aberrants were usually only out for less than a minute. Even though Bishop was human, the otherworldly rig he supposedly wore might mean that he would regain consciousness sooner.

There would be no time to take Justice into the Chamber. Victor grabbed the sharpest knife from the block on the kitchen countertop. He knelt over the fallen man and began to cut away the red, white and blue suit. It was difficult with his numb arm, and the suit was not a normal fabric. It seemed to emanate from the rig beneath. It tried to grow back until he started in on the rig.

With the suit gone, it was no longer Captain Justice on the floor. It was just Bishop.

The rig was a thin membrane of connected, pulsing, luminescent wires and nodes on Bishop's chest. It almost seemed a living thing. He began slowly unfastening the rig. It was delicate work, but he was able to remove it. He set the rig aside and focused on Bishop.

He returned to the kitchen drawer and grabbed plastic zip ties to bind Bishop's hands and feet. He'd just finished zipping the ties when Bishop started to come around.

"What did you do to me?" Bishop asked.

Victor picked up the knife from where it lay among the tattered remains of the Captain Justice uniform. "I saw you for what you are. And really, it's more about what I'm going to do to you now."

"We can work something out," Bishop said. He struggled against the ties, but he seemed to realize very quickly that his

power was gone. "I'm a very wealthy man."

Victor leaned over him, the knife poised to strike. He definitely wasn't going to write about this in *Angel City Beat*.

"I know the bad things you've done. I know the horrible things you are *going* to do. Your fear betrays you. I can smell the blackness on your soul, and I see your inhumanity flash in my mind's eye. You can't hide your corruption. No one can. And *that's* why you have to die."

*** *** ***

Victor didn't know why, but he tried the rig. Something within him, perhaps the darkness of his Aberrant nature, told him that he must.

The rig adjusted to fit him. Microscopic filaments burrowed into his tissue, sending electrical surges to every cell in his body. The pain quickly gave way to pleasure as the rig's unnatural power shot through him.

A bodysuit made of similar material to the one he'd cut off Captain Justice began to spread out from the rig and cover his body. No trace of red, white or blue. Victor's suit was a shimmering, liquid black. The suit looked similar to the ebony tendrils of his natural Aberrant power. He was happy to see there was no cape.

Power was a damned thing. He could be a dark god or a shining hero. He did not know where he would fall.

He did know one thing.

Miss Olivia, with her silky smooth voice and murderous crimson ways, was going to spend one more evening with him.

He knew the bad things she'd done…

BEDTIME STORY

PETER CLINES

DAD SET HIS BRIEFCASE DOWN AND STRETCHED. HE SLIPPED his shoes off. His toes grabbed at the carpet through his socks. Fists with the toes, fists with the toes, just like in that movie. Much better than when he used to end each day with a drink. He was reaching for his glasses to set them on the hall table when Mom stepped out at the end of the hall.

"He wanted to wait up for you," she said, "but I told him you were going to be late."

A few more toe clenches. "And?"

"I think he's still awake."

"He's a growing boy, hon. He needs his rest."

"I know. But there are some things you just can't get a seven-year-old to do. No one can."

Dad's mouth formed a half-smile. It was an expression

that conceded she was right but still refused to admit defeat. He gave her a kiss, clenched his toes twice more, and headed down the hall to Bobby's bedroom.

LEGO bricks covered the floor like so many small booby traps, and action figures sprawled across the undersized desk. A red-white-and-blue sneaker sat in the doorway while the other had made it halfway to the bed. As usual, in the last hour before bedtime, his son had displayed an amazing ability to wreak havoc and undo the day's cleaning.

The boy himself was sprawled across the mattress, not so much in the bed as on it. A pile of sheets and blankets by his feet showed his struggle to get under the covers. One arm was stretched out toward Mister Teddy, the well-worn bear he insisted he didn't need to get to sleep anymore.

Dad bent down and tugged the sheet up to Bobby's shoulder blades. The blanket came up next, just a bit lower, and he folded the sheet down over the edge so it wouldn't scratch during the night. He brushed a few strands of hair aside and kissed his son on the forehead. He lingered for a moment. The boy's skin was warm and smooth. Still so much like a baby.

The boy shifted, stretched, rolled over. "Dad?"

He tousled Bobby's head. Most of his hair was brown at this point, but a few streaks of towhead blond still ran through it. He looked so much smaller and younger than seven. "Hey, kiddo. What's up?"

The little boy sat up and blinked three times. He rubbed at his eyes. "I think one of the teachers said something bad in school today."

Dad smirked. Not a baby anymore. He'd been expecting something like this any day now. He remembered being seven, when he started to notice the off-limit words adults threw around now and then. To be honest, with the way some people spoke, he was a little surprised it had taken so long for this talk to come up. "Which teacher?"

"Miss Richmond."

Dad tried not to frown. He'd met Miss Richmond a few times at school functions. Each time, he'd restrained himself with some help from Mom. It wasn't that surprising to hear the young, overly-liberal teacher had let some profanity slip in front of the children.

He adjusted his glasses and glanced over at Bobby's bookshelf. A long-unopened copy of *Everybody Poops* sat on one of the shelves. He looked at his son. "Which one was it?"

Bobby took in a breath and let out a loud sigh. "Miss Richmond," he repeated. His tone said that his father had just lost a few points on the "smart parent" scale.

Dad smiled. "No," he said, "which bad word. Was it the S word?"

The boy shook his head.

"Was it the F word?" If it was, Dad might need to have a few firm words with Miss Richmond.

Bobby shook his head again.

"Hey," said Mom from the door, "so what's going on in here?"

"His teacher said a bad word today."

"Which one?"

"Miss Richmond," said Dad and Bobby together. Bobby

rolled his eyes at the realization he had two dumb parents.

Mom managed a small laugh and a smile. "Nothing too strong for his sensitive ears, I hope."

"That's what I'm trying to find out," said Dad.

"Not the S word?"

Dad and Bobby both shook their heads. "Not the F word either," Dad said.

Mom furrowed her thin brows. "What's that leave that he'd know? You don't think he knows…" She looked at Bobby. "It wasn't the C word, was it, baby?"

"Mommmmmm," he whined.

"You're always going to be my baby," she said. She leaned forward and kissed him on the head.

Dad patted his son through the blankets. "Okay, kiddo," he said, "do you think you could spell the word she said?"

Bobby frowned and looked at the ceiling. "No," he said after a moment. "There were a lot of them. She said a lot of things. One of the other teachers came in and yelled at her to stop."

Mom's brows went up. "Really?"

"Uh-huh."

Dad looked at his wife, then back to Bobby. "Do you remember some of the things she said? The words?"

His head bobbed up and down. It made his hair flop around. He needed a haircut.

Dad sighed. "Could you say some of them?"

The boy's mouth twisted and he studied his parents. "You won't be mad?"

"Nope."

"I won't get in trouble?"

"You can say them just this one time."

The boy's chin dipped in understanding. "She said none of us were free and that Omnes was evil. That he was one of the bad guys."

Mom gasped and covered her mouth. Dad sat up straight and looked up at his wife. "Are you sure?" asked Dad. "You're sure that's what she said?"

"Yep," said Bobby. "We were talking about the founding fathers, and she said that Omnes was a monster and a bad guy and he took away our ri—"

Dad's finger rushed up and came to rest across the boy's mouth. "You don't have to say anything else," he said. The finger trembled against the boy's lips, so he reached up and mussed his hair again. He took a breath and calmed himself.

Mom wrapped her arms around herself and shivered. "We'll have to call the school," she murmured. "They'll have to get rid of her."

"I'll take care of it," said Dad.

"Let the school take care of it."

Dad glanced back at her. "If the school was going to take care of it, do you think we'd be hearing about it from Bobby? They're going to try to brush it under the rug."

Mom stared at the floor. "I should call the other parents," she said, "and warn them."

"If they haven't heard already," he said.

Bobby set his hand on his father's. "Is it true, Dad?"

He looked Bobby in the eyes. "Is what true?"

"What she said. About Omnes."

The parents looked at each other. Mom crossed her arms and turned to the window. Dad took another slow breath. "Well, he isn't a monster. He's a person, just like you and Mom. And me."

"Really?"

"Yep."

"Than how come he can do all his stuff?" asked Bobby. "I mean, like, he can fly and see really far, and he's super-strong and super-fast, and nothing can hurt him, and he makes lightning with his fists and all that."

Mom's fingers fidgeted against her crossed arms.

"No one knows how he can do all those things," said Dad. "It's like the old movies, where only a few people know how the superhero got his powers."

"Is he a mootant?"

"I don't think so."

"Is he an alien?"

"I doubt it," said Dad, smiling and shaking his head.

"Does he get his powers from his suit or a magic ring or something?"

"No," Mom said. "It's all him. No one can take his powers away from him. They've tried."

Dad glanced back at her then scooted back on the bed so he could see his whole family at once. He tapped his fingers on the back of Bobby's hand. "I think… I think it was just an accident," he told the boy. "I think Omnes didn't want to get powers or expect them. I think one day, something happened to him at work or somewhere. Something that wasn't supposed to happen, like an explosion or a radiation leak. But instead

of getting hurt like most people, it changed him. It gave him his powers and made him into what he is today."

The boy nodded. "A superhero?"

"Yes," said Mom quickly. "A hero." She looked out the window again, up at the sky.

"The best hero," agreed Dad. "A hero for everyone."

Mom nodded without turning her head.

"That's what his name means," said Dad. "It means 'everyone.'"

"Yeah?" asked the boy.

"Yep," said Dad. "He saved the city a dozen times at least and the country two or three times. He even saved your mom once."

"Really?" Bobby's eyes lit up. He looked at his mother for confirmation.

"It was before," she said, and Dad looked up at her from the bed. "It was a long time ago."

"And then," said Dad, "he decided to save the whole world. So he got rid of all the bad people and made everything safe and happy and better for everyone."

"But if Omnes is a hero," said Bobby, "why's so many people scared of him?"

"I don't think anyone's scared of him," said Dad. "It's just…it's complicated."

"Why?"

Mom looked at Dad. Dad looked back at her. Her head trembled, just a small, side-to-side movement.

He sighed and shifted on the bed, careful not to put his weight on the small form under the blanket. "Well," he said.

He let the word hang in the air for a minute, and Mom stared at him. "Well," he said again, "you like orange soda, right?"

Bobby's hair flopped back and forth.

"So if I gave you orange soda, that would be a good thing, right?"

"Yup."

"But does everyone like orange soda?"

The boy shook his head. "Kevin says it tastes like aspirin."

Dad managed a smile. "Okay," he said, "so if I gave Kevin an orange soda, he wouldn't think it was good, would he?"

Bobby rubbed his ear. "But he doesn't have to have orange soda, does he? Can't he have Pepsi?"

Mom let out a little noise, almost a snort. Dad gave her a sharp glance and looked back at Bobby. "Okay, kiddo," he said. "Let's try this. You know how you can go to a birthday party and there's lots of stuff to do, like games and sports and toys to play with?"

The boy's hair flopped back and forth again. "Like Jack's party last month. It was really fun."

"Right, just like Jack's party," said Dad. "So everyone gets to have fun and do what they like, but then the cake comes out. And everyone has to have cake and ice cream, right?"

"Right," said Bobby with a nod.

"But everybody doesn't come right away. Usually, one of the grown-ups has to go get all the kids, right? They have to stop doing everything else so they can have cake and ice cream."

Another sage nod from Bobby.

"They *think* that they want to keep running around

or playing games or jumping in the bounce house," Dad explained, "but the grown-up knows that once everyone sits down, they're going to be happy with cake. So they have to give up all that other stuff so they can have cake and ice cream. Does that make sense?"

Bobby twisted his lips up again. "I think so," he said.

Mom rubbed her temples and looked out the window again.

"But there's always a couple kids who don't want cake," continued Dad. "Maybe they just want to keep jumping in the bounce house or maybe they don't like the flavor."

The boy gave a sage nod. "Nancy doesn't like chocolate cake," he said.

"Right," said Dad. "But the adults still make her stop playing and sit at the table with everyone else, right?"

"Uh-huh."

"Because they know that once the cake and ice cream's there in front of them, the kids will want it. It may not be the flavor they want, but it's still cake, and they'll all be happy. They'll be upset at first, but then they'll see it's all for the best."

Bobby shook his head and his hair swished to either side. "Nancy's illergic," he said. "She's not s'posed to have any cake."

"But they still make her sit down, right?"

The boy considered this. "Yup."

"Even though she can't enjoy it."

"Yup."

"Because it wouldn't be fair to the other kids. They're not going to enjoy their cake as much if someone else is running around and playing with all the toys. And the adults try to

find something else for her, right?"

Bobby thought about it for a moment. "At Jack's party, they got her a slice of banana bread I think," he said.

"And was she happy?"

The boy shrugged. "Guess so."

"See?"

Mom made another noise, and Dad shot another sharp glance at her.

Bobby weighed all the examples in his mind. "So Omnes gave everyone in the world cake?"

"More or less," said Dad. "And it made all the good people happy."

"Very happy," added Mom. "We were all thrilled."

"But Miss Richmond isn't happy," said the boy. "She's mad."

Dad pushed his glasses back up his nose. "Well," he said, "sometimes, good people do bad things. They only think about themselves and not everyone else. That's when they get scared of Omnes."

"Why?"

"Because they're being bad. And bad people don't get cake."

"But you said he got rid of all the bad people."

"Yes," said Dad, "he did."

Mom sniffed. She reached up and wiped her eyes. She sniffed again and then walked out of the bedroom.

Dad set a hand against the boy's shoulder and guided him back down. The blond-streaked hair spread out on the pillow. He really needed a haircut.

"Why's Mom crying?"

"Because…because she's so happy."

Bobby tugged at the sheet and twisted it between his fingers. "Omnes didn't give everyone real cake, did he?"

The corners of Dad's mouth went up a little. "No, he didn't."

"Was it something just as good?"

"Even better. He gave everyone peace."

"Peace?"

"It means no more wars," said Dad. "No more problems. Resources get spent on all the right things. Everyone has fun. Everyone gets cake."

Bobby yawned. "Even if they think they don't want it?"

"Yes," said Dad. "Even if they don't want it. Everyone gets cake because he knows it'll make them all happy in the long run."

The boy rolled onto his side. "Why'd he do it?"

"Do what?"

"Give everyone peace?"

Dad smiled. "Because someone had to."

"Why?"

"Because…" Dad paused to organize his thoughts. "I think it's like in the old comics. 'With great power comes great responsibility.' And Omnes is very, very powerful. So he feels very, very responsible. For everyone."

Bobby yawned again, and his eyes fluttered. His head shifted on the pillow. "Okay," he said.

Dad bent down and kissed him again. Bobby smiled, and his face relaxed. His breathing sank into a smooth rhythm.

Dad stood up, looked down at his son for a moment, and then took a few gentle steps into the hall. He tugged the door shut behind him.

The smile fell from his face as soon as the latch clicked. He walked down the hall to his study. Mom was there waiting for him.

"You're still angry," she said.

"Of course I'm angry," Dad said. He slid his glasses off his nose and folded them flat. He only wore them for show, but he treated them as if they were real. "Can you believe that bimbo's saying stuff like this, let alone in a classroom full of kids? Exposing them to dangerous ideas like that?"

"Please," she said, "just let the school deal with it. They've probably disciplined her already, docked her pay or—"

"Discipline?" said Dad. He set the glasses down on his desk next to the photo of his family. "If there was any discipline at that school, this wouldn't have happened in the first place."

"But just this once," said Mom, "we could let someone else handle it."

"I said I'd take care of it. None of the children will know."

Her face dropped.

Dad unbuttoned his cuffs and pulled his shirt off over his head. It was an old habit from when he'd have to change in a hurry. It had been years since he'd had to rush like that.

The shirt slid off to reveal the blue and gold uniform. He rolled his shoulders, and the cape unfurled, spreading behind him like angelic wings. His hands tugged at the belt, and his slacks and the last of his secret identity fell away.

"He's a good boy. He understands these things need to

happen sometimes." He walked past her, through the kitchen, and out the back door.

"But she's his favorite teacher. I think he even has a little crush on her."

"I'm sorry," he said, "but we can't allow this sort of thing. You know where it leads. You remember what happened to China." It wasn't a question. No one would ever forget what had been done to the Asian nation.

Omnes rose into the air. He circled the house once then headed for the west side of town, over by the community center and the graveyard. He knew that was where Miss Richmond lived.

He knew where everyone lived.

THE ORIGIN OF SLASHY

JEFF STRAND

KAYLIE WAS RAPED. IT WASN'T A PARTICULARLY BRUTAL RAPE as far as these things go. Oh, it was a rape all right—no blurred lines of consent here—but there were no weapons involved, and the violence was all implied. She was told to let it happen if she didn't want to be beaten to death, and since she didn't want to be beaten to death, she let it happen.

Kaylie knew the guy. Colin. Not a common name for somebody from New Jersey, but his parents were fans of British television. He lived in one of the apartments in her complex. At the time of the rape, she hadn't known which apartment even though he'd lived there for almost a year, and she'd lived there for eight. She didn't go outside much.

He was decidedly average in height and build. Not an intimidating figure unless, like Kaylie, you were four-foot-eleven and anorexic. Before he raped her, the only real time they'd spent together was one late night when they were both doing laundry. He'd tried to strike up a conversation, which hadn't gone well because Kaylie wasn't good at conversations, and when she thought about it later, there'd been a flash of an odd expression on his face when she folded her panties.

Three weeks later, he'd knocked on her door at two in the morning. He hadn't awakened her because she was always still up at two, but it took three different knocking sessions within ten minutes—each more insistent—before she let him in.

He was drunk and sad. He asked for a beer, and when she explained that she didn't have any alcohol, he said she was lying. *Everybody* had *some* alcohol in their refrigerator because it was rude to not have some to offer guests, and Kaylie offered to let him look through her refrigerator as proof.

Had he taken her up on that offer, she would have called the police while he was distracted, and though she might still have been raped, it's entirely possible that nobody would have died.

He did not take her up on that offer.

Instead, he took her by the hand and led her into the bedroom, telling her exactly what he was going to do to her and exactly what would happen if she made it difficult to get what he wanted. He still sounded sad even though he was presumably describing things that he would enjoy doing, and that should therefore make him happy.

She asked him not to do this. She told him she was a virgin. He laughed at her though not like she'd said something funny. She was at least thirty, he said, and he knew she was

lying just like she'd lied about the beer. Kaylie was actually thirty-two, and she was not lying.

In the bedroom, he did awful things to her. If she'd done them willingly, they might not have been such bad things, but with his hands around her neck, they were horrible, painful, disgusting things.

When he'd finished, he thanked her—*thanked* her—and left. He didn't even tell her not to call the police. Did he think she'd be too frightened of retribution to tell anybody what he'd done? Did his guilty conscience make him want her to turn him in? Was he too drunk to care?

She stared at the phone for a long time. All night. She cried a little but not too much. She felt revulsion and fear and shame all at once, and though she tried to throw up, she couldn't get the sickness out of her.

Maybe the sickness would never leave.

Why even live like this?

Just the thought of suicide filled her with relief. There was a way out. He could stain her body but not her soul, and if there was no soul, at least she'd be dead and wouldn't care.

She thought there were a couple of razor blades in a drawer in the bathroom, and she was right. Quickly, before she could change her mind, she cut a deep red line down each of her arms.

It barely hurt at all. Blood flowed.

And then, seconds later, the cuts healed.

She stared at her arms. Had she imagined that?

No. The blood was still there.

She cut again, in the same place, slicing even deeper. Once

again, blood spilled out onto the tile floor, but then the cuts healed. There wasn't even a scar.

Kaylie stared into the mirror and then slashed her cheek very slowly. The cut began to close itself up before she'd even finished.

What had happened to her?

Had Colin done this? Or had this happened before? She couldn't remember the last time she'd accidentally cut herself. It had to be a year or more. She tried to think of any major events that could have bestowed this power upon her and came up blank.

Was she immortal?

If she was immortal, she didn't have to fear anything, right?

Suddenly, she realized it was seven o'clock and time to get ready for work. She didn't have to leave her apartment, but the insurance company knew when she logged in and logged out, and her boss would be mad if she was late.

She turned on the shower as hot as it would go. It disturbed her to realize that she didn't need to take off her clothes because she'd never put them back on. As steam filled the bathroom, she stepped under the scalding water, which for about half a second felt like it was delivering cleansing and purification but then felt way too hot, so she turned it to a more reasonable temperature.

As she washed off her blood, she imagined the police taking Colin away in handcuffs. It was a mediocre mental image. She'd be glad that he wasn't around to hurt anybody else, but would she feel vindicated? Not really. Even when she added the image of the cops zapping him on the back of the neck with a Taser, it didn't make her smile.

Being completely drenched in Colin's blood? That was a better one.

By lunchtime, she realized that long stretches of her workday had been spent staring at her computer screen without really seeing anything but that the time wasn't completely unproductive because she'd made the decision to murder Colin. If she'd been gifted with super healing powers, why not try it? She'd do it as soon as she clocked out.

Kaylie didn't own a gun and didn't want to go that route because of the noise. She did own several knives. Obviously, she couldn't just rush at him with a butcher knife, but his size advantage wouldn't make a difference if he was asleep. You could be three hundred pounds of pure, steroid-enhanced muscle, and it wouldn't protect you from a blade in your throat.

She needed to know which apartment was his. The first option was to wander around the complex until she saw him, but that wasn't good use of her time. The manager would probably tell her since they would have no reason to be suspicious of somebody who'd lived there for eight years except that when Colin turned up stabbed to death, they'd probably remember that Kaylie had inquired about which apartment was his.

Maybe she'd just sit somewhere, being inconspicuous, and watch the mailboxes. Everybody checked their mail. Her other superpower was the ability to sit patiently for a long, long time.

So that's what she did. She sat next to the pool and pretended to read a book. She sat there until well past dark,

far too dark to even read, but Colin never showed up to collect his mail. Finally, she gave up and went back to her apartment. She ate a couple of bites of macaroni and cheese, slashed her wrist again to see if the healing still worked (it did), and then went to bed.

The next day, Kaylie decided that she didn't actually care if anybody suspected her of Colin's future murder. It wasn't as if she was going to be falsely accused of a crime she didn't commit. There were probably consequences to stabbing a rapist in the neck, and she'd accept them.

When she told the apartment manager that Colin had left his shirt in one of the dryers and that she wanted to return it to him, the manager explained that Colin had moved out early the previous morning. There was no forwarding address that would allow Kaylie to return the shirt. He'd mentioned moving to Los Angeles.

Los Angeles! She'd never find him there! And he'd probably lied about it, being a rapist and all, so that left the entirety of the United States for him to hide! Maybe even the world!

Even if she hired a private investigator who did find an address for him in California, she couldn't go there. She could barely force herself to go out for groceries. Maybe it would be easier to go out for groceries now that she was a superhuman healer, but California? Not a chance.

She went back to her apartment and cried a lot.

The mental image of being drenched in Colin's blood cheered her up a little. And as she thought about it, reviewing the mind-picture from all angles, she realized that it didn't necessarily *have* to be Colin's blood.

What if she got somebody else to rape her? Would sticking a knife into another man's neck make up for both crimes?

She went through her closet. She didn't own any revealing clothes, nothing to encourage lewd advances. Of course, she had the panties that had presumably set Colin off, but she couldn't go out only wearing those.

She did have her favorite turquoise blouse. Though it wasn't sexy, it looked nice on her, and if she kept it mostly unbuttoned...

Why hadn't she called the police? Colin could be raping some other girl right now. He could even be strangling her to death.

It was too late now.

No, it wasn't.

The police would want to know why she hadn't called them immediately.

So what? She was the victim. She'd tell them she was scared and humiliated and couldn't bring herself to tell anybody about it. Surely, there were plenty of other women who'd reacted the same way to this kind of violation.

But there'd be no closure. No blood.

She changed into the blouse and looked at herself in the mirror. Not bad at all. Her face was still plain—*no, ugly*—but if she let her hair down, she thought she looked relatively desirable.

Now what? She already had a perfectly good butcher knife, which would fit in her purse, so if she bought some sleeping pills and crushed them into a powder, she'd be good

to go. She knew there were date rape drugs out there that you could slip into somebody's drink, but she didn't have the slightest idea how to go about getting one, and she thought over-the-counter sleeping pills would work just fine.

Kaylie was surprised to discover that crushing pills into a powder was a challenging process. They kept popping out from under the spoon, and she had to keep picking them up off the floor. Since these pills were to aid her in a murder, she didn't worry about this being unsanitary.

Finally, she poured the powder into a snack-sized plastic bag and put it into her purse next to the butcher knife. There. She was ready to go. Now all she needed to do was figure out where the rapists lurked.

Waffle House?

No.

Under a bridge?

Probably, but her intent was not to be gang-raped and dumped into a river even with her magical healing powers. She had to remain in control of the situation.

A bar would be a good choice. Though she'd never been inside of one, there had to be some predatory men in there trying to get women drunk. That was the whole point, right? There were bars all over the place, so if she found no suitable candidates at the first one, she'd just go to the next one and so on until she achieved her goal.

Yes, that's what she would do. It was a perfect plan.

She looked in the mirror again, burst into tears, stripped off her clothes, and scalded herself in the shower until the hot water ran out.

She cursed her healing powers for keeping her in this agonizing world.

What if she cut off her own head? That would kill her, wouldn't it?

Kaylie didn't know how to go about cutting off her own head and didn't really want to try. She'd live for now. Vengeance before suicide. If the vengeance worked out, she might not want the suicide anymore.

She dried off, got dressed again, took her purse, and walked out of the apartment complex. She didn't own a car, but there were plenty of places within walking distance. In fact, there was a bar only two blocks away, a place called Abby's with a martini on the logo.

Kaylie cringed as she passed a couple of people walking in the other direction. Did they know she had a butcher knife in her purse? Did they know she was tainted? Did they know she could instantly heal wounds? Or did they just think she was some unattractive, emaciated girl desperately hoping to get lucky tonight?

She walked into Abby's, but the smell of smoke was so overpowering that she had to walk right back out. Her eyes already burned. That wasn't going to work.

She reached the next bar and didn't even go inside; a cloud of smoke practically billowed from the place when she opened the door. However, there was another one next to it, and though the place definitely reeked, it was at least tolerable.

There were about a dozen people in there, most of them sitting by themselves. She hesitated, unsure if she should go through with this or if she should just go home and cry some

more and then walked over and sat down on a stool.

The bartender asked her what she wanted to drink. What *did* she want? Not alcohol. She ordered a Coke, hoping he wouldn't get mad at her. He didn't seem to care. The drink was mostly ice and about six times as expensive as the soft drinks she bought from the vending machine by her apartment, making Kaylie wonder why anybody ever went into a bar.

Nobody approached her.

She stayed for about an hour, long enough to drink four overpriced Cokes, and then left. Why had no men hit on her? Was she too unattractive? Did she have a recently-raped scent?

At the next bar, she considered just getting a glass of water, but that would anger the bartender for sure. So she continued to buy Cokes even though she desperately had to pee and didn't want to use the strange (and probably horrific) restroom.

Just as she was about to leave, a man sat next to her. He looked old enough to be her dad, but he had a pleasant smile. He asked her name, and she decided to make up a fake name, so she said it was Dot. He said his name was Jim.

She told him that she couldn't stay anymore because she really, really had to pee, and he said that his place was two minutes away and that he had a very clean bathroom, and that's all it took.

It was more like eight minutes. Still, he hadn't lied about the cleanliness of his bathroom, and Kaylie/Dot was able to relieve herself while suffering only a minor panic attack.

Now that she no longer needed to sprint to the toilet, Kaylie came out of the bathroom and looked around at Jim's apartment. It was a nice place, at least twice as big as her own.

There were framed paintings on every wall though Kaylie didn't know if the art was any good.

Jim offered to make popcorn, which she thought was kind of charming.

After he went into the kitchen, Kaylie considered how she might get him to try and rape her. Should she just take off her shirt? No, if she was that blatant, then it might not be a legitimate rape. He seemed like a nice guy. What if he didn't try anything? What if she had to spend the evening watching a movie and eating popcorn?

He asked if she'd ever seen *The Princess Bride*. She had, of course, but lied and said that she hadn't. So they sat on his leather sofa and ate popcorn and watched the movie.

When the movie was over, he asked if she was ready for him to take her home. He said it with a smile, in such a way that she knew he would take her home if she wanted, but that he hoped she would say that she didn't want to go. So she said that she didn't want to go.

He asked if she wanted to move somewhere more comfortable.

It was a tentative, low-pressure question from a man who was clearly not used to having the opportunity to ask it. Not exactly the behavior of a savage sexual predator, yet at the same time, they'd barely known each other longer than the running time of *The Princess Bride*. Who did he think he was? Who did he think *she* was?

She said yes.

Though he was a bit shorter and thinner than Colin, she didn't think she could just lunge and successfully get a

butcher knife blade into him without putting her safety at risk. Her healing powers gave her the courage to try this in the first place, but she didn't want to strain them too much. She'd have to use the powdered sleeping pills.

She asked if he had any red wine since she needed a dark-colored beverage to hide the powder. He said no, he didn't drink, and she tried to think of a suitable substitute until he grinned, said that he was joking, and reminded her that they'd met in a bar.

They sat on the couch and sipped glasses of red wine. It was even grosser than she remembered from the time she'd tried it as a little kid, but she choked it down. Unfortunately, Jim never left his glass unattended. What was she supposed to do? Ask him to go take a shower? Was that allowed?

He asked if she was ready to go to the bedroom. She couldn't figure out how to create an opportunity to spike his drink, so she said yes, she was. She picked up her purse as he took her hand and led her into the bedroom.

Jim started to light a candle, but she said no, she liked it better in the dark. And then, though Kaylie was not good at coming up with spontaneous plans, she got an idea, and she told Jim that if he lay on his stomach, she'd give him a back massage.

He happily agreed to this. He took off his shirt, revealing a hairy chest and a small beer belly, and stretched out on top of the blankets.

Kaylie unzipped her purse. She told him that she was getting out a…she couldn't bring herself to say "condom," so she said "thing" instead. He didn't question her. Technically,

a butcher knife was a thing, so she wasn't lying.

She climbed onto the bed, straddled him, and ran her fingertips over his shoulders.

He let out a soft moan.

She clutched the handle of the butcher knife in both hands.

Had he truly done anything wrong?

Did she really want to do this?

Yes, he had, and she did.

She slammed the blade into that son of a bitch's neck. It didn't go in as far as she wanted, but his entire body went stiff, and she wrenched out the blade and stabbed him again, giggling at his high-pitched yelp. She shoved the blade in deeper, wishing it wasn't too dark to see the blood spurting from that fucking rapist's neck (she should have let him light the candle), and suddenly, he was up, bucking her off like a rodeo horse, but it was a mistake for him to turn around because she jabbed the blade in his goddamn throat, not a direct hit but close enough, and spatters of blood got all over her face and blue blouse, and he shoved her away, but she came right back at him, and the knife plunged into his chest, and he was weakening in a big way, and she couldn't wait for that motherfucker to burn in hell for what he did to her, and she stabbed him over and over and over. When he stopped moving, she just kept stabbing, and when she was positive he was dead, she just kept stabbing, and it wasn't until his head was most of the way off that she decided this was overkill and dropped the knife into the soaked blanket.

She ran her index finger along his ruined chest and

considered whether her burden felt sufficiently lifted.

Yes. It did.

Her rape had been officially avenged.

And quite honestly, even without the vengeance angle, this hadn't been such a bad way to spend an evening. Knowing that she was a superhuman healer had removed a lot of the stress. She wondered if she'd heal from a crushed bone. Maybe she should drop something heavy on her fingers to test it out.

She did. They healed.

Kaylie decided that she should kill more people.

She did.

After the third murder, involving a teenager who wouldn't be using *that* penis again even if he weren't dead, she realized that she had to become a transient or she'd eventually get caught. That was fine. After all this time, she was discovering that it was nice to get out of her apartment and go do things.

And besides, as long as she could find an internet connection, she didn't have to quit her day job.

Because she was careful, rarely murdered twice in the same state, and varied her methods, the media never caught on that there was a new superhero (or serial killer, or whatever) in the country. Which meant that she didn't get a cool nickname.

So she gave herself one: Slashy.

It was a silly name, but hey, it was silly when she played Tic-Tac-Toe on a man's stomach with a straight razor. Nothing wrong with a little silliness.

She's still out there, protecting the world from those who might have evil in their hearts.

And that is the origin of Slashy.

CONVICTION

EDWARD M. ERDELAC

"HELLO, ABASSI," THE LADY SAY WHEN I SIT DOWN. "MY name is Daniela Orozco. Now, can you tell me why you were referred to me today?"

I just shrug even though I know.

When she open the folder and slide the piece of paper with my drawing on it, I look down at my busted shoes.

"Your teachers are concerned about you," she say though I know really they just worried about they own selves. "Abassi?"

I look up, and her eyes are on me. I look away, but every time I come back, she still looking. She pretty.

"You're a very good artist, Abassi," she say.

Nobody never tell me I good at anything. It feel good. I wish the picture was something nicer.

I drew it in history class. We was learning about the

minutemen. In the picture in the book they wore GD colors, and they was all strapped in the street like they was bangin'. I thought about Lateesa. I drew the minutemen blowing up, like they swallowed bombs. Their triangle hats was on fire. Their heads come off, some of 'em. I drew my own punkinhead self in there too. I shouldn't have. If I'd of left that out, nobody would've said shit.

"You told the teacher these were the minutemen," she say with her pencil on the bloody bodies. "But who's this down here?" She point to the little boy with the big head and the busted shoes.

I don't say shit.

"Are you angry about something, Abassi?"

I shrug.

"Are you afraid?"

"Afraid?"

She wait.

M'always afraid. In the hall. In the street. In the stairwell goin' back to Grammaw's place up in the whites. I see 'em on the corners, in the doorways, lookin' out the windows. I don't go to the bathroom at school 'cause they in there. I hear 'em from the hall, and my back and my neck hurts I get so scared.

"Abassi?"

She looking at me.

"Abassi, I want you to sit up and take a breath. Breathe in very deep through your nose like this, and out through your mouth. Breathe with me."

I do what she say. My neck don't hurt so much after.

"Better?"

I nod.

"Can you tell me what makes you afraid?"

"I scared sometime," I say real quiet so they can't hear through her door. "They goin' gimme another PhD."

"PhD?"

"Punkinhead Deluxe," I say. "They beat you till your head get big like a punkin."

She look at me, and I look at my broke-ass shoes again. I know I ugly. I been ugly since the PhD.

"S'why I look this way."

"Who beat you?"

I shake my head.

"Abassi, I want you to be able to trust me. Will you tell me what happened?"

I like her. I guess maybe 'cause she pretty.

So I say.

I tell her how Lateesa was smokin' water all the time with the clique (I don't say who in the clique), and how she start in smokin' rock too. I tell her how Grammaw told me one night to go out and find her, that I was responsible for her.

I tell her how I found Lateesa out by the reds with the clique tryin' to get TreySix to sell her some rock. I seent 'em push her around. They say she got no loot, so she gotta pay the other way. I don't wanna tell her how she get on her knees, how she take TreySix's dick in her mouth. I feel sick sayin' that to Miss Orozco, but she tell me it OK, so I tell.

I tell how I stepped up to them, how I yelled at my sister to stop. They all told me to fuck off, but I din't listen. I hollered for Lateesa to come home.

Then I say how they bum-rushed me. I din't see nothin' but blue and silver and the black of they fists and they Tims comin' down, they gold chains swingin'. They shout, they laugh the whole time. I din't hear nothin' but my bones snappin.' The last thing I seent before I woked up in the hospital was TreySix laughin' on his celly with Lateesa on her knees in front of him.

But I don't snitch. I don't say TreySix. GDs kill me and my Grammaw if I do.

Just like they kill Lateesa. She OD'd while I was sleep. But it just like they kilt her.

"Breathe," she tell me.

I breathe.

"Abassi?"

I look at her.

"Do you feel responsible for Lateesa?"

I shrug.

"Grammaw said I was."

"You're not. She was your older sister. Anything she did, anything that happened to her, was because of choices she made, not you."

"Okay."

"I understand why you're scared and why you're angry. I want to keep seeing you. Is that alright?"

I nod.

"I want to talk to you about what the goal of our therapy is going to be. I want you to remember the breathing exercise and something else. I want to you to keep your head up when you walk. Don't slouch. Try not to hunch up your shoulders.

I see the way you carry yourself, and I see that you're afraid. There are people, like the ones who hurt you, that will see it too and jump on that fear. It's okay to feel afraid, and there are places that it's appropriate to show that, like right here with me. But you and I know that there are places out there that it's better to look like you're not. I think you'll find too that if you start carrying yourself like you're not scared, you'll be scared less and less. If you start to believe in yourself, you'll find you'll hardly be scared at all anymore."

"I'm always goin' be scared," I say.

"You only think that because of where you are right now. I don't mean just in this neighborhood. In this school. I mean in your life. You don't have to always be this way. I know you feel like everybody has power over you. The GDs, your grandmother, your teachers…but if you have conviction…"

"What?"

"Conviction. Belief. If you believe in yourself, I mean really believe, like, how you believe that every step you take your foot will touch the ground. If you believe like that—that you can change things for yourself—you can."

"I can't."

"Yes you can, Abassi. You can control it, you just have to convince yourself. I'll help you. But we'll talk about that later. Our time's almost up for today. I wanna give you some homework…"

I suck my teeth, and she smiles.

"Yes, I get to assign homework," she says. "I want you to practice visualizing goals that you want to attain."

I shake my head. I don't know what she mean.

"I mean making a picture in your mind of how you'd like things to be. I want you to draw me a picture tonight, Abassi," she says.

"Of what?"

"Draw me a picture of yourself."

"I don't wanna."

"Then draw me anything at all. And I'll see you tomorrow, okay?"

"Awright."

She stands up and shakes my hand. Her hand is clean and smooth and warm.

"It was nice to meet you."

*** *** ***

I walk home.

"Yo yo yo! Whatchoo want? Whatchoo need? 'Got that rock. 'Got that weed. 'Ay! 'Ay, my man! Give it up! 'Sup, folk? Got my squares? Yup yup! What up, nigga? Hangin' bangin' slangin' natamean? Right-right. Where my nigga Mike-Mike? Yo! 'Ay, yo! 'Sup, GD? 'Ay, here go Punkinhead. 'Ay nigga! Draw me a picture, nigga! Draw yo sista on my tip! Haaaaaaaaaaaah…bitch ass…"

I go up to Grammaw's.

"'Bassi! Where the hell you been? I need you to go to the 'sto! I need smokes!"

"The man at the store say you got to get them, Grammaw. He won't sell 'em to me no more."

"Well what fuck good is you then?"

I close my door. I get out paper. I draw for Miss Orozco.

I think about what she say. About believing I can change things. I make a picture about how I want things to be. I draw the projects, the reds and the whites all broke down and the GDs all up under the bricks. TreySix and Caveman, BillDawg and Mike-Mike. They can't shoot nobody. They can't jump nobody. I start to color in the blood, but I stop. I want to draw something nice for her, so I draw grass growing over the bricks. Grammaw say they used to be grass in the projects till the white folks paved it over to save money. I draw it green like I seent it on cartoons, not like the yellow shit that grows in the Killin' Field where the crackheads go. I draw pink flowers so thick you can't see the bodies no more. Pretty soon, the bricks look like a hill. I draw myself on top. I draw Miss Orozco too. I give her a pink and yellow flower. With the projects gone, you could see the sky in my picture. I draw it blue, and I make the clouds big and white. I draw a smile on the sun. That fucks it up kinda. Makes it look like a little kid's picture. I make the sun orange. That fixes it. I don't draw no po-pos. I don't draw no ghetto birds even though I hear one outside, see the light comin' down, lookin' for somebody.

I hear shootin.' Back back back. I should go lay down in the bathtub.

But I look at my picture. It's a nice picture. I hope Miss Orozco will like it. She say I'm a good draw-er. I think she will like it.

I breathe.

I fall 'sleep looking at it.

*** *** ***

At school, Mr. Wade tells me I won't see Miss Orozco no more.

I feel like somebody bust a cap in my chest. I ask how come.

He say somebody shot her in the parking lot after school yesterday. He say they found her car out by the reds. He say it was too nice a car to drive around Cabrini and she ought to have knowed better.

I get up and go. Mr. Wade tell me to come back, but he don't do nothing. Like always.

I go out to the parking lot. I see some yellow tape, but it rained sometime last night, and they ain't no blood. They ain't nothing left of Miss Orozco. It like I dreamed her. I feel worse than when Lateesa died.

I stare at her picture. I want to believe it could be like that. I got to believe it.

But she say the picture got to come from my mind. So I leave her picture layin' in the parking lot. The water makes it gray.

I go home and I wait. I breathe like she taught me, till the hurt in my chest and in my neck hurt less.

I wait in the Killing Field between the reds and the whites, where the crackheads go and the po-pos won't 'cause they get shot at from the windows. Them windows is like hundreds of eyes, and the red and white buildings be like giants looking down on you. I wait by the wet mattresses and the busted stones and the bottles and the pipes and the crinklin' chip bags and the yellow grass that ain't never been green.

I stare at the ground while I wait. It's wet from the rain. Rain s'posed to make things grow. They ain't no reason it

shouldn't be green. They ain't no reason they can't be flowers.

Yes they is. The poison. The poison in the dirt from the blood and the rock and the puke and the dog shit and the people shit and the glass, which is the only green they is.

I think about the grass bein' green. I breathe.

From where I sit, it turns green like it always should've been. The green spreads out across the whole lot. The grass drinks up the rain and spits out the poison into the street where it belong. It grows up my ankles so thick you can't see the glass and the garbage no more. There are pink and yellow flowers like the ones in my picture.

I get up. I know what I can do now. I got conviction.

I go to the liquor store.

*** *** ***

"Know what I'm sayin? This is how we do, folk. All day every day, nigga. Right-right. LK Killa! 'Ay nigga! Who this 'lil nigga? Who you steppin' to, nigga? What set? What set? Man chill, BillDawg. S'that trick nigga Punkinhead. Whatchoo lookin' at, Punkinhead? Ugly ass bitch! God-*damn* you ugly! Go on in, nigga, get yo grammaw's diapers."

They laugh and jump. They pound they fists and twist they fingers and throw signs.

The pictures are in my mind. I breathe, and I think about the field, how I made the picture real.

They stand there lookin' at me. They stand in front of the wall. They tags is all on the wall like dog piss. They stars and pitchforks and sixes. The upside down crowns, dissin' the LKs who don't even come around Cabrini. They wearin' they blue

and silver, they Georgetown gear and they nice big coats and they jumps, all bought with dope. They saggin', and I can see they straps. They like the minutemen on the ave. Grinnin, laughin, like they own me. Like that night with Lateesa.

But I ain't afraid, 'cause this ain't the picture in my mind.

I start with Caveman 'cause he the biggest. I scratch him out like that smile on the sun. I color over him. I use red. They hate red. They jump you just for wearin' it. Red for Vice Lords, red for Kings. But Caveman goes all red. I use his blood to color him with, and the pencil's in my mind. To get at the color, I open him up right in the middle and dip my mind in his chest. He screams, but it sound like he underwater, the blood bubbling up in his mouth, runnin' out his eyes, over his face, all down his expensive gear.

Caveman's big. I need more red for the others. Most of his is all over the wall and the street. I pull Mike-Mike's skin and clothes off him like a glove. He falls down screaming, painting red wherever he rolls.

This all goes down as fast as I can think it.

TreySix and BillDawg are still laughing when Mike-Mike rolls over their kicks, paintin' em. They kill you for that, but killin' Mike-Mike would be the best thing they could do for him now. He wanna die. He cryin' like a bitch to die.

"What the fuck, Dawg?" TreySix say.

I don't want him to die yet.

BillDawg gives me an idea. He takes out his strap, a big silver one, shinin' like ice cream money from his belt. He don't know it's me he needs to shoot. He looks stupid, looks up and down the ave, tryin' to figure out what poppin'.

I think about him eatin' his own gat, and just like that, he does it. I think about him painting TreySix, and he does. He blows red from his dome all over TreySix.

TreySix takes out his gat.

They found Miss Orozco by the reds, the Extension building of the projects where TreySix and his clique slang. I don't know if it was him, but I bet it was. I want it to be. I take his gat away so fast and so hard his whole arm comes off with it and flies off down the street.

He falls on his knees like Lateesa, the blood pourin' out his shoulder.

He looks at me, and for the first time, that loud mouth nigga ain't got shit to say.

I know how to do this now. It's easier than breathing. All it takes is conviction. I like it. I put up my hand like they do on Star Wars, and TreySix floats off the ground, the blood slappin' on the curb sounds like when the pipe bust under the sink at Grammaw's. Believe your feet touch the ground with every step, Miss Orozco said. But I believe TreySix's don't, so they don't.

I do like they do in them movies. TreySix hits the wall hard. I bring him back, and I push him to the wall again. Again. I smash him against his stupid GD sign in the middle of the stupid star and the pitchforks and all the shit they tag on the walls of everything they see. Their stupid ass cartoon drawings of big-tittied g-queens with fat onions that look like a baby drawed 'em. I'm a better draw-er than any of 'em. I spread my fingers and turn the star into a red sun, and parts of TreySix come apart and out like a map of the planets.

The man at the liquor store looks out the window. His eyes is all white. He on the phone.

I let what's left of TreySix slide and drip down the wall.

I go home to Grammaw's. I hear the sirens, and a ghetto bird goes across the sky. The light shines down on the liquor store and the picture I made there.

"You get my smokes?"

I go to the TV.

"You know that mo'fuckin' thang's broke, you dumb shit," she say.

But I turn it on, and it does work. Because I want it to.

They show the liquor store on the news. They's lots of yellow tape and flashin' lights. The man on the news talks a lot but don't say nothin' cause he don't know what happened. The man at the counter din't say shit. I know he din't 'cause wouldn't nobody believe. The writing on the screen say 'Gang Violence At Cabrini-Green.'

I don't like that. I ain't in no gang.

Then I think about Miss Orozco's picture. All the GDs under the red bricks with the grass over 'em. That's what I want to happen. That's the goal I visualize.

*** *** ***

I don't go to school no more. I walk the projects all day and night. I go to the reds first. On the left of the building by the street is where they slang weed. I go there night after night, and the po-pos come night after night with they yellow tape to clean up the mess. Pretty soon, they ain't enough GDs in the reds to slang weed no more.

Then I go to the front gate. The GDs are scared now, but they don't know what to be scared of. They smoke water, and they carry shotties and zoo-zoos and Tec-9s out in the open like soldiers.

"Whatchoo want, nigga?"

"Rock," I say.

"Who know this nigga?"

"That Punkinhead. He live with his grammaw up in the whites. He ain't no crackhead."

"The fuck you want, son?"

"Abassi."

"The fuck you say?"

"My name Abassi."

They don't want me to go in. They shout and they holler, but I take the iron gate off, and I go in anyway. When the elevator opens, the one inside starts shooting soon as he peeps all the red. I make all the bullets stop in the air and go back into the end of his Tec. It blows his hands right off.

I ride the elevator up to the fourth floor where the crack is. I pull the drippy ceiling down on the crackheads, and I push the GDs through the walls and through the floors like nails. When I'm done there, I go up to the ninth, and I get rid of the heron and all the slangers and bangers and hangers there too. I send 'em through the bars the white folks put over the balconies to stop us from throwin' each other over, and they drop out in little pieces on the other side.

They ain't no livin' GDs in the reds when I finally leave.

I go to Miss Orozco's field, and I sit on an old chair with the pink flowers and watch the po-pos across the way. They

all in blue and silver like the minutemen too. They stand around a lot. More come and go. They lights bounce between the buildings, and the hundreds of eyes look scared. Others come and clean up the pictures I made. It takes till morning.

I go upstairs and watch TV.

On the news, it say Gang Massacre At Cabrini-Green.

"Fuckin' animals," Grammaw say. "Somebody ought to kill 'em all."

"Maybe somebody is," I say.

"Shut the fuck up, boy, and go buy me my smokes."

I go but not to the store. I walk around all day. I walk away from the projects. I don't think about going back. Pretty soon, the houses get nicer. It's crazy how short a walk it is. It's crazier that I never been here. Everything is so clean, and each house got its own patch of green grass and flowers. I would eat off the streets here before I'd eat off Grammaw's kitchen table. White faces turn to look at me.

Pretty soon, the 5-0 roll up.

Two big, fat one-timers get out, so big the car sits up when they get out.

"You lost?" one of them say, steppin' up to me like he own me.

"Naw."

Then he say what he mean.

"You're *lost*, boy."

"Get in the car," his partner say. "We'll take you home."

But that ain't my home no more.

"Come on," he say.

I keep on walking.

"Hey, motherfucker," say the first cop. "Get your black ass back here."

I keep walking.

"Get the fuck back here, or I'm gonna light you up."

I turn around and look at him. Minutemen. GD. Blue and silver. All the same. Always fightin' the red.

He point somethin' at me. Look like a space gun.

"Go on, Carl," say the other one. "Fry that stupid nigger, and let's haul his ass back."

Somethin' come outta the space gun, slower than a bullet. It's easy to catch. It's a pair of hooks on wires. They hang in the air for a minute, then I turn 'em around and put the hooks in the fat cop's eyes. He screams and jumps around, and I hear this fast clickin' sound. I make it faster. Hotter. He starts to smoke.

The other cop don't grab a space gun. He pulls his strap. I wave my hand at him and paint him red, so red there ain't nothing left of him but his gun.

Across the street, a white lady screams.

I sit down on the curb. I pull up my hood. It's cold.

The fat cop shakes on the ground, blacker than I am now.

More one-timers come. More than came to clean up the GDs even. They close off the street. They come in big vans, and I crush 'em like pop cans. They climb up on roofs where they think I can't see, but I seen movies. I do to them what they try to do to me, and they roll off the roofs with no heads.

I never even get up off the curb.

Night comes, and the ghetto birds buzz around in circles over my head like the hungry, baldheaded birds in the cartoons

when somebody's dyin' in the desert. They shine they lights down on me.

I paint the light red, and what comes down is on fire and smashes through the roofs of the nice houses. Ain't nobody inside. The white people have all run away. I let 'em go.

On a dead man's radio, I hear them say they goin' send soldiers next and tanks. I never seen a tank, but I seen soldiers. I think about how they tanks'll look comin' apart.

Over the roofs of the burning houses, I can see the reds and the whites a ways off like big mountains.

The moon is behind 'em. I can see the light, but I can't see the moon, so I put up my hand and I pull the projects down.

When the dust clears, I see the moon real nice. It's not the sun, but I put a smile on it anyway. I think about the moon shinin' down on the green field, of the pink and yellow flowers openin' up to catch the light. I know flowers ain't s'posed to open at night, but the ones in my picture do.

Miss Orozco would've liked that.

THRESHOLD

KRIS ASHTON

THE PAIN IS ONLY MILD NOW, A FAINT THROB BEHIND THE eyes. But it won't stay like this.

Eighteen hours was the longest I lasted. How to describe the agony? Imagine your skull shrinking until it felt like the contents might spurt out your nose.

Painkillers don't help. Believe me, I've tried.

I have a talent, and the pain is a symptom. Another man might get off on the talent. I don't, but I think that's the point—I'm not supposed to. Or maybe the person who gave me this ability is incompetent, and I'm just one unlucky son of a bitch.

*** *** ***

I was twenty when it first happened. I don't think it was a

coming-of-age. Sometimes, shit just happens when it happens.

I was on my break in this seedy little diner down the road from the hospital where I work. I was pulling a double shift to cover for a colleague. The rims of my eyelids felt like cracked earth, and I still had to slog through another seven hours when I went back. I opened my throat and tipped some coffee into it, trying not to taste it.

A guy exited the men's room and went by my lifted elbow. I got a flash of pain—a microsecond at most but enough to make me gag on the coffee.

Then the facts fell on top of me like old shoes tumbling out of a cluttered closet.

He had abducted a girl one night. Dragged her into a dark spot, held her down, and raped her. When it was over, he closed his fingers around her windpipe and watched on as she thrashed and waned and then finally died. He had then bundled her into a garbage bag, added some rocks, and tossed the package in a river.

I knew that. I also knew where he lived and where he would be at any particular time on any given day. It was as if the information had been hibernating in my mind and suddenly woken up.

I also knew something else: I was supposed to avenge the girl's death. Eye for an eye, death for a death.

I twisted around in my booth. The man was pushing open the door now, and I got a brief but clear look at his profile.

When he was gone, I shook my head and drank some more coffee, wondering not for the first time if shift work was slowly killing me. It seemed I had the makings of a headache

too. Odd since I hardly ever got headaches.

I walked back to work and set about cleaning and dressing an old lady's leg wound. But after an hour, the headache started to worsen. I stopped by the nurses' station and popped some paracetamol then continued on to some obs. I got through two wards reassuring myself the drugs would kick in, but then the pain dialed up. That's the best term for it. It was like someone had attached electrodes my forebrain and begun shocking its jelly with increasing voltages. Each pulse also brought a reminder message: I was supposed to kill the guy in the diner. I didn't know his name, but I knew where he was. In my mind's eye, I could see him sitting at his terminal and scratching the back of his neck. Like most murderers, he held down a steady job and threw the occasional dinner party for friends.

I was supposed to be stitching up a skateboarder's gruesome knee when the pain hit a new high. Dark things sparkled in my eyes, and I dropped the tweezers, which clattered into a tray. When I could see again, the skater looked worried. I didn't blame him.

One of my workmates walked in, and I told her I had come over ill. She offered to assume the job, much to the skater's (and my own) relief.

I stumbled down the hallway, masking my eyes, and lurched into a quiet room. I closed the venetian blinds, already subconsciously aware my condition had nothing to do with the sun, and collapsed into an armchair. I persisted for another ten minutes, trying to control my breathing, but the pain refused to abate. Large-bore drill bits were now screwing into

my temples, and it felt as though my teeth had come loose in their sockets.

Between the layers of agony, soft voices wheedled, assuring me I could be free from this torture in a second…

As I unwrapped the syringe and drew cleaning fluid into its barrel, I did wonder—as well as I could in my high state of misery—whether I had lost my mind. But I didn't feel insane. I felt as an ant must feel when an impossibly huge human hand herds it away from its chemically-determined task.

I didn't tell the nursing unit manager I was leaving. For that, I could have been reprimanded or even fired, but rational concerns were far down my priority list. What mattered was the pounding in my head and the capped syringe in my shirt pocket.

As I drove my car from the hospital parking lot, the pain relaxed a little. Only a notch or two but enough for me to feel the difference—a grim reward.

The guy from the diner worked in a call center, one of a hundred cubicle dwellers fitted out in pants and a collared shirt. My nurse's uniform attracted attention, but I strode amongst the cubicles as though I had important business to attend to.

Which I did.

I knew where the men's room was even though I had never entered this building, and I also knew the guy from the diner had a full bladder. I hid in a toilet cubicle for perhaps thirty seconds before he stood at the urinal and unzipped his fly.

I walked out, staying on my toes so my shoe heels wouldn't click, and plunged the needle into his neck.

He cried out and batted my hand away before I could press more than half the cleaning fluid into him, but a small dose of that shit in your bloodstream goes a long way. I do not intend to describe his death.

The moment Diner Guy's heart ceased to beat, the brutal pounding in my head did also. Heroin users claim their first experience is like kissing God, and this neared that: a sudden absence of pain coupled with a sense of immense achievement as if killing this man had done the universe a favor.

I walked out unmolested and returned to work. It was a quiet day, and my departure had gone virtually unnoticed.

So now you know what it's like. There have been more than fifty incidents since that first day, and they've all gone down much the same way. I'm not writing this from a jail cell. I should be. After all, a nurse in a call center does not go unremarked, and the most dunderheaded detective could link my absence from work and my appearance at the murder scene. But I'm put in mind again of that ant, giant fingers briefly steering it on a new course…

Not what you might expect from a vigilante, huh? Righter of wrongs, scourge of evil, apathetic fatalist.

But this is not just about me. This humble posterity is also about a girl called Claire.

When they're not eviscerating innocents, murderers like Diner Guy maintain the semblance of normal lives. The murderers of murderers do too. I had three full-time girlfriends before my "power" kicked in; the occasional kill urge did nothing to stem the more socially acceptable ones.

I met Claire, of all places, in a bar. I was alone with a

beer, my eyes glued to a game on TV. Claire was two tables over with a group of friends. On the way to the bathroom, she stopped to look at the TV and asked how we were doing. I said, "Not too good."

As a tree grows from a seed, love grew from an offhand remark about a ball game. Claire had strawberry-blonde hair and blue eyes and long eyelashes that seemed to wave at you when she blinked. I don't know…what makes you love a person? It can be a few things or everything. How it happened doesn't matter anyway—just that it did.

We moved in together after six months, and in the first year I killed only two men: one had molested and finally poisoned his stepdaughter, the other liked to bait dogs.

I passed the first man in the hospital halls. He had his arm around his distraught wife and was working hard to suppress a smile. That time, the pain barely got past a regular headache. I just followed them home, waited until he gave his wife a sleeping tablet, and then strangled him with a length of rope while he writhed in an armchair with a bowl of macaroni tipped over in his lap. I told Claire I had been held up at work.

The dog-baiter, however, was messy in every sense. I tracked him to a park and watched as he threw rat bait around like chicken feed. As he returned to his car, I leaped out from behind a hedge and plunged a scalpel into his throat. It's human instinct to touch the site of an injury, but dog-baiter was cut from unusual cloth. He threw his arms about my neck and pulled me into a bear hug. My face pressed against his jetting neck. Warm blood trickled into my eyes and onto my shirt. I managed to escape his manic grip, but by then, it

was too late. I looked like one of the car accident victims that arrive in the ER most days.

I left Dog-Baiter choking in his own blood and made a dash for my car. I wiped my face with my shirt sleeves and then put on a jacket that I always kept in the back seat. As drove off, I glanced at myself in the rear-view mirror. My ears and eyelids were still smeared with drying gore, and I wished the car had tinted windows.

Arriving home, I sprayed bleach on my shirt's stiffening, red-brown patches and tossed it in the washing machine then went upstairs to shower. As I scrubbed the blood out of my eyebrows, it occurred to me that Claire might one day be home, and I would have no safe-house should another "directive" go awry.

Two weeks later, I decided to confess what I was and what I had to do. Better to be upfront and have her leave than be deceitful and suffer the same fate.

We were eating breakfast on the back deck, the autumn sun shining on us. I could not imagine a better time to say what needed to be said, so I put down my toast and took a sip of coffee.

"Claire," I began. "I have something to tell you."

An expression flashed across her face. At the time, I thought it was worry or concern, but in hindsight, I believe it was guilt.

"What's wrong?" she said.

"There's something you don't know about me." I hated the stupid cliché as soon as it left my mouth. "I have a certain… calling, I suppose you'd say."

Her face fell. It tore my heart to see it. "Please don't say you're leaving me."

"What? God no. That's the last thing I would ever do. No, I'm not leaving you. But after I say what I have to say, you might leave me."

The forlorn softness left her face, and the bright-eyed, no-nonsense Claire returned. "Just say what you have to say."

I decided to leave the supernatural out of it. It seemed like the right thing to do at the time.

How many rueful men have spoken or written those words?

"I kill people," I blurted out. "Bad people. Not often. Only when I have to. But there it is."

She stared at me for a long time, perhaps trying to gauge whether I was messing with her. Then she shrugged and said, "If they deserve it, I don't see anything wrong with that."

Relief gushed into my veins. It was not as intense as the post-kill euphoria, but it was definitely sweeter. I picked up Claire's hand and kissed it.

Love kills logic.

With Claire providing a shoulder to rest my head on when I needed to, I almost felt like a normal person again. Hell, excepting an occasional head-splitting directive, we led the most normal lives imaginable. We got married eight months ago with all our friends and family in attendance. On the desk where I'm writing this, there's a wedding photo of Claire and I. She looks gorgeous with her hair up and her shoulders exposed above the fitted curves of her dress. She's smiling.

Smiling.

Our happy life ended at seven o'clock this morning. I was engulfed in a somnolent bliss after a week of night shifts. I rolled over and placed my hand on Claire's hip. A familiar sliver of pain lanced through my head and burst an information sac, spilling it into my brain.

I gasped and sat up, windless with horror as I learned things in a manner no mortal person has a right to.

I saw my lovely Claire, an IT consultant in her more pedestrian moments, fixing a telescopic sight onto a rifle and shutting one eye to check its aim. I saw a portly businessman's reddened face appear in the sight's crosshairs. I saw the hair on the back of his head fly out like a bad wig in a breeze and his brains follow an instant later.

I saw an ethnic man, perhaps Greek or Italian, standing near a steel door in a dark alley way. He spoke to someone for a few seconds. Then the door closed, and he started toward the street. A red dot appeared at the back of his head, and then a bullet punched through it. He fell forward, and the red dot moved to the left side of his back, roughly where his heart would be, and three more shots ripped through his jacket's black material.

My wife Claire: the hit woman.

Why the directive happened then is another of those ant-questions. Some particular victim, some critical mass—it could be either or neither. Whatever the case, a dull throb set in behind my eyes.

Terror clinched my heart—terror beyond words. I retched and almost vomited in my lap. When the nausea passed, I reached over with a trembling hand and shook Claire awake.

She made a sleepy sound and regarded me with half-closed eyes.

"You have to get out of here," I said. "Get as far away from me as you can. Right now."

Her eyes opened wider. "What? Why?"

I thought about going all nineteenth century and telling her not to ask questions and ordering her from the house. Then I considered what she did in her spare time and almost cracked a bitter smile.

Almost.

I sighed. "Claire, you know how I said I kill people from time to time? Bad people?"

She nodded.

"Well, I don't do it by choice. Someone…something… forces me to do it."

Her face hardened. I wondered if that was the face her victims saw as they cowered against the nearest wall. "Who forces you to do it?"

"I don't think they exist on this Earth. Or maybe they do, just not in the same way as you and I."

Claire sat up, scrunching the bedclothes in her lap. "What are you talking about?"

"This is why I didn't tell you about this part the first time around. But you need to know now." I rubbed a hand across my eyes. "You're a…what? A hit woman? A hit person? Does political correctness apply to assassins?"

Claire's mouth fell open.

"You got into the gig through one of your brother's friends, who first showed you how to shoot a rifle. You made your first kill when you were twenty-one. A right-wing politician that a gay activist wanted dead. You've made eight kills since then, three since you met me. One of them was last night."

Claire tried to draw breath, and it stuttered in her throat. "Who…who told you this? Who ratted me out?"

I shook my head. "I rolled over in bed this morning, and whoever gives me these directives gave me one about you. I don't know. Maybe the last person you killed was innocent or something. Bad info, you know?"

"He was a gangster," Claire protested. "He was responsible—"

I held up a hand to shush her. "It doesn't matter now. The directive's been set in motion. The pain is going to get worse and worse, unimaginable. And only one thing can stop it."

"Isn't there pain relief that—"

"Trust me, morphine couldn't take the edge off this thing when it really gets going. So before that, you have to get going. Pack some stuff and get as far away as you can. Another state, another country if possible. And don't tell me where. Believe me, in a few hours, I'll be dying to know."

Claire must have thought she was humoring a madman, but she got dressed and began to stuff clothes and toiletries into a large sports bag. I sat on the bed and watched her do it, feeling the tight pulse behind my eyes.

When she was done, she came over and kissed me.

"I'll try to trick you," I said. "I'll say anything and everything to get you back here. Don't buy it. In one week, give me a call from wherever you are. Don't tell me where it is. I'm hoping if it's somewhere I've never been, I won't be able to

track you there. When you call, keep me talking. It shouldn't take you long to figure out whether the kill-urge has passed."

"Okay," she said in a strained voice. A tear spilled onto her cheek. She looked like she was about to say she loved me and then appeared to think better of it.

I understood completely.

So that's it. She left more than two hours ago. She's in a plane flying west. I know that for certain even though it feels like tiny needles are piercing my optic nerves.

I need to stop. The screen is blurring, and every third word is a typing mistake. The writing helped take my mind off it for a while, but soon, nothing else will matter. When it feels like my overgrown brain is about to crack its casing, I'll need to make a decision.

Which of us has to die?

OILY

A.D. SPENCER

THE MARBLE IN ITSELF WAS NOTHING SPECTACULAR: AVERAGE in size; clear, opaque glass; and a smooth, iridescent finish. When the light from the swaying, fluorescent bulb above danced across the surface, a hazy rainbow appeared on the orb. Almost an illusion but not quite. It was a simple thing, polished and lacking the small chips that would have marked it as a game piece, yet it sat inside a wooden box upon a black, pillowed bed of velvet like a fine piece of jewelry.

The father, Jim, had hands that were as flat as rolled dough and rough, the skin splashed with white and pink scar tissue and brown and leathery liver spots. He closed the box's lid and handed it to his daughter with no preamble.

"Just an oily?" Cin asked because she knew the type and knew her father's craft well. She had seen him sculpt glass, pull colored strings of it across the length of a room. She had seen him make swirling artwork out of crystal balls no bigger than the tip of her thumb. This little marble, this oily, though, was more toy than masterpiece.

She smirked. "Kind of plain for our taste, Poppy."

He scratched the steel bristle along his weathered jaw line, trying to hide a proud grin when he recognized the compliment inside her words. "Not my work actually. Just a little something I found in a box of your old toys." He put distance between those words and the next ones, his lips curling with each syllable as if they had a sweet taste: "Figured you'd find a good use for it."

This was the way it began.

Cin knew what was hidden in the comment. It was a request. Usually, she was the one asking him for favors, but this wasn't entirely new to her. She swayed slightly, as if a wind were pushing against her, and found balance on the balls of her feet. Fingers grasped the box tightly, taking it. Accepting it.

"I will." It was her promise, the only one she ever made.

The heat off the craftsman's oven met her back when she turned away from him. It drifted out the garage, following her into the house, unlike her father. This was a winter evening, and he would stay, she knew, working the glowing glass rods until long after nightfall, waiting for her to go out so that he could pretend he didn't have a chance to see her change. Or to protest whatever it was she did when she finally left. Cin wasn't sure which assumption was correct, and she'd never ask him.

A two-day-old newspaper had been left on the breakfast table. This was the second part of the request. The paper was thin, not the city's Journal but a county rag. Cin snatched it up on her way past, boots pounding the laminate checkers below. She found her room, closed the door, and went to work.

It was good to have a job.

The last one had been months ago. Too long ago. Crime, as the temperature dropped, had risen as if the thieves and cut-throats of the city had suddenly realized they were in need of stocking stuffers. Yet Cin had found herself home, recovering, the only reminder of the last marble she'd given away, the last request she'd fulfilled, the long, surgical scar running down her thigh.

But that was the past. A different time, a different marble.

Cin flexed her shoulders, rolling out a kink, and pulled her stool out from beneath her wooden vanity, sparing the mirror's reflection only a sideways glance. Only one eye moved of course. The other stayed constantly ahead, its false pupil always smaller than the living eye, especially in the dimly lit confines of the bedroom. It was her most unusual feature, yet the everyday passers-by never noticed it, due, no doubt, to her trained stare. Cin had learned long ago to look at people straight-on, to turn her head with every movement instead of drawing attention to the fixed glass iris.

"Never let strangers see what makes you different," she quoted. Her father had told her those words a dozen times before. They were, perhaps, the closest he ever came to advising her to keep up a façade for the general populous.

She turned her focus to the wig sitting to one side of the vanity, balanced on a faceless foam head. The dark hair was natural, not synthetic. Expensive but worth every penny.

Heavy bangs hung low. It was cut into a bob that lowered in the back and tapered up to kiss the chin with a soft curl. Cin reached out, ran her fingers through it.

The caress finished, her body stiffened once more. She flipped through the paper, glancing over each column and looking for the answer. It could have been made simpler for her. Jim could have circled the article. Heaven forbid he actually told her which one he'd intended her to see. But her father, for whatever reason, never spoke to her much at all. In fact, he never actually acknowledged what she did with the cryptic messages sent her way. Such a realization might have given another woman pause.

Cin only continued her search. Finally, she hesitated, her fingertips hovering over a bold word that had caught her eye.

"Oil," she whispered. She read the rest of the title aloud, "*Car Crushes Local Man During Oil Change.*"

An innocent enough accident. Two slipped jacks and Mr. Paul Ortiz was found dead hours later in his attached car garage. It didn't stink of criminal activity. Cin had seen a similar article not a year ago in a national paper.

"These things happen," Cin said with a sneer, certain she was quoting an official who'd been on the scene.

She lifted the marble out of its casket, staring at the colors reflecting off its surface, just like oil floating over water. In that moment, she knew there was more to Mr. Paul Ortiz's death. Her father had, somehow, known as much too.

Cin let her fingers stretch out, the oily rolling to the center of her palm. It sat in place only a moment before it began to spin. She smiled, leaning over it, willing the marble to continue. The glass orb lifted off of her skin, hovering a few inches above.

"No strings attached," Cin said, losing her grin.

The marble slapped back down into her palm.

It wouldn't fly any higher, not yet. Not until she felt that old fire inside her. That rage. When it came, when it filled her, she'd be able to do more than make the toy hover. She'd make it fly, make it dance—make it shoot out of her palm at the speed of a bullet.

First, though, she needed to know more about Mr. Ortiz. Anger would come on its own.

She pulled her bag of makeup from the top drawer and turned to face herself. It was time for a night out.

*** *** ***

Cin stayed in over the next two nights, but Cat's Eye made her long-awaited return to the shadows. She wanted to go into the city, to play amongst the factories and skyscrapers, to be spotted by thugs and would-be rapists. To hear the villains whisper that she had risen as if from the dead. Mostly, though, to hear them say her name with fear.

Instead, Cat's Eye stayed hidden in the suburbs. This neighborhood was not her own. In place of dilapidated sheds and blue collar workers were the commuters with their clean lawns and tight schedules. Over those two evenings, she watched them, families in mini-vans, fathers in suits returning home late. Her main focus, though, was Mrs. Ortiz. In the daytime, Cin would drive by the neighborhood, visit the local library, eat lunch at the diner where Mrs. Ortiz liked to take

her ten-year-old son for pie after a long day at school. Study, observe, know your enemy:

Mrs. Ortiz.

Mrs. Ortiz didn't work, a stay-at-home mom with a television as her companion. With her youngest, the pudgy-cheeked devourer of sweets, at school and her oldest away at college, it appeared loneliness was part of her job. Mrs. Ortiz spent her days and her evenings the same way, in a constant cycle of cooking, tidying, and sneaking off to the fenced-in seclusion of her backyard for a few pulls off a cigarette. Most of all, though, Mrs. Ortiz smiled. In fact, she smiled far too much for a woman who'd just lost her husband in a tragic accident.

When Mrs. Ortiz thought no one was watching, when the smoke was unfurling from between her lips, when she doused a pan in soapy water, the woman's sorrowful mask slipped. And she grinned, a quiet joy in her sparkling eyes. Mrs. Ortiz was a woman at peace.

After the third day of researching her target, Cin was growing tired of seeing the expression on the woman's face. The timing couldn't have been better either. At the diner, the youngest Ortiz had been babbling nonstop about Tommy McAdams' new game system. The boy would be spending the evening at the neighbor's, testing out the toy. A perfect opportunity for Cat's Eye to make a special delivery to Mrs. Ortiz.

At sunset, Cin locked her bedroom door, slipping on a uniform of black street clothes that hugged her body and left no room for clumsy slip-ups. Military boots clapped the floor as she crossed it, tying up her stringy, blond hair and tucking it beneath the black wig. She sat down at the vanity, spreading waterproof make-up three shades too dark over every patch of exposed skin. But she was still Cin. Even though she now looked far more like her late mother than her absent father, she remained Cindy Burrows.

A brown contact lens covered her right eye, her living eye. There was only one more element of her transformation. She tapped her left eye with one finger, feeling nothing but the perfectly sculpted rise of the glass. Using the nail of her index, she pushed beneath the bottom lid. Lashes fluttered at her intrusion. The false eye slipped out. Its touch was a warm token against her palm.

She blinked, the absence leaving her with a pink, empty slit.

The new eye was heavier than the last, sculpted by her father. There were a slew of its clones stored like precious gems in a lock box below the vanity. Each and every one was a masterpiece, each and every one distinct, varied, if only slightly, from the other. Cin held it up to the light, and the light loved it. Cat's Eye was the common name for this type of marble, and the narrow channel of black swirling against a tunnel of gold made it look the part. What she held between two fingers, though, was only part of such a marble, its magnificent curve set in clear glass with a black setting.

She pulled up her brow, resisting the need to flinch as the cool glass hit barren flesh. The effect was both terrifying and mystifying. A colored orb floating in black space.

When she stopped a criminal in his tracks, it was this

feature alone he was always able to recollect: "She had a funny eye… Looked like a damn cat's…"

Cat's Eye stood from the stool, leaving Cin behind. She slid the oily into her pocket, forgoing all other weaponry. She wouldn't need the rest tonight.

*** *** ***

Cat's Eye went in through the back. The sliding pair of doors led to Mrs. Ortiz's favorite smoking hide-away, a folding aluminum chair tucked out of sight along the hedges. Two nights, and the woman had taken her escape at the same time every evening, right before she was ready to retire, and this third night was no different. Cat's Eye slipped in behind her and past another opening before the woman could come back from brushing the taste of tobacco out of her mouth.

Mrs. Ortiz returned to the glass doors, opened them, sniffed the fresh air as if to ensure that all evidence of her little habit was blown away, and shut them again. She slid the joke of a lock down, oblivious to the one eye following her every movement from behind the pantry door. The curtains fell into place.

Cat's Eye followed her to the bedroom.

Mrs. Ortiz stopped at the bed but didn't bend to pull back the covers. Instead, she stood perfectly still, her hands loose and at the sides of her robe.

"Figured something like this might happen," she said.

The voice was so soft that, for a moment, Cat's Eye thought it had been her imagination.

Mrs. Ortiz turned, the movement deliberately slow. She

squinted, the yellow lamp light playing games with her vision. The older woman straightened.

"I know you," she continued, but it didn't sound like an accusation. "The papers call you Cat's Eye when they call you anything at all. I thought you stuck to the city."

Cat's Eye cocked her head, looking every bit her namesake. Untouched by wind or force, the door behind her slammed shut.

"I go where the crime is," she replied.

Mrs. Ortiz sat down on the edge of the bed, crossing her legs modestly. There was weariness in her gaze, but the peace, the undeserved peace, remained in the small grin at her lips. Seeing it, Cat's Eye felt an old, familiar heat crawl over her skin. When she raised a finger, the blinds over the windows slammed down with a clap.

If the ghostly movement bothered Mrs. Ortiz, it didn't show on her face. "Haven't heard much about you in a while."

"Been on vacation." Cat's Eye realized she'd snapped with the words and regretted it not because it was wrong but because this housewife sitting in front of her, knowing and at peace, was too damned calm, calmer than any criminal Cat's Eye had ever taken down.

Cat's Eye slipped two fingers into her pocket and withdrew the marble. She let it hover in the air between her gloved thumb and index finger as if it were being held by a string.

"I know what I did was wrong," Mrs. Ortiz said, beating Cat's Eye to the punch line.

"And I bet you're real sorry," Cat's Eye said. The marble was spinning now, picking up speed. "Or, at the very least,

sorry you were caught."

"I should have to pay," Mrs. Ortiz agreed.

"You really should."

The lamps beside the bed began to shake with a tremor they alone felt. Mrs. Ortiz ignored them, staring up at the young woman. The silence between them stretched tight before it broke. The lamps went still again. Cat's Eye had a hard time holding back a sigh of frustration.

"We'll do this the right way," Cat's Eye finally said. "A full confession. No mention of my…persuasion. You'll go away. You'll pay."

"Sure." Mrs. Ortiz nodded. "Alright."

"You're not going to put up a fight?" Cat's Eye asked. The marble had stopped spinning. She was losing it, the anger. The rage. "This isn't how it usually works."

"I'm done fighting," Mrs. Ortiz replied. "I won my fight. I didn't have to do a thing either. Not a thing. Winner by default."

Cat's Eye raised a brow, her body tense, alert. Her brain registered the sound a split-second after her foot had already lifted, ready to deliver a kick to the door.

But it opened only a crack, a trembling voice from the hallway pushing past the opening. The words were high-pitched and muffled, but Cat's Eye recognized the voice.

"Please don't."

The boy wasn't supposed to be home.

Fingers clenched around the marble, holding it still. Cat's Eye sucked in a breath. A part of her knew she should still kick the door shut, block him from whatever he was about to say, but she waited too late. His fingers were clasping on to the frame and in her way.

Mrs. Ortiz stood, and the mattress wailed. "Go to bed, James," she said.

The child didn't listen. He pushed his way into the room, wide-eyed with drowsiness. But he didn't flinch when he saw the stranger in his mother's room. If anything, his back straightened. He stared up at Cat's Eye with the same tired intensity as his mother. He recognized her eye.

"Don't," he repeated. "Don't take my momma away."

"Go to bed, James." Mrs. Ortiz squeezed his shoulder, trying to steer him back to the door, but he stood still. "James, baby, Momma's busy right now."

"I'm not a baby," he said, pouting. His brow wrinkled. Cat's Eye could see the wetness in his eyes. As much as they shined, they didn't leak. "I know what she's doing here. I know, Momma. I do." He turned from his mother to the stranger. "She didn't do it." And back again. "Tell her, Momma. Tell her."

Mrs. Ortiz slid to her knees, holding the child.

"I did, baby," she whispered.

The tears fell. "It was an accident." But the statement quivered with his bottom lip.

Mrs. Ortiz smiled her peaceful smile. "It was, baby, but leaving him there was the same as killing him. I watched him die. I waited for him to."

James huffed, holding back a sob. He pushed away from his mother's soft hands, glaring up at Cat's Eye. "This is your fault!" he snapped. "You're 'posed to get the bad men, and you didn't. You didn't help." He pushed his sleeve over his wet

nose, his round face red with the effort to continue. "It's not fair. My momma's a better hero than you! She saved us when you… *you* never even came."

James let out a sob, disappearing back out of the room. Cat's Eye could hear him, just one room away, his body shaking against the plaster wall. She gazed down at the woman sitting on the floor. Studied her. Two days and two nights, Cin and Cat's Eye had watched and waited. Neither of them had seen the dark bruising over the woman's chest, right below the modest neckline of her blouse. Tonight, the robe showed too much and too little. The marking was nearly healed. Several days old.

Probably about four if Cat's Eye ventured a guess.

"Tell me," Cat's Eye said. It was not a request. This was not Cin's teasing voice. These words were orders. "Tell me now. Justify it."

Criminals were experts at justification. Those were her father's words, and they were true. As always.

Mrs. Ortiz shook her head, unmoved by the authority in Cat's Eye's voice. "It doesn't matter, does it? It was wrong. Two wrongs don't make a right." She paused, a small laugh taking her breath. When she recovered, her hand was raised, open and cupped. Asking for it. "I'll call the cops myself. I promise."

Cat's Eye squeezed the marble before unfolding her fingers. This was it, the part where she left her calling card behind, left the criminal with something to think about. Something to remember her by. The rainbow over the clear glass looked wet, polished by the glove's hold. Cat's Eye gave it a final glance before sliding it back into her pocket.

"It's not meant for you," Cat's Eye said even though she wasn't sure of the truth behind those words. She had read the newspaper her father had left out twice. She knew the articles, knew what to look for when it came to her father's subtle hints. This, this story of a tragic accident, it had been the one he'd wanted her to see.

Mrs. Ortiz didn't reply, and Cat's Eye didn't ask for more answers. She would never ask for those answers, even the ones she needed. The ones her father held. Had he meant to teach her something, sending her here, after the justified?

The question wouldn't leave her lips.

When Cat's Eye finally returned home, her father was still in his shop, his oven glowing hot. She put the marble back in its box, not mentioning its imperfection, and left the toy sitting on his work counter. He didn't speak, as usual, his eyes straying so that he wouldn't have to see her black uniform, see his shining workmanship in her eye socket.

"I won't," she finally said and left him to his craft. Cat's Eye hoped the frown at his lips was not one of disappointment.

Sometimes, even Cat's Eye didn't keep her promises.

HERO

DR. LANGE STOPPED THE RECORDER AND STUDIED THE MAN on the other side of the desk. Robert Hanover looked broken. He was wrecked with exhaustion, his lips purple, his skin a pasty gray and filmed with sweat, yet even still, he fought against the restraints that held his wrists to the chair.

Dr. Lange sighed.

This was yet another recording he'd have to erase.

Hanover suddenly rallied. He fought against the restraints. "God damn you!" he shouted. "You let me go. Let me help her. For God's sake, Gene, let me go!"

Dr. Lange's expression soured when Hanover addressed him by his first name, but he quickly forced his distaste down. Correcting the man would do little good. Hanover was a clinical narcissist—as close to a textbook case as Dr. Lange had ever seen in fact—and refusing to address doctors by their proper titles was but one symptom of his inflated sense of entitlement and self-importance. He also needed constant praise and reinforcement. He set unrealistic goals. Social clues went by him unnoticed. And, of course, his self-esteem was fragile as an eggshell.

All of which was routine. Just about everything about Robert Hanover was routine. Only his delusions of power were exceptional. More precisely, the nature of his delusions set him apart, for Robert Hanover believed he could see exactly seven minutes and twenty-two seconds into the future.

But not all the time.

When he was calm, he would always qualify his claim.

He couldn't do it on command either. His premonitions came unbidden. They were violent and painful. They were like lightning, sudden and unpredictable. And when they did come, they left Hanover exhausted and frantic.

Like now.

Dr. Lange studied the man, remembering when Hanover had told him about his supposed visions. He had barely been able to contain his smile in fact. The fantasy was thoroughly banal and absolutely unoriginal, straight out of a Stephen King novel and half a dozen episodes of the Twilight Zone. It was such a tired conceit that Dr. Lange was less intrigued by the delusion itself than by the very precise timing involved.

Seven minutes and twenty-two seconds.

Exactly.

But why that length of time?

Dr. Lange expected Hanover to have some pat answer.

A fragile ego like Hanover's, one that believed itself superior to everyone else around it, should have had a ready retort to explain why that amount of time was important. But Hanover insisted he had no idea, and nothing in his history, and nothing in their sessions, offered any clues.

Still, Dr. Lange knew there was something there. If there was a key to unlocking Robert Hanover's condition, that odd length of time was it.

Dr. Lange began cataloging the events Hanover claimed to have predicted, hoping that he might shed some light on the problem that way. Most of Hanover's visions were insignificant and ultimately unverifiable. His mother running over a cat in front of their house. A bird flying into the kitchen window. His dog killing a squirrel in the backyard. With no way to prove those claims, Dr. Lange was forced to dismiss them.

But there were some that could not be dismissed so easily.

When he was nineteen, Hanover saved a three-year-old little girl from getting hit by a taxi. Half of the lunch crowd gathered on Boston Common had been there to witness his heroism.

He'd once called 911 to report his elderly neighbor's heart attack, which seemed to have just started when the ambulance arrived.

He'd saved at least four people from drowning.

He'd once pulled a woman from a burning shop on Boylston Street.

Dr. Lange had the newspaper clippings for all of them. In fact, he'd been able to verify a total of forty-seven incidents where Robert Hanover had clearly saved another person's life.

For a time, the Boston *Herald* was calling him the Miracle Man.

The news show *20/20* even did a segment on him.

The man's record was nothing short of incredible, and personally, Dr. Lange believed the media would have fallen head over heels in love with Robert Hanover if he hadn't been such a self-absorbed prick. He was twenty-five, a good-looking guy, at least when he wasn't acting like a raving lunatic, and fairly well-spoken. But he loved the adulation that came with saving lives.

No, Dr. Lange thought, love wasn't the right word.

Robert Hanover's motives were decidedly less pure than that.

He craved adulation and fame like a glutton. He swam in it. Wallowed in it like a pig in slop. There was something greedy and repellent in the way he begged for praise and recognition, and people had a tendency to back away from him, sensing instinctively that there was something wrong with him. Dr. Lange had even caught himself doing it a time or two.

The media, in an unusual example of discretion, marginalized him.

And just like that, the greatest American hero turned into a zero.

The predictable downward spiral of failed personal relationships and financial disasters that followed led Robert Hanover to the Paulsen Institute and to the ministrations of Dr. Lange. And Robert Hanover might have remained a pathetic, failed narcissist—at least to Dr. Lange—had he not made a fateful prediction during one of their sessions.

"The man's got poisonous shit!" Hanover had shouted as the orderlies dragged him away. "You have to listen to me!"

They were in the hallway outside of the common room. Patients were milling about, but they all stopped and stared after the raving Hanover. When he was gone, they turned back to Dr. Lange, questions lingering in their drugged expressions.

Dr. Lange smiled back at them, assuring them it was alright. Then he'd smiled at Ms. Reynolds, the stunningly gorgeous young nurse on watch at the time. In fact, his gaze lingered for a long moment on Ms. Reynolds. It was easy for the eye to linger on her. Even in baggy scrubs, her body made Dr. Lange's mouth water.

Suddenly, a patient stumbled out of the shadows. He was a middle-aged man in green pajamas. His eyes rolled crazily from side to side.

"My bowels," the man said. His voice had a tremulous quality, making him sound like some mad Baptist preacher calling forth hellfire and damnation. "It comes out of my bowels. My bowels!"

As Dr. Lange and the gorgeous young Nurse Reynolds stared at the man, he reached into the seat of his pants and rooted around in the crack of his ass like he was digging clams out of the mud.

Dr. Lange didn't understand what was happening until he saw the clod of shit in the man's hand.

Then he remembered what Robert Hanover had said. The man's shit was poisonous. Hanover had raved that the man was going to throw his feces into Dr. Lange's mouth, and

suddenly, Dr. Lange knew what he had to do. Beside him was an autistic woman with an intense fear of being touched. He stepped behind the woman, who in her bovine-like stupor had no chance of reacting.

Bowel-Movement Man hurled his waste at the spot where Dr. Lange had just been standing. It splattered against the autistic woman's face, bits of it landing in her mouth, in her eyes, up her nose.

Late, shaken, but nonetheless convinced, he confronted Robert Hanover.

"Your premonitions," he'd said. "Everything you've told me indicates that they only concern life-threatening incidents. Having a handful of waste tossed in your face is disgusting, but it's not life-threatening."

"It is a life-threatening matter," Hanover had said. "That man is dying."

"But how do you know?"

Hanover just stared at him, angry and bitter yet poignantly sad.

Two days later, when a court-ordered test of Bowel-Movement Man's blood came back positive for HIV, Dr. Lange finally understood the bullet he had just dodged. He started keeping a separate file on Hanover's premonitions, one he nicknamed Cassandra, the young woman from *The Iliad*, who was destined to tell the future and cursed never to be believed.

For Robert Hanover was such a figure, a latter-day Cassandra.

From the moment Bowel-Movement Man hurled his

clod of shit, Dr. Lange was sure of that. He believed, without reservation, that Robert Hanover could foretell the future.

Yet Hanover was not credible and never would be. His status as nutcase prohibited any sane man from believing in him.

It was a tough nut to crack.

Still, Robert Hanover, the Miracle Man, had just saved his life.

What was he to make of that?

What would any sane man make of having his very own private oracle…and the intoxicating knowledge that he alone could control its fate?

Hanover's screams jarred Dr. Lange back into the moment. "For God's sake, Gene! You have to believe me!"

Dr. Lange smiled graciously. Then, he looked at his watch and was surprised that two full minutes had gone by. He had to hurry.

Orderlies were banging at the door.

Dr. Lange let them in.

"It's okay," Dr. Lange said. "Everything's fine. Just take him back to his room."

"Gene, please!"

The orderlies ignored his shouts but were careful not to release the hold they had on him. "Any medications?" one of the orderlies asked.

"Aprazolam ought to do it. Let him sleep it off."

The orderlies dragged Robert Hanover out of Dr. Lange's office and down the hall, the man's screams echoing into the recesses of the Paulsen Institute's winding passageways. A

lull settled over the patients in the common room. "It's okay, everyone," Dr. Lange said. He smiled and waved, and soon, the patients went back to their routines, milling about as though nothing at all had happened.

A nurse came up to him.

"What is it?" Dr. Lange said.

"Doctor Pendergrass is on the phone for you, sir."

Dr. Lange grimaced. Wayne Pendergrass was the Paulsen Institute's director of operations and, ostensibly, Dr. Lange's boss.

"Tell him I'll call him back," Dr. Lange said to the nurse.

"But sir, he said it was urgent."

"It always is, Nurse—" he made a furtive glance towards the woman's name tag, "Cowell. Unfortunately, I have somewhere I have to be. Tell him I'll call him back."

And with that, Dr. Lange walked toward the stairs.

He glanced at his watch. He had exactly three minutes and eighteen seconds to make it the gorgeous Nurse Reynolds' new station on the second floor. Robert Hanover's latest premonition had been of her and of the raving lunatic with the snapped-off broom handle who was about to bludgeon her beautiful, blonde head into a bloody mess.

Dr. Lange had a life to save.

He smiled, thinking how very appreciative the pretty young nurse was sure to be.

Afterwards.

PRIDE

WAYNE LIGON

I WAS IN LINE AT THE LOCAL CHINESE BUFFET WAITING FOR A free cashier when the robbery went down. They weren't pros; that much was apparent right off. It's just two of them, and they do way too much yelling and screaming. "Down on the floor! You move, you die!" That sort of thing. And of course, they're robbing a Chinese buffet instead of a bank. Maybe they were working their way up to that.

I squeezed the bridge of my nose. My therapist says it helps relieve tension. This was going to make me late back from lunch, and I'd probably get canned because of it. I did not get down on the floor. It was damp outside, and my left knee was giving me problems.

Thug One stuck a gun against my head and screamed, "You a fuckin' hero, man?"

Well, as a matter of fact…

Two seconds later, both of them were screaming like little kids as my telekinetic field flared up and clamped down, blue foxfire light flickering along their bodies. I twisted the guns around and into their mouths, forcing their fingers to stay on the triggers. They give off muffled screams as they go to their knees, fighting not to blow their own brains out. "Down on the ground!" shouted a Concerned Citizen of Detroit, pointing his Second Amendment penis substitute at me.

"Do not pull that shit with me, Cornfed. I am not in the mood," I said. "I'm regis—" BLAM! I go for my card, and apparently, it's not slow enough, so Barney Fife shoots me. The bullet hits my reflex field, and there's a little show as I bleed off its kinetic energy into waste light and heat. Then, I let it drop. He stammers, and I pretzel his gun before he shoots someone's mom.

I flash the bright red card since none of them will be able to tell it's worthless. "Do Not Panic," I say in a calm, steady voice. "I am a registered freelance law enforcement specialist. I am also off-duty. Can I please get some orange beef to go?"

For once, things go my way, and the manager takes care of my food. The cops are there by then; I release the would-be robbers to them and avoid the looks the rookies give me. At twenty, I'm not old enough to join the force even if that was allowed, and I put away a good fifty or so guys like these before my license was placed "under review." They didn't know that though. I slip out the side door before I have to talk to one of the plainclothes. It'll take too much time.

It doesn't much matter though because I'm still ten

minutes late. I trot outside and push off from the sidewalk, the flickering light surrounding my body as I vault into the air. I wince at the sound of a fender-bender below. Another looky-loo whose inattention is going to make my metahuman tax (sorry, I mean "insurance") go up another five bucks. I hopscotch over rooftops and drop down into an alleyway to wolf down cold orange beef and rice.

It's 12:13 when I go over the back fence of the construction area. Immediately, I pick up a pile of bricks and have the mass follow me like a dog. Calm, casual, just been around the back of the site and already diligently at—

"I got my eye on you, Carmichael," says a gravelly pack-a-day voice.

"I know you do, Matt—Mr. Foster," I correct hastily. I put on that neutral smile I've been cultivating and meet the man's eyes square on. "Sorry, I was just looking for these for the facing. They need 'em up on third." Butter would not melt in my mouth.

Foster's left eye twitches, and I think this might be the day he goes for me. He likes to mess with me because he knows he can take me in a fair fight—powers aside, I'm just a skinny slacker kid—but if I hit back with my gift, I blow my probation and do life in Leavenworth for powers use on a normal. I keep the smile neutral. It does not move a millimeter.

Foster's boss saves about ten thousand a day using me as an illegal substitute for earthmovers and other machinery and their operators. My alpha-class gift means I can juggle I-beams if needed, but union rules were strictly pro-norm. No super-strength, no robots, no cyborgs, no alchemists, no

teeks like me.

Hundreds of class-action suits were still grinding their way through the legal system like huge paper glaciers along with all the other meta-rights legislation. We were people; wait, no, we were corporate property; no, we were classed as WMDs. In nine states, we could marry. In six, we were barred from coming within a hundred feet of any concentration of children. I could not eat from a salad bar in Rhode Island. Every school kid in Alabama was required to be tested for "genetic abnormalities" before the onset of puberty, when most metanormal gifts got a kick in the backside from the hormone stew and decided to manifest. Fear of just this kind of shit is why heroes wore masks for real before JFK convinced them otherwise.

"Ask what you can do for your country," my ass. In twenty years, I might be able to work legally somewhere. Probably flipping burgers ten at a time with my mind.

Foster looks me over and walks off. I keep up the neutral smile until he's out of sight. He'd love to bust my balls on general principles because I was everything he wasn't—slim, young, able to get a date—but he got a bigger cut under the table than normal because of me, so he usually let it slide.

I walk around to the side and stack the bricks. One of the Mexicans crosses himself, and I shake my head. I try to explain in halting Spanish that it's just a talent like anything else, but he's not having any of it. He spits out "*brujah*," witch, and gets in the lift. I shrug and send the bricks up after him, ten at a time, to the third floor. He sends down a huge hawk of spit that I flick aside. I snap one of the bricks in half and then quarters with the strength of my mind, keeping my eyes on him. I give him the same smile I gave Foster. He pales and backs off into the interior, muttering curses.

"Carmichael! Peterson wants you. Emergency," comes over the loudspeaker. I leave the remainder of the bricks behind and bolt for the basement. Peterson isn't someone to cry wolf, and he's trying to get the plumbing into shape. I levitate down an open shaft and fly through the narrow maze of maintenance passages, dodging valve wheels and other workers. Most of them are heading the other way; a couple point the way, and I give them a nod as I blur past.

I flash into a flooding basement room, and Bill Peterson screams at me, "Pressure valve is broken; this whole set of pipes is going to blow! Please, can you—" He's cut off by the squeal of metal even as I reach out with my gift.

I usually say it's like a small electrical shock that keeps going, which is a barely adequate description of what it feels like to use my power at its peak. I reach out and clamp down on the entire assembly, letting my power permeate the metal into the rushing water behind it. I brace and strengthen the pipes from the inside and the outside, but the welds are not going to hold.

My power flares out from me, light strobing gently around me like a fluorescent bulb about to go out. The room shakes. Some of the onlookers scream and run. Yeah, you better run, you monkeys. This is what an alpha-class gift is really like.

Alpha-class or not, there's nothing I can do. The whole assembly starts to break apart in my grip: substandard metal, faulty welds, parts forced to fit together that shouldn't be

within a hundred miles of each other. It all comes to a head. I throw Bill and two other guys out of the room and let go. The valves burst apart, and the pipes explode under the pressure, shards of metal flying out like spears shot from a gun. I sink waist-deep in water, nothing left to levitate myself, and throw up a shield across the entire length of the room. Shrapnel floats, caught in nothingness. Water surges and batters against a barely-visible, flickering blue wall. My eyes are glowing white by this point.

I wave my hands like fucking Harry Potter and then make fists so tight my palms bleed. I know, intellectually, it doesn't do a damn thing, but it helps my concentration. And that's all that counts. Half of the room fills with water as the pressure eases, but then it starts to mount again. Shouts come from behind me.

"Get everyone out! I can't hold this for very long!" I yell, already hoarse. I start to back out, the wall sliding with me. I can hold the door better if the physical walls will hold. I send feelers out into the concrete and steel, sensing the weight of tons pressing down on them from above. The walls will hold at least. I back out, eyes closed, hands up and open. The sound of evacuating workers dies away. Slowly, I pull back on the wall, sliding it across the room and then contracting it until I'm just blocking the door. I can feel blood running down my face: nosebleed.

Then I'm trapped. I can't leave without the plug fracturing, and I can't fly fast enough to outrun the water that's going to come erupting out of there. So I stay, trembling slightly.

"Are you shutting the mains off?" I yell. No response. I

wait—wait for the panic to subside and someone to remember what needs to be done. They'll need to call the city guys, get a crew here, all that. It takes time.

What the fuck am I doing? I don't owe anyone anything. The City of Detroit shafted me good and hard already, back when I wore a mask as a member of Detroit's Teen Corps One.

I was drafted into the Teen Corps after "an anomaly" showed up after a routine doctor's visit. I'd been keeping my power a secret from everyone exactly like you are not supposed to do, so right away, that put me on every watch list in the country. It wasn't literally a federal offense like it is now, so they put me into a pair of tights and told me I was an apprentice.

I was a sidekick. It was worse than driving school. Due to federal regs, I wasn't allowed to go solo until I was twenty-five, so I was paired with an older paranormal who would train and oversee me.

A day shy of my sixteenth birthday, my mentor messed up a simple bust and put a woman in a wheelchair for the rest of her life. She sued the city for millions and won. My mentor blamed the whole thing on me. He told me that since I was a minor, they'd go easy on me whereas he had a wife and kid to support and a pension to protect. A year or so in therapy, and I'd be free. I was an idealistic fool and signed the papers saying I was at fault.

I got my year in therapy all right courtesy of a federal supermax facility. The ACLU went to bat for me and won my release on some technical grounds, but things didn't get much better. I was out of prison but not free. Any paranormal that

messes up and hurts a normal with his powers gets put on permanent probation. One strike, and you're back in prison forever. Depending on your ability, they also dope you up so you're not a public nuisance. Your parole officer comes by once a week to give you a shot, and you get to play normal for the rest of your life. My gift was too powerful to blunt with the drugs they had at the time without killing me, so they did the next best thing.

They took my mask.

Most metahumans wear masks for the same reason narcotics cops do: to prevent retaliation by the people they bring to justice and to give plausible deniability to their higher-ups in case something goes wrong. "Kid Kinetic" became simple Calvin Carmichael of such-and-such address. My family was put into Witness Protection, and I haven't seen them since. Most of my rights would never be reinstated. If I ever moved from the federal housing project they installed me in, I'd have to get signatures from everyone in the neighborhood after explaining I was a potential metahuman threat. There was a lot more. I lived under a set of restrictions that made me yearn for the freedom of a repeat sex offender.

"Cal, what the hell is going on here?"

His voice paralyzes me for a second. I guess I knew they'd send him. I take a deep breath, pretend I'm having trouble maintaining the plug.

I look to my side, sweat pouring down my face. Black Saber, head of the Detroit Defenders, the state-and-local-backed team of emergency-response metahumans. He was taller than me by a head and was dressed in his working clothes: black, skintight Preflex uniform with gold and white highlights and accessories. He wore a crossed-swords emblem over his broad chest.

Saber is a super-speedster, able to run about fifty times the speed of sound. The only other alpha-level talent in the city besides myself. My former mentor. He trained me, and then he betrayed me. He was also the guy they sent when there was a mess to clean up.

"Ah, just another day on the job, Saber. Holding back about a hundred tons of pressurized water. Everyone out of the sub-levels?"

"They are," he said casually, eyeing the water surging against the doorway. He smiles tightly. "You always tried to do the right thing. What's your plan here?"

"You grab me and super-speed out of here, and their basements flood until the city gets around to shutting off the mains. Nothing is wrong with the foundations, so everyone wins."

"No can do," Saber says casually. "The mayor is heavily invested in this building; it's the centerpiece of his renovation initiative. If it's late going up, he stands to lose a bundle."

I set my jaw. "Dude, really? It *is* going to flood. Nothing can stop that…" I paused. Oh.

He saw the look on my face and nodded. If the building flooded and they spent six months pumping it out and exposed all the substandard plumbing, the mayor would lose both his shirt and the next election. On the other hand, if the building were damaged by a metahuman terrorist, then it was ice cream and insurance payments for everyone. Guess what industry

the mayor's brother had in his back pocket? Hint: He didn't own a Baskin-Robbins.

"So," I said way more casually than I felt, "They really just need a body."

"A trial would take too long, Calvin, and it would certainly blow up into a federal matter."

"Can't have the Feds sniffing around the Defenders program," I said, my voice carefully flat and reasonable. That I did know. Just the kickbacks and under-the-table benefits coming to light would bring a squad of federal super-soldiers down on Detroit. The entire program would revert to federal oversight, and it would be the end of the gravy train.

A small voice said, *At least you won't go back to prison.*

No. No, I was still in prison, and I was damn tired of it.

Slowly, I expanded my plug against the arch, pushing microscopic cracks down and out as far as I could through the concrete. I closed my eyes and bowed my head like I was resigned to my fate, was waiting for the blow that would save face for everyone. Actually, I was pushing myself further than I ever had before. With each heartbeat, I pushed harder and harder, extending those cracks while keeping the concrete solid.

Black Saber smiled, his mouth and jaw visible, the armored cowl rendering his eyes into unreadable white slits. Any split-second, he'd go for the Mach-4 snap-punch and break my neck, the way he used to do to crackheads on Eight Mile. In his mind, he was doing me a favor For Old Time's Sake by not letting me drown.

"I knew you'd understand, Kid," Black Saber said softly.

I dropped the plug the same instant he tried to kill me, my reflex shield shunting the energy of his multi-mach punch off into the surrounding walls. They shattered like glass, sending an earthquake-level shockwave ripping through the entire structure and down into the very bedrock. The foundations and every load-bearing support turned to gravel. Then, the mains and sewers blew upwards, turning everything to quicksand. There was a blaze of pain, and the world disappeared into a tornado of muddy water as I fought to keep my shield intact.

Here's a little-known fact: When your paranormal power is "I run really fast," being underwater sucks balls.

If the mayor wanted a body so badly, let him have one.

I rose out of the wreckage flaring like a star bright enough to throw shadows in the suburbs, the energy of the domino-effect collapse feeding into my own. Emergency crews fled as I threw two of the backup Defenders through a nearby office building. The looky-loos scattered. See the monkeys run. Run, monkey, run.

I didn't bother going back to the shitty fed apartment. The only thing waiting for me there was a lifetime of four walls and shock therapy.

I'm not going to live like a prisoner anymore. Not me and not the thousands like me and not the thousands waiting to be born. Paranormal Pride, bay-bee.

It feels good to put on a mask again.

G-CHILD

AS I FREEFALL FROM THE UH-60L BLACK HAWK HELICOPTER, I point my chin to the ground and my toes to the sky. The shit is hitting the fan on Oglesby Avenue below. Homes have been reduced to splintered wood and rubble. A steady stream of small arms fire flashes from a house to my left. I smile. Finally, a true test of my abilities.

The PR people for the Institute of Psionics thought giving us code names would be a cute and easy way to gain public sentiment. They call me Bliss. That big, bald, black dude in the middle of all the carnage down there is Rayge. Looks like Ray J is living up to his code name.

Just before I hit the ground and splatter into yet another grease spot on the streets of Jeffrey Manor, I manipulate the air flows around me to slow my descent. My sleek, black and yellow carbon fiber titanium suit aids the aerodynamics and—arms outstretched, palms up—I descend to Earth like a goddess from on high.

Usually, when Ray J or I go to the South Side of Chicago, someone always bumps Wiz Khalifa's "Black and Yellow" like it's our theme song. But not this time. It's quiet except for the occasional rat-tat-tat of gunfire. Folks or Vice Lords or Gangster Disciples. I should know which gang, but I never paid attention during the gang training the Institute gave us. All I care about is the social dynamics of the North Side and the north suburbs. I figure since the South Side is Ray J's territory, he should know.

Speaking of which, he disappears into that house I saw coming in halfway down the block. Almost immediately, an explosion levels it. Nothing moves.

"Is he dead?"

I turn and see Kee-Kee. Ray J's baby-mama. Their little boy Ray-Ray clutches her, his chubby fists trying to find good purchase on her too-tight jeans. He looks at me wide-eyed and then hides his face in her hip. I put up a telekinetic shield around the three of us and frown at Kee-Kee.

"What the hell are you doing?" I ask her. "Go home! Get out of here!"

"I ain't got no home no more." Kee-Kee points behind me to where her house used to be.

Shit. I rotate my wrist and speak to the inside of it. "Mother Bird, I need an evac. Two civilians. Mother and child." I look around. I hope there are survivors in the burned out garages and under the overturned cars. "Possibly more."

My wrist communicator crackles. "Roger that, Bliss. We're on our way."

Ray-Ray peeks out at me from behind Kee-Kee. I bend down and smile at him but speak to his mother. "What happened?"

"They killed Ray J's father." I raise an eyebrow. "It was a drug deal gone bad." Ray-Ray presses his face into his mother's hip again. Kee-Kee looks down at him. "Ray J hadn't seen him since he was Ray-Ray's age." Tears stand in her eyes. "He told Ray J he was clean."

Ray J is from the Manor. He grew up on Oglesby. Today is his day off, and he got a special day pass to go see Ray Sr. He was nervous. He'd told me last night that he didn't want his father inside the Institute around all of those government people, so he was going back to his old stomping grounds to meet him. And is he ever stomping the shit out of it.

The wind picks up as the Black Hawk lands behind us. I lower my shield and motion Kee-Kee and Ray-Ray toward the helicopter.

"He'll be all right," I shout over the rotor blades. "I'll make sure of it."

Two tears roll down her cheeks. She doesn't believe me. She sees the destruction he wrought. But she puts Ray-Ray on her hip and goes to the 'copter because there's nothing she can do here.

I throw up my shield again, a crackling dome of mental energy, and walk toward the inferno that was a house just moments ago. It's up to me to stop him. I've never been able to in our training exercises, and that's with him pulling his

punches.

I'm almost at the burning house when an enormous streak of fire slams into me. I come to one street over in someone's living room. Shit. My shield barely saved my life.

*** *** ***

When my mother was five months pregnant with me, her obstetrician suggested she participate in clinical trials for an experimental prenatal supplement at Great Lakes Naval Hospital. She'd been having complications from pre-eclampsia. Headaches. Hypertension. Problems with her kidneys and liver. For African-American women like my mother, pre-eclampsia was more likely to result in death. But that was something my mother was willing to risk if it meant she could bring a happy, healthy, beautiful baby girl into the world.

*** *** ***

I stagger to my feet and wipe away a trickle of blood from my nose. My fists glow blue with psionic energy. Fine. If Rayge wants to have a slug fest, then let's have a slug fest.

*** *** ***

I was her first child. Her only child. It had taken my mother and my father fifteen years to conceive. At first, my mother refused to risk her only chance at having a baby for an unproven drug that probably wouldn't even work. She told my father that if something went wrong because of the prenatal experimental supplement—that if she lost me—she would never be able to live with herself. My father reminded my mother what she always said: She was a tough old bitch, and the Good Lord Himself didn't have the balls to mess with her.

*** *** ***

I can see Ray J's fury before he gets to me. It manifests itself as two malevolent, violet-black probing tendrils as big around as my thigh. Ray J's schtick is to take all of his pent-up anger and unleash it as physical rage. When we train, it always takes everything I have to hold off his blows with my telekinetic shield long enough to flip the calm switch in his brain. But never before have I seen his fury this massive.

*** *** ***

Eventually, my father convinced my mother to participate in the clinical trial with tears. He had grown up with Dr. Shimada and told my mother he trusted her with his life. When my mother asked him if he trusted Dr. Shimada with the life of their unborn child, the only child they would probably ever conceive, my father, who had taken a few performing arts classes during undergrad at Sophia University in Tokyo—where he met my mother—answered her with tears on his cheeks.

*** *** ***

I can sense the two purple-black tendrils probing the half-destroyed house, looking for me or someone that Ray J can lay the smack down on. The tendrils search down the hall and go into the bedrooms, hesitant, careful, and sneaky. They move slowly. They search thoroughly. They peek around corners. I

close my eyes and take a deep breath to clear my mind. Send out my own tendrils. They're slender. They're bright blue. And they're badass.

*** *** ***

It was a big deal for my father to show emotion. He was raised Japanese old school. Not like these sensitive Japanese boys today. My father was taught that Japanese men weren't supposed to cry, and they damn sure weren't supposed to cry in front of their wives. But that was exactly what my mother needed. She showed up at Great Lakes Naval Hospital with ninety-nine other pregnant women happy and smiling. But two months later, when twenty women miscarried and another twenty women bore odd, squalling, premature babies, my mother told my father she wasn't going back to the hospital.

*** *** ***

But not badass enough. Ray J's tendrils seize mine. My eyes snap open. Roll back into my head. The pain is excruciating. Like nothing I've felt before. My tendrils turn black. Begin to rot. Decay creeps down their length. Toward my mind. I'm awash with intimidation. Fear. I can't pull away. I can't shake free. I can't order my mind. So I do the only thing I can. I open my mouth and scream.

*** *** ***

My mother went back to Great Lakes Naval Hospital though. How could she not? Her headaches were gone. Her kidneys and liver were stable. Her blood pressure was down. But

she wasn't happy. Every night, she woke to the screams of misshapen, grotesque babies. My mother dreamed about them so much that she was surprised she carried me to full term and I came out normal. And that's how I stayed. For twelve years. And then I turned thirteen and linked my mind to my fifty-eight-year-old mother while she was having sex with my sixty-year-old father.

*** *** ***

My fight-or-flight psionic response allows me to break free of Ray J's rage and intimidation. I need to get out of these people's house before it's destroyed any further. When I step out the front door, Ray J is standing there. He smacks me three blocks over to Luella Avenue. My psionic shield takes the full brunt of the impact. But something is wrong with me. I should have known he was there. I should have sensed him. And then I do. I look up and see Ray J coming in feet first, hard and fast, ready to get his stomp on some more.

*** *** ***

My mother told me I couldn't live at home after that. It was just too weird for her. I knew my mother's orgasms. I knew her every thought, emotion, and experience. She sent me to the Institute of Psionics in Hyde Park with the other eighty prenatal supplement children who freaked out their mothers. I didn't want to go even though knowing her so intimately was weird as hell for me too. I kicked and screamed and bit and cried. My mother told me it was for my own good. My father just looked away. That was five years ago, and I haven't

forgiven either of them since.

*** *** ***

Dazed, I manage to drag myself out of the way as three hundred fifty pounds of Ray J smash through the street where I just lay. My fists blaze blue again. I try to stand, to pick myself up off the ground, but Ray J does it for me instead. The street beneath me erupts, and we arc toward blue sky and sun, human rockets launched high. Ray J snatches me to him in a wicked embrace amongst the chunks of flying concrete. As we begin to level out, he crushes me against his sixty-two-inch-chest with his thirty-five inch arms. The breath is forced from my lungs. I see bright spots. My vision fades. Stupid me. I didn't put up a shield.

*** *** ***

I don't call the North Shore home anymore. But I can't bring myself to call the Institute home either. What bothers me is I'm starting to like the Institute and its rigor. Scientists from Great Lakes Naval Hospital train and teach us from a curriculum sanctioned by Homeland Security. We're separated into four classes. They call the preemies beta children. Us drama kings and queens are gamma children. The smelly kids are delta children. And the normal kids are epsilon children. (The dead babies—God rest their souls—are alpha children.) I met Ray J the first day at the Institute. He told me his mother died of breast cancer. I told him my mother could go fuck herself.

*** *** ***

Two ribs break, and my spleen lacerates before I can put a buffer of psionic energy between me and Ray J. The makeshift shield won't hold long though and starts to buckle under his strength. I can't tell if the coolness on my face is the wind rushing past or blood Ray J has squeezed from my ears, eyes, and nose. I need to end this before he kills me, so I do the one thing I've wanted to do since the day I first met Ray J. I kiss those wonderful, full lips of his.

*** *** ***

I can't bring myself to hate my father as much as I hate my mother. He didn't carry me for nine months, love me from the inside, and then cast me aside thirteen years later ashamed, embarrassed, and horrified. He just abandoned me, his baby girl, when I needed him the most. But I have enough hate to go around. My mother's cervical cancer is now stage two. And the tumor in my father's prostate won't be getting smaller any time soon.

*** *** ***

I throw all of my psionic energy into the kiss, and for a few moments, it's just me and him. No rage. No hatred. No fear. No intimidation. Ray J relaxes his bear hug. One humongous hand goes to the small of my back. The other goes to my ass. His mouth opens. It's warm and moist. I press into him: mouth, breasts, crotch. I tell myself it's to sink my tendrils deeper into his mind. Our tongues touch.

And then the shit really hits the fan.

Ray J stiffens. His face contorts with pain. He lets go of me and plummets back to Earth with frightening speed. I try to reach for him with my mind to stop him, to slow him, to catch him, but I can't. I'm too fatigued. I don't have the mental power to heal my injuries, ravage my mother's cervix and my father's prostate, slow my fall, and save Ray J. Besides, at this height, falling with this velocity, he's more likely to survive.

But everyone on the Black Hawk helicopter won't. Ray J is lined up just right, and they don't see him coming down. I try to direct some of the swift air flows around me, slowing my descent to Ray J as a last ditch to save Ray-Ray and Kee-Kee and the others on board, but they're just too far in my weakened state. Ray J smashes right through the Black Hawk as it takes off for Great Lakes Naval Hospital. Bodies and medical equipment are flung end over end by the impact.

I quickly scan the mental signatures within the hurtling debris and fireball for Kee-Kee and Ray-Ray. But there's nothing I can do for them. They are already dead. And then the concussive wave from the explosion hits me, and the world goes black.

*** *** ***

My bedroom is exactly as I left it five years ago: Rihanna poster to the left of my white Ikea dressing table. Nelly Furtado poster to the right. Clothes hamper overflowing next to the closet. Pajamas crumpled on the floor.

I sit on the bed in the three a.m. darkness. I had been wrapped in a blanket cocoon of warmth and laziness the day I mind linked my mother as she was having sex with my father.

Outside, my window had looked like a Christmas postcard. Everything was pristine and white. I had been drifting in and out of wakefulness while big, fat snowflakes hushed the world as they fell.

At the time, I didn't know what was happening. My mind had grown wide as if a small hatch in my head opened. It spread throughout the house, expanding, roving, and—

My mother knocks on the door. Her knock hasn't changed in the five years I've been gone either. It's still tentative, cautious, apologetic.

"I thought I heard you come in."

She looks old and frail in her nightgown. There are new wrinkles at her throat and scored into her face. The ones around her eyes and mouth are the pain wrinkles.

"Hi." I don't know what else to say.

"Did they kick you out?" She hovers in the doorway, hands clasped before her, not sure if she should stand there, sit at my desk, or next to me on the bed.

"They've decommissioned us."

"For how long?"

"Indefinitely."

"I'm sorry."

"Don't be."

"But I sent you there."

I pause half a heartbeat. "It's a good place for us."

"TMZ said the Institute wants you and Ray J to give your performance bonuses back."

I frown. When did my mother start watching TMZ? "Loss of innocent life clause," I explain.

"They also said that you spent your bonus money on a 10,000-square-foot French Provincial home here in Lake Forest with eight bedrooms, eight baths, a tennis court, indoor and outdoor swimming pools, and eleven-foot ceilings."

I give a sullen shrug with one shoulder, feeling like I'm thirteen again. "They pay us well."

"And Stella said in her column that Ray J's father was a crackhead, but Ray J is a good boy. He'd been paying his father's rent and car note all of these years."

I nod. "He's the nicest, angriest boy I know if that makes sense. He's just misunderstood. Stella is the only one in the media who has tried to look past his rage and my psionic abilities and understand us for who we are."

We fall silent and look at each other. My mother wants to say something to me, but I make a conscious effort not to read her mind. It's more of a strain than anything I've ever done with my abilities.

Finally, she says, "I saw coverage of the funeral on Channel 5."

I don't trust my voice not to hitch and crack, so I don't say anything. I couldn't bring myself to look at Ray-Ray's coffin as the cemetery groundskeepers shoveled dirt onto it. It was so small and perfect and white down there in the grave next to Kee-Kee.

My mother sits next to me on the bed, puts a hand on my knee—still hesitant, still tentative—and then gathers me in her embrace.

"Oh, my Aieesha," she whispers, and I lose it. I sob and heave and snot on her bony shoulder until I'm too tired to

cry anymore.

I never liked my real name. It seemed so stupid to me. I know it represents the duality of my multiculturalism—a combination of the Japanese word for "love" and a ghetto suffix my mother thought I needed just in case people couldn't tell I was half-black from my skin color—but I hated it because I hated my mother and father.

And now, to hear my mother say my name with such love and sorrow and hurt after not being able to sleep for a week because I keep dreaming of Ray-Ray's little broken body cartwheeling through the air has utterly destroyed me in a way no psionic strike could.

"I'm sorry," I whisper to her.

"For what?"

I'm too much of a coward to say, "For hating you and giving you and Daddy cancer." So instead, I say, "For everything."

But I'm not too spiteful anymore. I can't continue to allow their cancer cells to run rampant, so I release my mother's cervix and my father's prostate. My mother gasps, and her eyes go wide. The two slender, pointed tendrils that retract from their bodies back to my mind are black and viscous.

My mother looks at me for a long moment. Again, she wants to say something to me. But again, she takes me into her arms, guiding my head to her shoulder, stroking my curly-curly hair.

I guess you can go home again.

PAST IMPERFECT
—A SCORPION STORY—
WARREN STOCKHOLM

"HERR KURT, WE SHOULD DO AN EDITORIAL ON SUPERHEROES," Benny Herzog suggested, popping his head into my private office.

I looked up from the proof copy of the latest edition of *The Inquisitor*, Benny all fuzzy because I was wearing my reading glasses, and said, "Superheroes? Why?"

Benny stepped fully into the room, the milk-glassed insert door with my name on it hitting him on the rump as it closed behind him, cutting off the frantic sounds of my secretary Olga's typing and the other clattering office noises of the bullpen at eight o'clock on a Monday morning. There were days when I propped the door open with my rubber plant just to let it all in. There's something very soothing about the noises of a busy and successful newspaper office. But this morning, I'd needed some privacy or I was never going to get the issues worked out of the latest edition. I'd had a long, busy night and no sleep.

Benny held up several grainy photostats, delivered via one of my correspondents in the city. I could just make out a humanoid figure hanging suspended over a busy line of traffic. If I hadn't known it to be impossible, I'd have said the figure in the photostats was *flying*. Benny smiled broadly, showing off his nicotine-stained grin, the grin that always said *money shot*. "It looks like Steeltown finally has one. Its very own superhero."

So that's how it started. A little adventure that nearly cost me my life, not that such things were unusual, considering my history and line of work. There are people out there who dislike me, who want to kill me. I take great offense to that. This city is American through and through from its tallest spires to its lowliest slums. This city is not Germany under the iron fist of the Reich. This is not the America held hostage for almost sixty years by the Axis Powers. Germany nearly destroyed a third of the world before it was brought low by the most embarrassing of circumstances: financial depression. People do not live in fear here. They have freedom. And when someone—anyone—threatens that freedom, when they threaten *me*, they answer to the Scorpion.

Steeltown is his territory. His city. And here, there be monsters.

I set the proof aside and started going over the photostats one by one. If forgeries of some kind, they were so damned good even *I* couldn't find the wires and special effects using

my special magnifying monocular.

I was still examining them, Benny hovering excitedly at my elbow, when Olga tapped on my door. She had the morning edition of *The World*, my number one newspaper competitor in the city.

The World is run by real estate mogul Farnon Pendrick, who owns more properties in Steeltown than anyone else, myself included. *The World* is merely a hobby of his, or so he's been known to state in public. But then, seven years ago, when I'd finally made *The Inquisitor* the number one paper in town, I'd learned through various channels that Farnon was pouring nearly all his assets into *The World*. The price of a wounded ego, I suppose. It had since become a white elephant that Farnon couldn't let go. Call it a cold war if you will—or maybe Farnon is just a poor loser—but I have to keep an eye on him every minute. As such, one of Olga's duties is to fetch me *The World* the moment it hits the newsstands.

"Your paper, sir," Olga said cheerily, depositing it on my desk. It was an inside joke between us that she gives me the world every day. But today, I wasn't laughing.

I glanced at Farnon's paper, looked back at the photostat I was trying to authenticate, then looked back at the paper. A very similar photograph graced the front page of *The World*, a man in dark blue, skin-tight body armor and an honest-to-God cape was apparently flying free-style over Jump Bridge, only a few miles from this very building. I dropped the monocular to my desktop and grabbed up the paper. Farnon had gotten the drop on me today.

I was both angry and impressed. Yes, it's possible to be

both. I disliked Farnon, but I also admired his chutzpah at running such an absurd story. So for the next two weeks, I had my best correspondents in the city covering the many sightings of the vigilante who called himself Morningstar.

The reason I say *vigilante* is that he seemed to be bent on insinuating himself into the nightly activities of Steeltown. The chump had the misguided belief that by preventing crimes from happening, it somehow made him a hero worth celebrating. I had my doubts. I had long ago lost my faith in God, government, and superheroes. I was a big boy now, my youth and ignorance far behind me—long since buried in a prisoner-of-war trench in Nazi Germany. No one did anything without expecting something in return. It went against human nature.

The truth would come out. In time.

All I had to do…all the Scorpion had to do…was watch and wait.

*** *** ***

For the next two weeks, I had my people watch and report on Morningstar's many nocturnal activities though I didn't print any of his stories. Or, if I did, I cut Morningstar's part in the fiasco out. Farnon did the same thing anytime there was a Scorpion sighting. It was a longtime joke between us. Only *The Inquisitor* reported on Scorpion activity. *The World*, up until a few days ago, reported so-called "real" news—car wrecks, gangbangings, murders, rapes, and the occasional terrorist act.

I'm nothing if not a patient man. I waited and watched. It was little things at first. Morningstar was sighted stopping

a pair of youths from assaulting a cab driver. Later that same day, he collared a purse-snatcher. Small beans, crimes almost laughable in their insignificance. Then again, those were the types of crimes that the Scorpion had cut his teeth on. If anything, it seemed Morningstar was more of a showman than a hero. He certainly enjoyed being photographed as he went about his nightly duties committing acts of Boy Scout heroism. The Scorpion, on the other hand, usually took pains to avoid publicity—unless he knew that publicity would raise readership of my paper. In that way, he and I often work together.

Two weeks to the date of the first sighting, I got my chance to talk to Farnon. We were part of the same gentleman's club, and we did our teeing on Lakeside Greens. We met up on Saturdays twice a month, but I had missed the last game. I had been recovering from a slug I'd taken in the shoulder when the Scorpion put one of mobbie Gil "Black Fingers" Blackman's lackeys through a plate glass window. He'd gone over the edge backwards, pulling his manstopper as he did so. He was an amazingly accurate shot up until the moment he died, splashed across the fresh concrete outside Gil's new high-rise apartment complex.

"Hallo there, old boy. You're looking fit as usual," Farnon said as he came up the hill, towing a valet, two security personnel, and his teeing partner and fourth wife Belinda, a bottle blonde who was young enough to be his granddaughter. Farnon greeted me the same way every time. He hated me, but he was a gentleman about it and preferred to launch his assaults at me in true passive-aggressive editorial style.

Belinda Pendrick smiled insouciantly at me, her golf slacks indecently tight. The one and only time we'd been alone, Belinda had climbed into my lap and tried to dry hump me. Since then, Farnon only let her out of his sight fully chaperoned by one of his heavies. The guy standing on Farnon's left was for his security. The one on the right, nervously picking his nose, was there to keep Belinda out of trouble. I smiled and kissed Belinda's hand.

Farnon did not reciprocate the gesture with my own teeing partner, Suzaku. Despite being the most stunning thing on the green in her flowing white kimono full of flocking red cranes, her hair bound up in a bounty of small braids and her face painted as exquisitely as a fine porcelain doll, Farnon treated my Suzaku as if he might catch a communicable disease. Farnon believed in the science of eugenics. He thought it scandalous that I should be keeping a Geisha. That was another point we disagreed on.

Suzaku was my sensei, not my Geisha.

We'd only just teed off when he said, "I know what you're thinking, old thing, and you're completely off base, as usual."

"What am I thinking, old thing?" I asked as we hefted our bags and started down the hill where our balls waited. Well, I hefted my bag. Ironically, Farnon had his wife carry his. I figured she'd done something wrong and was being punished.

"I know what you're thinking, but I didn't hire him, the chap with the cape. Awful melodramatic, wouldn't you agree?" Farnon wrinkled up his tanned face like a Pekinese.

"Yet you insist on running stories on him."

"I'm considering it an experiment."

"Oh?"

"I wanted to see if this theory of yours is right, if all this vigilante humbug is capable of selling papers."

"Paper not selling, old thing?" I raised my eyebrows at Farnon, but he wouldn't answer me.

Belinda sashayed past us, giggling.

Later that evening, as I prepared for bed, I told Suzaku, "I'm not entirely certain old Farnon's behind it."

I stood in the lavishly tiled, Byzantine-inspired bathroom off my bedroom, peeling off the Scorpion's bloody clothes bit by bit while trying not to stare at myself in the mirror. It had become something of a ritual. Obviously, I needed the mirror to shave in the morning, but I resented it bitterly and avoided it when possible. The man in the glass was tall and gaunt, almost stoop-shouldered tonight. He looked sallow and unwell and sported dark, haunted rings under his pale, gray eyes. I did not like my eyes of late, the way they flickered uncertainly around a room like silver bugs. The way they never rested—never *looked* rested—anymore. It made me want to put the Scorpion's veiled fedora back on.

After the hat and long leather coat had come off, I went to work on the bloodstained gauntlets and various bits of body armor. I pared the Scorpion down until he was only Herr Kurt Reinhardt again, a man, a German ex-patriot, and a newspaper mogul, someone most people in the city figured was dirty but only in terms of sex and money. They did not know about the blood. No one knew about the blood except Suzaku.

It had been a rough night. The brother of Black Finger's dead mob lackey had called a challenge, threatening to blow

the top portion off a bank building if the Scorpion didn't arrive and turn himself over for execution. The Scorpion had arrived on time but not in the manner the man, a nervous little fellow, had expected. Instead of walking into the trap, the Scorpion had rappelled down the side of the building and shot out the plate-glass office window. The glass had shattered and knifed into the man. He'd been little more than a bloody heap by the time the Scorpion had put a mercy bullet in his brain.

Dressed only in my trousers, I pulled the band from my hair so it fell in long, tired strands against my cheeks and the back of my neck. Even my hair hurt tonight.

I went out into the adjacent room, where Suzaku had prepared my bed. She stood by my bedside with a collection of small pots of creams she herself had made from ingredients she did not divulge to anyone. On nights like these, she applied those creams to my shredded muscles and ligaments then went about the distasteful work of sewing up any wounds that had not healed of their own accord. They would be manageable in the morning, I knew, the Frankenstein stitches all gone. But whether this is due to Suzaku's exotic salves or my own inner queer clone anatomy, I've never discovered.

"Why do you say that, K-san?" she said in response to my statement about Farnon.

I sat at the edge of the bed as she began working her magic creams into various muscles. The creams burned at first then slowly stole away the low-grade agony snaking venomously through my back and shoulders. It was perhaps her touch more than anything else that helped, that eased the pain. It felt good to be touched with something other than bald-faced violence.

"Farnon knew I would suspect him of being behind this Morningstar business. He almost seemed annoyed by it all." I grunted as she examined the gaping, mouth-like wound in my side where a shard of glass had ripped into my flesh. My genetics were struggling to mend the hole but not succeeding very well. Suzaku opened the case that contained trauma needles and sutures and went to work on it while I lay on the sheets, bleeding and grunting with every stitch.

"You do not think he is inclined to such subterfuge, K-san?" Suzaku asked. I was acutely aware of the soft press of her breasts as she worked over me. It made the experience that much more pleasurable, I have to admit.

"I think he finds such things beneath him. He seems almost…reluctant, like he's only doing this on advisement from someone else. He has that board of investors, doesn't he?"

"I recall you saying something to that effect, K-san, yes," Suzaku answered, cutting a suture wire with her delicate, sharp teeth.

"I wonder if his investors are forcing him to run the stories, hoping to increase circulation."

"Perhaps you ought to run the stories as well."

"I like to think my readership is more interested in terrorists and the Scorpion than in some idiot in tights and a cape." I glanced down where Suzaku's hair blanketed my lower half like a silken, blue-black shawl as she finished trimming the last stitch with her teeth. Eighty-three stitches—something of a record for me.

Suzaku massaged her healing creams into my wound then climbed back up my body and lowered her face so her

long, perfumed reams of hair tented us in together. "Perhaps an opinion piece about the possible identity of the vigilante," she suggested demurely. "It might draw him out."

"It might make him want to kill Kurt Reinhardt."

"If there is a mind behind all this, it may force that person to show their hand. Either way, K-san may unsettle the party involved."

"You may be onto something," I agreed. The pain was edging away, leaving me aching and sore and empty. Our lips were mere centimeters apart. I looked deep into Suzaku's eyes and saw darkness, flames, chaos. Hell. If I looked closely enough, I could see her rising up from a nest of phoenix fire, eternal, un-killable, unlike myself. It made me want to mourn. I wished she was real as I lay there on my pillow, touching her hair, which felt delightfully soft to my callused hand. I wished she were a real woman.

But the one creature drawn to me was only female on the outside. Inside, she was a shikigami, a guardian beast, older than rocks or trees or earth. Just a raw force of nature made flesh. Making love to Suzaku is like being drenched in a lightning storm: exhilarating, overwhelming, sad, unreal. It's all I want at the time, but when it's over, the loneliness and doubt are redoubled, reminding me of how impossible it is to carry on a relationship with a real human woman. The Reich who manufactured me poisoned my body and blood with their chemical venom; there is no fluid in my body not caustic on contact with human flesh.

Suzaku came unto me, covering me in her light, fragrant, lily-soft body. She opened her obi belt to me, and I slid my

hands beneath the silken material, stroking her breasts until she arched her back and sang the sweetest song in a voice not human at all. Her entire body flushed, and I could feel her skin warming under my touch. When she looked again at me, her eyes weren't human at all. They looked like portals into Hell, that place I had sent dozens of criminals over the years. Suzaku smiled as if sharing some intimate knowledge with him. Not for the first time, I wondered if I wasn't simply a tool of the gods, here to dole out the punishments they were apparently too busy or too damned lazy to take care of themselves. I wondered if I wasn't food for Suzaku, feeding her souls and chaos to fill her eternally empty soul like the victim of some hungry, eternal vampire.

Suzaku kissed me, and all my doubts vanished for the moment. "My little K-san," she said sweetly, like a mother rewarding a child for an act of obedience. She stroked my cheek. She kissed my throat then moved steadily downward, the imprint of her rose-red lips lifting my body like a puppet on strings, writhing to the will of a greater force. The wound in my side didn't hurt at all. Nothing hurt so long as I stayed within the circle of her arms.

*** *** ***

The following day, I had Miss Emily, our opinion columnist, run a small article speculating on the possible origins of Morningstar. Letters immediately began flooding the office, thousands of people trying to guess at the identity of our masked local superhero. Some expressed doubts that he was real, claiming he was nothing more than a collection of special

effects. There were even people proposing a duel between Morningstar and the Scorpion and theories as to who would win in a fair fight. No one bothered to mention that the Scorpion seldom bothered to fight fairly.

Suzaku had been right. The exercise did in fact propel Morningstar, or whoever was behind him, to act more boldly because the following night, the caped vigilante intercepted an armed bank robbery, taking three direct gunshots in the chest before flying off—or so various witnesses claimed. His flying had been erratic, but he *had* flown off. Obviously, he was stepping up his game in a way he was unprepared for.

The Scorpion gathered blood samples that I then examined under the high-powered electron microscope in my private lab at home. I was a child of the Reich. The Reich had created me, educated me. I knew mutated cells when I saw them. Morningstar's cells were similar to mine, the only difference being that they had been mutated at some later point in his development. My own mutation was induced on an embryonic level; I never had normal cells. These cells were forcibly altered. Morningstar's cell mutation was random rather than uniform as in my case—the hallmark of forced mutation.

The cells also looked self-regenerative, which explained how Morningstar could take three direct shots in the chest and still fly off. I sat back on my lab stool and thought about that a moment. I knew that sooner or later, the Scorpion and Morningstar were going to have to meet, and it would likely be in the Scorpion's best interest to be careful. The Scorpion wasn't nearly as durable or regenerative as his caped rival seemed to be.

It came as little surprise to me that a week later, during the NFL playoff at The Steeltown Stadium, halftime was interrupted by a message on the digital scoreboard that read:

SCORPION MEET ME NOW

Suffice to say the missive, wedged between a wedding proposal and a get-well greeting, upstaged the show, which was something of a shame because the Steelers were leading Baltimore by 6-4.

It was a Sunday afternoon, and I was home in my office, the television on in one corner. I was poring over a number of files that a man who owed me a favor had retrieved. They contained Farnon's various bank statements, including all the off-shores no one else knew anything about, even the IRS. I was looking for a withdrawal of a large sum of money, or even a series of large sums that might indicate a payroll, but most of the activity on his statements belonged to his wife. Belinda was bleeding him dry. And—to my utmost glee, I admit—his paper wasn't doing nearly as well as I'd thought.

I looked up when I heard the announcer talking about a showdown between the Scorpion and the city's newest vigilante, Morningstar. Two and half minutes later, I was upstairs in my bedroom, changing into my gear. Suzaku swept forward, virtually floating in her blood-red kimono, bearing piece after piece of body armor, various recent injuries aching from the pressure of the Kevlar I was sporting under my trench coat. Never say I'm not prepared.

"Do you think it will be enough, K-san?" she asked. She sounded concerned as always.

I slipped on the veiled Fedora. The Scorpion chambered

the Sting and sank more ammunition into his pockets than he probably needed. "It better be," he said.

He left the estate and cut across the city. He knew every hidey-hole, every shortcut, and every dead-end alley. In less than ten minutes, he'd reached Steeltown Stadium. The game-watchers were likely expecting a bloody match to the death in the end zone, but the Scorpion had no desire to make this a spectacle.

He moved stealthily around to the back of the stadium building, keeping to the shadows and out of the sallow, yellow pools of security lights. He reached up to the brownstone wall behind the concessions stands and placed his gloved hand upon it, the diamond-tipped fingers digging deep into the rough brick, then reached up again, kicking against the bricks, climbing steadily up the face of the building until he'd reached a window ledge. Balancing on the ledge, the Scorpion caught the bottom rung of a fire escape and swung himself over. The next four stories were easy climbing as the crowd roared its approval down in the Coliseum-sized field. The Steelers must have made another touchdown.

"You came," said a voice as the Scorpion reached the top of the concession building.

He already had the .50 caliber Sting out, which made climbing over the edge of the building awkward but not impossible. He wasn't about to approach Morningstar unarmed.

The man who was Steeltown's newest sentinel was tall, taller than the Scorpion, and perhaps twice as wide. Body armor and/or biological mutation had granted him a towering, wrestler-type physique further emphasized by the dark, midnight blue suit trimmed in places with white. It wasn't a very good suit for the purposes of stealth in the Scorpion's opinion. Then again, Morningstar wasn't especially fond of stealth. His face was half-masked with a hood, and he trailed a long cape behind him. The first thing the Scorpion did was calculate all the things that could go wrong with a costume like that. The second thing he did was cock the Sting and take a bead.

"Who are you working for?" he asked the man.

Morningstar looked briefly taken aback. "That's not much of a greeting, friend."

"I'm hardly a friend," the Scorpion answered, leveling the gun with the bridge of Morningstar's nose. "Answer the question, or I'll shoot your brains out the back of your fucking head, asshole."

Morningstar looked appalled. The eyes in the hood were much younger than the Scorpion had expected. Morningstar raised his hands to show he was unarmed. The Scorpion knew that already. There was no way he could carry weapons on such a spotty outfit, which made it just another bad idea. "I just wanted to talk to you!"

"Really." The Scorpion smiled grimly behind the veil.

"Really," Morningstar confirmed. He had no German accent that the Scorpion could detect, but that meant nothing. Kurt Reinhardt could hide his accent very well when he needed to. "I'm new to all this," he said, indicating the city without moving too much. "I thought I might benefit from speaking to you, learning from you."

"You summoned me here because you want to *chat* with me?" the Scorpion asked.

Morningstar flinched. "I know I can learn a lot from you. I know you have great wisdom to impart."

"You must be fucking joking." The Scorpion charged forward and side-kicked Morningstar in the breadbasket. The man went down surprisingly easy. The Scorpion was disappointed. While he was still down, the Scorpion pistol-whipped him across the face. Blood and teeth spattered across the concrete like red dice.

Morningstar groaned.

"Who sent you?" the Scorpion demanded to know, jabbing the nose of the gun into the soft pouch of flesh under Morningstar's chin. "What's his name, asshole?"

"I don't know what you're talking about! Are you fucking nuts?" Morningstar screamed through blood, loose teeth, and terror.

The Scorpion shifted the gun exactly five inches to the right and jerked the trigger. The shot exploded into the asphalt roof in the tiny space between Morningstar's neck and shoulder, filling the night with hot ozone. The whole thing made the young man scream and wet the front of his outfit, which further disappointed the Scorpion. He waited until the deafening rapport faded, and the young man lay there limp, shaking like an electric wire carrying a charge, tears filling his eyes and spilling over his cheeks. He was making small gasping noises like a man fighting badly not to hyperventilate on the spot. The Scorpion stood back though he kept a bead on Morningstar's forehead. The Sting could turn the young

man's head into a Hula Hoop. It might even be interesting.

"I'll ask you again," the Scorpion said, his voice dead, emotionless. "Who are you working for? Is it the Reich?"

Morningstar shook his head. "I told you! I don't know what you mean!"

The boy sounded hysterical, in no state to lie. The Scorpion lowered his gun but kept it close at hand.

Slowly, Morningstar sat up, wiping at his bloodied mouth with his sleeve. If the Scorpion hadn't known any better, he would have said new, shiny teeth had already replaced the broken ones in his mouth. That was interesting too.

"How did you come to be this way?" the Scorpion asked, genuinely curious.

"I don't know!" the boy sobbed as he fought to get his composure back.

"You don't know? I find that hard to believe." The Scorpion started raising the gun again.

"I'm telling you the truth! *I don't know!* I answered an ad in the newspaper for a modeling position. That's what I am, you see…what I used to be." He gasped for breath and smeared away the rest of the blood. "It was an address downtown, at some warehouse. I should have known better I guess. The moment I was in the door, someone hit me. The next thing I knew, I woke up in a lab. I was there a long time…months at least."

The Scorpion watched him carefully. "And what went on at this lab?"

Morningstar shook his head. "They never told me anything. It was all so painful, and it went on and on. They

kept injecting me with this stuff that burned. It hurt so badly, but it also made me stronger. It made me survive all the things they did to me." He stopped, and his eyes turned inward as he seemed to relive the memory, not a pleasant one. He looked genuinely shaken. "Then, one day, I was able to break the straps they used to hold me down. Even the bars on the windows of the lab were no problem for me. I wanted to go home, you see. I wanted to see my girl, my parents. I fell from the window and into the sea. I think I was being held on some remote island somewhere."

Assuming the boy was telling the truth, he could easily be talking about a Reich-run lab. The Scorpion knew there were still many in operation, labs secreted away in remote Costa Rica and on Polynesian islands, places owned by private investors, places almost no one visited.

He'd go with the boy's story…for now. "And what happened after you fell into the sea?"

"I drifted a while until this fishing boat found me. After I got home, I thought everything would be all right, but then things started to happen. I started to change…"

"Mutate."

"What?"

"I've examined your blood, boy. Whatever those scientists shot you up with, it mutated your DNA at a core level."

The boy looked interested. "That's why I can fly? Why I can't be hurt?"

The Scorpion studied the boy's tear-and-blood-streaked face under the hood. If he was lying, acting, he was doing a damned fine job of it. He felt a twinge. "Why this?" he

asked, indicating the costume with the gun. "Why become Morningstar…whoever you are."

"Mark. My real name is Mark."

"Why become Morningstar, Mark?"

The boy climbed shakily to his feet. "I…I don't know. I guess I didn't want what happened to me to happen to anyone else."

The Scorpion laughed. It just burst out of him like staccato gunfire from the muzzle of an automatic. Laughter nearly doubled him over. "So altruistic! So naïve! I think I'm going to be sick!"

Mark looked wounded. His eyes darkened, becoming broody pits into an unknowable hell. "I thought you would understand, but you're just as messed up as I am! I guess what they say about you is true." He looked at the blood on his hand and clenched it.

"What do they say about me?"

"That you're insane. That you're worse than the criminals you kill."

The Scorpion laughed that off as well. The sound was bitter and nearly hysterical as he jumped up and down and aimed the Sting at pale, round mother moon hanging high overhead. Play a little hardball with the criminal underworld, and everyone thinks you've taken the bend! Suddenly, *you're* the villain, *you're* the menace, even though crime was down 60 percent in the city since the Scorpion had laid claim to it. The Scorpion knew that because Kurt Reinhardt had done the research for an exposé years earlier. Fucking ingrates. The Scorpion wanted to shoot them all—and he would have

except that would make readership deteriorate, and he couldn't let Kurt Reinhardt's business fall to pieces. They worked too well together.

"It's true, though, isn't it?" Mark said, sounding disappointed. "You're not a hero. You're just some evil shit with a gun a head full of loose parts."

"Boy," said the Scorpion, his laughter dying along with his little dance, "you don't *know* what evil is." He flung himself at Mark, and the two of them went right over the edge of the building. It was a surprisingly long drop; in the course of it, somehow, Mark got on top. The impact felt like a sledgehammer to the Scorpion's spine though the Kevlar probably saved his life. He felt the vibration of the impact in his teeth and a sharp pain cut down one hip, probably a hairline fracture. Mark landing atop him further drove the breath from his lungs.

Mark's face was twisted, not young at all. He slammed his fist into the Scorpion's shoulder like a kid having a temper tantrum. The Scorpion grunted and heard the distinct snap of his shoulder dislocating on impact. A bolt of pain jigged through his body, but the pain felt so good!

The Scorpion giggled, brought his knee up, fully intending to drive it into Mark's groin, but Mark launched himself into the air and hung suspended above him like a man on invisible wires. The Scorpion took a moment to admire the feat before rolling away and rising shakily to his feet. He tottered like a broken toy. Seconds later, Mark slammed his big fist into the ground, breaking the concrete.

Mark screamed.

The Scorpion laughed, snapped his shoulder back into place like a Lego toy, and brought his gun up. But before he could find his target, Mark flew right into him, driving him into the wall of the building behind them. The Scorpion heard other bones crackle, and the sweetness of nearly unendurable pain swept over him, making him groan in appreciation. Now this…this was a good conversation!

Mark held him effortlessly against the wall. His strength was enormous. He gut-punched the Scorpion so he sagged against the wall, coughing and spitting up gobs of blood. Mark pushed his face close, so close that the Scorpion could smell the blood from his once-broken teeth on his breath. "You're not so tough now, tough guy. Just another lowlife piece of shit to clean up…"

The Scorpion lunged at him, snarling and biting off the tip of his nose. Mark hadn't expected *that*. He screamed and yanked his head back, letting his enemy go and retreating as blood gusted over them both from the bloody hole in Mark's face. "I know they sent you!" the Scorpion laughed hysterically as he savored all the blood in his mouth. In the back of his mind, he knew he sounded like a hyena, like his clone brother Wolf, a man so evil and erratic even the Reich would have nothing to do with him. "I know who they are!" He tried to lift the heavy Sting, but with his injured shoulder, he could find no purchase.

"You are one fucking crazy motherfucker!" said a man who had suddenly appeared beside the two of them. He put a gun, cocked sideways, to the Scorpion's cheek.

The Scorpion stopped and moved his eyes analytically in

the direction of the gun. The man standing beside him was dressed in a security uniform, but he recognized him easily enough. It was Gil "Black Fingers" Blackman. The chickens always came home to roost at the oddest of times!

"And what do *you* want?" the Scorpion asked coolly, his laughter dying.

The gun barrel nudged the Scorpion's cheek behind the veil. "What everyone wants. I want your fucking skin on my wall for taking out my boys, freakshow."

"You'll have to get in line for that, chump."

In that moment, Morningstar flew at the two of them, roaring. The Scorpion moved aside. Blackman squeezed off two direct rounds. Morningstar sucked up the slugs like a sponge, barely reacting. The two wound up on the ground with Blackman on top at first, then Morningstar as he delivered a number of stunning blows that reduced Blackman's ugly face to ugly face soup.

"You kill me, and I'll have my boys blow this whole stadium, kid!" Blackman gargled. He grinned brokenly through his facemask of blood. "The whole place is wired with plastic explosives. That's ten thousand lives on your head, kid!"

The Scorpion struggled to sit up with all his broken parts, wondering what Morningstar planned to do.

Morningstar drifted back, eyeing the man as if he only half-believed him. He was used to petty thieves, not terrorists. Blackman was the big time. The mobbie climbed unsteadily to his feet, weaving but not down for the count. He was a big man, a former dockworker and heavyweight boxer who'd never lost a match even after he'd turned to organized crime.

He smiled at Morningstar and mumbled out of his crooked, mushed-up mouth, "Now you're gonna do exactly what I tell you, big boy." He turned and pointed one bloody finger at the Scorpion. "Kill that freak of nature, or everyone here dies."

Morningstar thought about that but only for a moment. He turned, eyed the Scorpion, and lunged.

The Scorpion shot Mark through the brain. It cleaved off the part of his head that was hooded and bathed Blackman in bloody gray matter. Blackman hopped back as the body fell toward him like a downed tree. Blackman looked at the Scorpion and blinked as if confused.

The Scorpion shifted the gun to track Blackman. His hip was mending. His arm was good enough to put another bullet in another brain.

"You shoot me, I'll have my gunmen take you *down*, freak," Blackman said, raising his hand to point erratically at the bleachers high above them both. "I have snipers. I have…"

"I hate it when a guy can't keep his bluff straight," the Scorpion said. He shot Blackman through the head too.

*** *** ***

Later, at home, I sat listening to the newscaster on TV as he recapped the events at Steeltown Stadium, Suzaku sewing up the sizeable fifteen-inch tear down my back. With the game going strong and the Steelers in the lead, no one had noticed what was going on until halftime. That was America for you. After that, it was all a muddled confusion though police investigators and medical examiners were struggling to piece the story together.

"They can't identify the boy, Mark," I told her. "If that was even his real name. No one knows who he was or where he came from. There's no record of him anywhere."

Suzaku started rubbing her special creams into my stitches and various contusions. It was pretty obvious I wouldn't be playing the green with Farnon this coming Saturday. More's the pity.

"He was, in fact, a mutant, but they can't identify him," I further explained "He wasn't on Farnon's payroll. He was probably one of *them*. One of the Reich. They always are."

Suzaku's painted fingertips stroked my shoulders and down over my chest, soft and persistent.

"It's always the past that gets you, Suzaku. Always."

She leaned down to kiss my shoulder softly.

"I did the right thing, didn't I? Killing Mark…or whoever he was?"

Suzaku's hair brushed my cheek like a perfumed cloud, and her voice purred in my ear. "K-san, let's go to bed."

KARINA L. FABIAN
ILLUSION

SLEEP WAS GOOD, WAS PEACE, WAS A BLESSED OBLIVION. Dreams, when they came, were merely dreams, phantoms Deryl could sometimes control. Even the dreamtime training sessions of the Master, which sometimes left him with visible bruises upon awaking, were at least linear and thus understandable. And when the Master finished his lesson of the night and Deryl faded out of dreams and REM sleep, his mind could finally rest. Sleep was healing.

Deryl woke into nightmare.

Even before he opened his eyes, the assault began: discontent about leaving a warm bed to put on the chilly school uniforms, dread at another day of facing bullies and disapproving teachers, eagerness to hang out with friends, fear of a math test, excitement about the math test, eagerness for the week to end and see parents, sisters, girlfriends. So many thoughts.

None of them his.

Think about the sheets: soft and warm, the blanket nice and heavy over me, like a cocoon. Smell the laundry soap. Laundry soap, not deodorant. Cotton sheets, not polyester blend pants. Dark and dry, not echo-y and steamy. My name is Deryl Stephens…

He pulled the covers over his head and fought against the dizzying onslaught of thoughts as his dorm mates prepared for the day. This early upon awakening, the chaos of their minds brought nausea more than pain. He'd learned that if he breathed slowly though his mouth and concentrated on physical sensations and his mantra, he could usually stay calm and fake sleep until the room cleared. It didn't matter if he missed breakfast; he'd be too sick to eat anyway. Later, when his waking mind had better control, the queasiness would leave, and the headaches would start. Enough medicine and he could bear those. Besides, if the Master had taught him one thing, it was how to handle pain.

There'd be less pain if I did what the Master wanted.

He felt himself scowling even though no one could see him. If disobedience meant pain, he'd deal with the pain. He was not going to attack other humans, not even in his dreams. He'd already learned how easy it was to lash out at others, how much he could enjoy it if he let the Master lead him down that path. He couldn't always keep track of who he was anymore, but he knew one thing: He was not a killer.

The distant hum of thoughts told him the room had emptied. At last, he could get up, shower, and steel himself for the day.

As the cool water struck his back and plastered his hair to his scalp, he began the mantra: "My name is Deryl Stephens. I'm thirteen years, four months, and seven days old. I'm in eighth grade. My favorite subject is science. I like meteorology best. My worse subject is Social Studies. I like raspberries and hate chocolate…" Every detail he could think of that was his, he muttered aloud, forcing himself to hear it above the wants, needs, pains, and thoughts of the population of the George Weinmann School for Boys. Sometimes, it was enough.

Once showered and dressed, he reached under his bed and pulled out the bottle of Motrin hidden there and poured eight into his hand. The bottle rattled. He'd have to buy or steal more soon. He took two in anticipation of the headache to come and stuffed the rest into his pocket. He shoved the bottle back into the mattress, through the tear, securing it among the filling, then pulled out a small, framed photo. He ran his fingers over his mother's hair, traced her smile. Her eyes looked wrong in the photo; they always did. No camera could capture the life that shone from them or the hidden knowledge that darkened their depths. She would have understood what he was going through; she would have helped him. But it was too late. He couldn't talk to her now, and he couldn't imagine what she would say. He shoved the photo back next to the painkillers then went to wash the tears off his face.

He checked his schedule and his homework, making sure they held his name and not someone else's. He recited his mantra along with his first hour classroom number. Finally, with a deep breath, like a swimmer about to jump the high

dive, he pulled open the door and forced his feet to take him to his—and not someone else's—first class.

Social Studies went okay—a film about the civil rights movement kept everyone focused enough that he could focus too. He even managed to take coherent notes.

Algebra proved harder. Even when they were supposed to be paying attention to the problem on the board, some of his classmates were still trying to catch up in the book; others were going on to the next problems; some were just baffled. A couple did homework from another class. Numbers and operations swirled in his mind along with boredom, exultation, and confusion. He closed his eyes and rested his head in his hands to try to cut down the visual stimulus until he could straighten out the rest.

Please. Make it stop!

"Mr. Stephens, please pay attention."

Make it stop. Make it stop! Makeitstopmakeitstop—

"Mr. Stephens, I said would you please come to the board and solve this problem?"

I am Deryl Stephens!

Deryl jerked his head up and looked at the board. *I am Deryl Stephens. I'm thirteen years, four months, and seven days old. I'm in eighth grade, and I am in algebra. I need to find the area under a curve.*

"You can do this, can't you?" Mr. Lane's voice was laced with sarcasm, and his pessimism thrust at Deryl like one of the daggers the Master used in training. Deryl wrapped his arms around his ribs against the phantom pain, but the teacher took that for obstinacy. He opened his mouth and said something.

Deryl didn't hear it. Around him, the room had focused on him. *Loser Deryl. What was his problem anyway? How'd this retard get into algebra in the first place? Kid's just weird. Wonder if he'll do something crazy again?*

Deryl sprung out of his seat, desperate for a reason to put even the slightest distance between himself and his classmates. He went to the board, but the numbers refused to resolve themselves. Chalk up to the blackboard, he hesitated. People thought he was stupid. He thought he was stupid. *I am not stupid!*

He heard his mother, clapping her hands over some school assignment he'd brought home and hugging him, telling him he was brilliant. He heard the Master scolding: *Of course, you are not stupid. Now, show them. Use your abilities intelligently!*

Mr. Lane couched his voice in boredom to mask his growing irritation. "Anytime now, Mr. Stephens. It's really a very simple problem."

And suddenly, it was, and Deryl's hand flew across the board, etching out the process and the answer without his having to think. Which, of course, was the problem.

When he stepped away from the board and his focus left the problem, he felt confusion from the class, mixed with amusement, and a combination of suspicion and surprise from Mr. Lane.

"Well," Mr. Lane started then cleared his throat and tried again. "Yes, that is indeed the correct answer—if we were in calculus and not algebra."

He looked at the board—with his own eyes as well as the class'—and realized he had no idea what he'd written. It had

happened again. He'd mistaken the teacher's thoughts for his own. He wanted to cry, but the kids started laughing—hard, cruel laughter—and helpless, he laughed with them.

He was late to gym because he had to wait until everyone cleared out of the locker room so that he could stare at his reflection in the mirror and recite his mantra. "I am Deryl Stephens. I'm thirteen years, four months, and seven days old. I'm in eighth grade. I am learning algebra. I do not know calculus…"

Gym class should have been easy. They were training for the fitness test: sit-ups, push-ups, chin-ups—so many ups!—then a run and the rope climb. Simple, physical, mechanical; even when minds wandered, they never strayed past the pounding of feet and the counting. Counting was hard, but even if he missed a number, they'd chalk it up to everyone else counting at once.

Then Gordo Villanova fell from the ropes and cracked the back of his head, and Deryl felt the blow as if it were his own. Only the training from the Master—or rather, learning to think past the pain of the training—kept him from crying out. He only paused for just a moment to grimace, easily mistaken for effort on his forty-second sit-up. His partner yelled encouragement, and he absorbed his excitement and plunged on. Afterward, he excused himself to go to the restroom, and when no one was looking, he swallowed down four more pills.

One would have thought the hallways would be the worst of all, but with so many minds thinking in so many directions, Deryl's went into sensory overload. Sometimes, he'd actually

 ILLUSION

shut down and have to lean against the wall and force himself to breathe until he could see with his own eyes again; but today, the mellow mood of the students and the painkillers had caused everything to fade to a kind of roar of psychic white noise, and he rode it along, reciting in his mind his name and the room number of his next class.

A thought pierced through the rumble. Barry Whitewater, anticipating the mayhem when he bumped Andy Bernstein into one of the meanest seniors in school. A memory—his own memory—of being on the wrong end of that trick flooded his mind along with the words of the Master: *You have an advantage none of your peers have. Use it!*

Barry stumbled and pummeled into the jock instead. The senior snarled an obscenity and grabbed Barry by the collar and shoved him against the locker. As the others, including Barry's intended victim, crowded around, shouting jeers or encouragements, Deryl hurried away before he got caught up in the thrill of the violence. Still, it was the best part of his day.

In the middle of French class, he was called to the school counselor.

Again, he had a few minutes of relative solitude, and he made his way down the great staircase and through the hall slowly, letting the clacking of his shoes on the marble floors sooth him. He recited his mantra until every word came out in English. He paused at the water fountain to take the last of his Motrin. He heard (or rather, Gordo heard) the nurse scolding him that if it really did hurt that bad, he could take that and ibuprofen together. Maybe after he met with the counselor, he could go to the nurse and coax her into a couple.

The thought cheered him enough that he even managed a sincere "Good afternoon," to the secretary and managed to fend off her irritation, imagining them as ants and brushing them off his arm before he knocked, then entered Counselor Phelps' office.

He found Dr. Peterson in the office too. That came as no surprise. Even if he hadn't felt the psychiatrist's presence, he'd expected it. They always talked to him as a team if only to corroborate that they heard the same bizarre things from their most trying student. He forced himself not to hunch defensively as he greeted them and took a seat between the psychiatrist and Mr. Phelps.

Their judgment and their concern made him want to cringe. It would help if they didn't believe themselves so sincere. If they really cared about him, they'd believe him, wouldn't they?

"So, Mr. Stephens, how are we feeling?"

As he had many times before, Deryl answered Dr. Peterson's question literally. "You woke up at two this morning with a toothache and are counting the minutes until you can get to the dentist because the ibuprofen you took isn't cutting the pain. You could try some Motrin; that's what the nurse is telling Gordo Villanova to do for his head. Mr. Phelps had been having a good day until Mrs. Whitewater called to complain about the treatment of her son. In the office, Mrs. Meriweather is upset because she and her husband got into an argument because she wanted to buy new towels, and now, she's torn between crying to her sister, buying the towels anyway, or getting something even more expensive

for herself. And I have my usual headache because I can feel your tooth, and your frustration, and her anger, and where Gordo hit the back of his head. He's not faking like the nurse thinks. It really hurts."

Believe, he begged. *Please, this time, believe that I really am psychic. Help me!*

The two gentlemen traded looks, and Deryl's heart sank as he felt their skepticism. He knew it was his heart—no one else could possibly feel as desperate as he did.

"Why did you trip Barry Whitewater?" Mr. Phelps asked instead.

"What?"

Mr. Phelps just gave him a stern look. However, he saw it in his mind: Barry insisting that Deryl shoved him as he walked by; two students saying they never saw a push, but he did fall just as Deryl passed, and that Deryl hurried off right after.

"I didn't—"

"Are you certain?"

You have an advantage your peers don't. Use it! the Master said.

Had he?

He shook his head, but in that moment of confusion, he dropped what little guard he had, and it all came flooding in: Mr. Phelps wondering how long he could walk the tightrope between pleasing the two biggest supporters of the school; Dr. Peterson running through the next possibilities of medication; the snappy comebacks Mrs. Middleton knew she'd never have the guts to say; the jock in the cooldown room, wondering if

he would get suspended and what he'd tell his parents; Barry's swollen lip, which throbbed in time with his pulse but made him hope that maybe this time his mom would get tired of it all and send him home to his real dad; the drama class laughing over one boy's comedy routine—it was so funny, and Deryl didn't know why...

Inside his mind, in the small part that he knew was Deryl Stephens, he screamed. In the shell he presented to everyone else, he fought to keep himself from gibbering, to keep his tone even; but the part of him between his inner self and the outer shell was full of teenage boys with their mood swings and their doubts and the sarcasm they wore as a shield against the hurts real and imagined.

"Well, Deryl? Have you anything to say about Barry Whitewater?"

He felt himself shaking and clenched his fists on his knees in an effort to regain control. Nonetheless, words tumbled from his mouth. He prayed they were his. "Barry's last name is Carlton. His mother remarried, but Barry doesn't care that his stepfather adopted him—he thinks the man is a jerk and only adopted him as a power play, and every time someone calls him 'Whitewater,' Barry feels like he's betraying his dad. And maybe if you talked to him about that, you could find out why he likes to push other people into the football players. All I did today was give him a taste of his own medicine in the process."

"So you admit to doing it."

The counselor's feeling of triumph sent Deryl over the edge—for once with his own feelings. "I may as well! It

wouldn't help if I denied it—or even if I were innocent. The Whitewaters own half this school. Barry could lie through his teeth, and it wouldn't matter. Principal Williams is afraid of them, and that makes you afraid. I know what I am to you: the bastard son of a mentally ill woman. My uncle has plenty of clout, which is why I'm still here, but apparently not enough that you'd actually believe me!

"Well, she was not crazy; she was psychic. But she found people to believe her—believe in her. That's what I need: someone to believe in me and help me learn to control this! And no!" He whirled on the psychiatrist. "A new medication is not going to help!"

Without waiting to be excused, he tore from the room. He wanted to sigh. He wanted to change his name. He wanted to go buy new towels. He wanted to call his girlfriend and get her to bring some friends to the party…

Make it stop! Make it stop!

He ran out of the school building and past the fields. He wanted to make a touchdown—a real Hail Mary move—so the recruiters would be impressed and he could get his dad off his back. He wanted the weekend to come so he could go home and party with his friends; now that he was eighteen, Mom and Dad didn't care.

My name is Deryl Stephens. I'm thirteen, and I am an orphan!

He made it to the small garden shed on the far side of the school grounds. The door creaked open to a mental command he didn't realize he'd given. He dashed in and pushed past the rakes and tools to a small corner and tucked himself in. *I am Deryl Stephens, and I am an orphan. My mother died three years,*

two months, and five days ago. She is dead, and no one else believes what's happening to me, and I just hurt someone without even thinking. Grief washed over him, and it was his. He clung to it and let himself cry, real tears, his tears, until he fell asleep.

Sleep was good; it brought relief, brought oblivion, but healing was an illusion.

SABRE

SABRE DUCKED LOW AND THEN HOOKED RIGHT AS THE anti-matter blasts exploded around her. The wall behind her creaked and groaned as it crumbled under its own weight. With no way out, Sabre did the only thing she could: she curled into a ball and let the suit take the brunt of the blow. For the umpteenth time that night, she was glad of her suit's contained atmosphere. It was bad enough to be engaged in a super-powered brawl with some low-level IQ reject that fate had deemed worthy of being able to shoot anti-matter energy blasts without having to deal with the fumes or the smell.

"Give it up, Hero. You're no match for me." Why did they always have to go for the canned dialogue? It was a dead giveaway for amateur hour, which just made Sabre's position under the rubble, hiding from the villain's stray blasts, all the more humiliating.

"Freeze, dickhead! Put your hands behind your head. Now!" A new voice joined the fray. A cop from the sound of it. Sabre sighed in exasperation. She appreciated the thought, but you'd think that the police in a city under the protection of over ten superheroes would understand that their standard-issue side arms just weren't good enough when the cutting-edge, three-generations-ahead, power-armored hero was being thrown through walls like some sort of cheap toy.

So much for catching her breath.

Sabre launched herself out from under the rubble just as the villain turned to face the cop. Her timing wasn't spot on, but it was close enough to get the job done right. She caught the villain mere moments before he could fry the cop and took him with her through the far wall and back out onto the street. A charged left straight put his head into the ground hard, and Sabre jumped back to create some distance. When she got through with this, she'd have to put some serious thought into completing the Broadsword suit.

"Get out of here. Keep the civilians out of the area. I'll handle him," Sabre commanded the cop. He was kind of cute. At least in an "I'm young and enthusiastic but in over my head" sort of way. Movement from the villain pulled Sabre's attention. The time for pleasantries was over. "Go!" she called to the cop before turning back to the rising villain, "If we're going to be doing a long dance, I think I should get your name."

"You can call me Anti-Matter," the villain growled before unleashing a bolt of energy from both hands. Sabre braced and shielded her chest with both arms. She couldn't risk the bolts hitting the cop. Property damage was fine, but an officer dead in the line of duty would be a tragedy. Unfortunately, even being braced and with her suit's shields at full, the discharge was enough to send her careening backward through yet another wall.

Flat on her back again, Sabre looked around the building she was in and smiled under her helmet. It was about time the fight had gotten here. She pulled herself back to a seated position and let her external speakers amplify her laughter. "Seriously, you call yourself Anti-Matter? I mean, sure it fits with the blasts, but you couldn't think of something more original, more you? Here, I got one. Let's call you Hand Job. You like that one?"

The roar of anger from Anti-Matter was almost amusing, and the villain wasted no time in charging forward. Telemetry readings popped up on Sabre's heads-up display, tracking Anti-Matter's progress toward her and counting down how long she should wait to get maximum effect out of her hand blasters. Sabre shifted, feinting low, and Anti-Matter jumped over a blast that never came. Sabre grinned.

"You really are stupid. Aren't you, Hand Job?" The air filled with a dull whine before raw force erupted from the blasters in both of her armored palms. The force caught Anti-Matter in the air, launching him straight up and through a hole in the crumbling ceiling, ending with the villain embedded in the wall.

Sabre, assisted by her suit's jets, hopped up through the recently made hole and caught the villain as he fell from

the wall. Perfect. Out cold just as planned. Sabre took a last look around to make sure she'd gotten the room right then grabbed Anti-Matter's unconscious form and headed back outside. Two minutes later, she deposited the villain's body for the gathered police to take into custody right in front of the throngs of gathered civilians and reporters.

"Sabre! Sabre! Does your presence here indicate dual sponsorship from Hildeman and Aegis? What was the criminal after? What do you have to say to others wanting to be a hero?" The questions flowed from the crowd faster than Sabre could follow, and even the suit's audio processors were having a hard time making sense of it. Not that it mattered. The questions never changed much, and she had a script to stick to.

"Now now, I'm not taking questions at this time, nor do I want to distract from the real heroes here: your local police, EMTs, and firefighters who are all working around the clock to keep you safe. I'm just glad I could be in the area to help when help was needed." Sabre held up her hands in placation to the crowd as she spoke. Not that the words ever did anything to calm the reporters down, but it kept the general public image up, and that was what really mattered.

"Ms. Shields, if you're about done down there. There are reporters here gathering for a statement. Shall I postpone?" The voice came over the private radio in her helmet, and once more, Sabre found herself smiling. Several members of the press had made it a personal crusade to prove that Sabre was tied to Aegis Inc. and thus had shown up at her doorstep every time Sabre was seen doing anything in public. Postponing a meeting with them would just play into their hands even more.

"No, Max, I'll be there in a second. Update my twitter feed to show me at home. Make a claim that I actually am a super hero or something."

"Very good, ma'am."

Sabre nodded to herself then looked over the crowd. "Sorry, folks; that's all the time that I have right now. Duty calls!" There was a general air of complaint as she launched off into the sky and then cut east. The opposite direction from her office and her home.

*** *** ***

"Ms. Shields? Ms. Shields!" Leandra Shields stopped just short of sliding her card through the access reader and turned to face the woman calling her name. Another reporter. The woman was wearing a power skirt and blouse that fit her well but was cut to distract her usual male prey. It was an appealing sight even if it fit an appetite that Leandra couldn't sate right now.

"Our official statement was already given, and I don't do personal interviews without an appointment," Leandra said. To the woman's credit, she was undeterred.

"Do you honestly expect me to believe that song and dance you just gave them?" The woman held up a sheaf of papers as she talked. When she gesticulated, Leandra caught sight of the picture on the top: the new exoskeleton her company had developed for the government.

"It sounds like you've got something to say, Ms.?"

"Pierce. Katy Pierce, with the Informer."

"Ms. Pierce." Leandra smiled and turned back to swipe

her card through the door reader. "Why don't you come with me, and I'll see if I can answer a few of your questions." Leandra pushed the door open and stepped aside for Katy to go through ahead of her. The view was more than worth the effort.

Katy walked a few paces down the hall before beginning to speak. "So you still deny any tie between your company and Sabre?"

"Only because there is no tie, yes," Leandra responded. The reporter's head was on a swivel as they walked, looking for anything extra she could find. Leandra smiled. She was starting to like Katy. "This way." Leandra led Katy into an elevator then hit the button for her top floor office.

Katy didn't wait for the ride to stop before continuing, "Then perhaps you can explain these photos?" The reporter handed over the top two pictures. One of them was the exoskeleton that Leandra had caught a glimpse of earlier, testing out the "new" shielding system that Sabre had grown out of three suits past. The other was a photo of Sabre herself with the same shielding system running.

"What am I looking at here?" Leandra looked over as she spoke. She wanted to see Katy's reaction.

"That, as if you didn't know, is a picture of the army's new exoskeleton doing a field test. But what is interesting about it is that the shield system it is using looks the exact same as the one that Sabre uses." Katy shuffled through her paperwork and handed over another pair of papers. "Then there is the fact that every time Sabre does one of her hero gigs, your stock goes up. Not a lot, no, but enough to be noticed."

Leandra wasted time by looking over the papers and two photos. The elevator chimed and opened into her office, and she lead the way out. She didn't speak until after she had settled into the large, leather chair behind her desk with Katy across from her. "There are several suits of power armor out there with shield units similar to these. More to the point, once an engineer sees something is possible, it is a lot easier for him to design something similar. As far as the stocks go, wouldn't I want to admit that a hero in such good standing was tied to my company to get my stocks to go up?"

"Then what about the fact that your company's plastics division sells to the company that makes the toy line for Sabre?" Katy fired right back. It wasn't hard for Leandra to maintain her smile. She liked the direct approach.

"We sell plastic to a lot of places, and that company does more than just make Sabre action figures. Now, you're just grasping at straws." Leandra steepled her fingers in front of her face and leaned back in her chair.

"Companies don't get as big as yours did overnight, Ms. Shields. Six years ago, you were nothing. Now, you're one of the largest companies in the world. I'm supposed to believe that it was just luck that you showed up at the same time as all these heroes?" Katy leaned forward, on the attack.

"Shortly after, actually."

"I'm sorry?" The response wasn't what Katy had been expecting, apparently.

"We showed up shortly after. It's not a secret. We existed before, yes, but as a smaller company with dreams of being bigger. Once the heroes showed up on the scene, I saw an

opportunity, and we gambled. We bought in on the insurance company that protects against damage from metahuman fights. Sure, it was costly at times, but with more and more metahumans showing up, it wasn't long before every city in the country, and then the world, wanted in on it. That makes for a lot of bank, especially for the small company looking for funding to attempt some of the projects we knew we could do."

Katy took a few moments and shuffled through her papers. When she deflated back into her chair, Leandra knew she had her. Still, Katy was nothing if not defiant. "I know there's more to this than that. You're too involved. It's just a matter of time before I find the connection."

"I look forward to when you do. In the meantime, what are you doing tomorrow night?" The look that crossed Katy's face would've been worth being caught out as Sabre right then and there. "Do you have plans? Maybe we could do dinner? My treat."

"I…I'll think about it," Katy stammered as she gathered her things. "Thank you for your time, Ms. Shields. I'll see myself out." Leandra nodded and held the smile as Katy made her way back to the elevator. As the doors closed, Leandra touched a button on her desk. A moment later, her monitor lit up with the security camera feed from the elevator. The reporter was even cuter when her face was flushed. It was a shame really.

Leandra waited for the reporter to make it back past the secured area, watched all the way by cameras, before moving from behind her desk and toward the inside wall of her office. Leandra's hand trailed along a nearby table as she moved and then up and over a small bust that she'd had for years. Her fingers tapped quickly over the eyes of the bust, and a panel in her wall opened up, revealing a small hallway and a more heavily secured door.

The room beyond, her real work space, was already lit up when she entered. Several previous and current versions of Sabre's armor were stored in transparent cylinders around the room as well as a large number of tools, a multi-monitor work station, and a large work bench with the still in-progress Broadsword suit on it. The monitors caught Leandra's eye. Several of them were showing various networks' coverage of Sabre's earlier fight as well as the related press conferences and speculation; the other monitors showed various internal security feeds, including one of her office and elevator.

"Should I be jealous?" Fox's words murmured in Leandra's ear just a moment before a pair of leather-encased arms wrapped around Leandra's torso and pulled her back. Even through her clothes, Leandra could feel the texture of the leather catsuit her "uninvited guest" wore as work clothes.

Leandra turned around in the thief's arms and struck her best innocent look. "What would you have to be jealous of?" It was impossible to pull her eyes away from the full, ruby lips of the woman holding her.

"I know you, Leandra. You're always horny enough after a fight that you'd have sex with a chair if you could figure out how. You were practically humping her leg by your standards." The hands drifted down Leandra's back, grabbed her ass, and lifted. Leandra purred as she sat down on the work bench, her lips stolen in a quick kiss. All thoughts of work left her mind.

*** *** ***

An hour later, Leandra extracted herself from the tangle of the other woman's limbs and climbed off her work space's lone couch. Once free, she paused for a moment and allowed herself to appreciate the lithe form of her still-sleeping lover. Leandra's lips curled up; it was a very pleasant sight and more than a little tempting to stretch back out and go for round two, or would it be round five at this point?

Unfortunately for Leandra, she had work to do, and that meant pleasure would have to wait. She didn't bother to get dressed before sitting down at her work station. A small USB drive caught her eye, and Leandra found herself smiling once more. Fox always delivered when it counted. Without a second thought, Leandra plugged the USB drive into her computer.

The smile stayed on Leandra's face as she looked through the files. Fox had done good. The USB stick had schematics and blueprints for Hildeman's newest R&D projects, the locations for those projects, and even better, Hildeman's bids for several upcoming government contracts. Leandra could do a lot of good with that information and make a lot of money.

She kept the locations of Hildeman's R&D facilities up on one screen and pulled up a list of contractors on another. Anti-Matter had been a joke. Good for her needs at the time, sure, but not enough of a threat or challenge for what she'd need next. Besides, it would look suspicious if he showed up at a Hildeman facility after attacking one of her places tonight. Not that the man could break out of jail with a seven-man team and fifty pounds of plastic explosives to help him out. "Hmm, maybe Omega would be up for some paid destruction?

He always seems to like putting on a show."

"Omega can be a tough nut to put down. You sure you got the juice to do that safely?" Fox's voice came from the couch, putting the lie to her earlier appearance.

"Definitely. Especially if I add this mass driver that Hildeman has been working on." Leandra brought the device's blueprint up as she spoke.

"Just like that?"

"Well yeah. It gives me a chance to build and test how they did it, and then I can fix it, improve it, and modify it for my own patent. I've got everything I need here to build it, and if Hildeman complains or tries to file a motion, that virus you put on their system will make it look like they stole from me and not the other way around." Leandra grinned to Fox. "Easy peasy."

Fox laughed and stretched out on the couch. "See, that's what I don't understand. If you had me working the building, why'd you bring your fight with that doofus in there?"

"Plausible deniability on where the target was. Besides, now when the city contractors fix the building up as part of the insurance rules, I can get more eyes in on what they're doing. Keeps us isolated and in the know. Which reminds me, that woman who was here earlier, Katy Pierce? I need you to take care of her before she gets too close."

Fox stood and then leaned against the back of Leandra's chair, letting her hand run through Leandra's hair as she spoke. "You've got to be the worst super hero in the world with the shit you pull."

"I'm providing a service. The fights are real, and those

thugs would have attacked somewhere else if not for me. I'm minimizing the damage they do and keeping it all under control. People should be thanking me for that, not trying to expose it like a crime."

"Right, and all the theft, sabotage, and corporate espionage that goes along with it. Just icing on the cake, right?"

Leandra grinned and looked up to Fox. "Of course, you've gotta take opportunities where you find them. It's the American way."

CROOKED

LEON LIGHTE WATCHED THE SWIRLING SNOW. IT WAS ALMOST

pretty when the streetlamps caught it, but in truth, this was a callous deceit. Winter was death, and Leon knew it. He despised the cold. He felt it worse on the left side—always the left side. Even beneath the woolen scarf and the thick hood covering his face, his cheek ached where the muscles slackened beneath his drooping eye. Soon, the numbness would come, and his arm and leg would stiffen beyond use, frozen like this place.

Leon noticed his footprints in the alley between the houses. They wouldn't do.

No traces, he thought as adrenalin kicked in.

He focused on the snowdrift, maybe three feet deep, piled on either side of his trailing prints. He cleared his mind, ignored the cold. It wasn't as natural as breathing yet, but it was getting easier by the day. He felt ready. He forced himself to reach out although his arms remained perfectly still. Suddenly, the snowdrift shivered and then shifted, collapsing over where his footprints had been.

No traces.

Satisfied, Leon turned his attention to the floodlight above the back door to the house. A ghostly tentacle emerged from his chest. It twisted through the night until it penetrated the cover of the lamp and wrapped around the bulb. He visualized an intense pressure and smashed the glass. Leon sagged, and the tentacle dissipated, swallowed by the falling snow. He walked to the back door, gave a cursory glance at the neighbor's house to ensure nobody saw, and scrutinized the glass panes. There were no alarm points. Not that it mattered. House alarms were child's play.

He steadied and delved inside the door's mortise lock. Invisible fingers reached inside it from somewhere deep within him. He aligned the barrels and slid the locking mechanism apart.

Leon drew a wobbling breath. It was more tiring than he remembered, but part of that was the cold. He almost leaned on the door for support but stopped in time.

No traces.

A thought and the handle depressed. The doors swung open into darkness.

Leon hesitated. He considered Dale Howard and his square jaw and tousle of blond hair. Then Willa. He felt unexpected regret until anger closed around it like a steel fist.

He stepped inside Dale's home.

*** *** ***

Leon wheezed, sweat sticking his shirt to his back. His breath was gray mist. Willa's house was a few hundred yards up the hill, a shadow beyond the snow. It was almost six weeks since she asked him to leave. *Not far*, he thought grimly although the pain in his legs didn't agree. The house might as well be on the other side of the world.

He managed the hill and noted the black saloon with opaque windows, parked on the corner nearest Willa's. His eyes lingered on it, wondering…

Leon clenched his teeth, continued on, grateful for the scarf, the Wellingtons, the mittens, and his thick winter coat. In his jacket pocket was a trinket from Dale's. It was an old habit, keeping something from every burglary he did for Jimmy. They were his good luck charms.

I'll have earned a cigarette when this is done.

Smiling bitterly, Leon approached Willa's door. The hike wouldn't have been a problem for a normal 35-year-old, but it was for him. It took him close to a year following the stroke to learn to walk again.

He paused and gathered his breath. The house glittered like it was caked in a skin of diamonds, and the garden was buried beneath a white shroud. Willa's home was still, picturesque, a photo on a Christmas card. He remembered snuggling Willa on the couch, the warmth of their bodies as one.

A callous deceit.

His world ended in that house.

Leon pretended to reach out his right hand, his left close to useless with the cold. It was for effect just in case any of the local curtain twitchers were paying attention. He hid, always hid.

The door opened, and he stepped inside the house and quietly slid it shut. He stayed in the porch, removed his scarf and his coat, and shook snow from himself. He was about to start a monumental struggle with his boots when he noticed the unnatural cold. His stomach fell away. *This was it.* He limped into the living room and saw through the arch leading to the kitchen. Pale moonlight shone in from the patio doors and cast the room in an eerie glow. One of the doors was broken with shards of glass scattered on the tiled floor. Snow drifted in from the yard, and the thin net curtains flapped in the breeze.

Leon felt strangely afraid. He hobbled to the door and traced footprints in the snow leading to and from the house. There were longer marks, like something had been dragged across the yard, and worse, a thin spatter of blood stained the snow. He dizzied, slumped against the wall. He thought maybe it would have come to a head here—but no. They'd taken her. Daggers stabbed his brain.

Not now, he thought. *Not another stroke for Christ's sake.*

His left side tingled. He wobbled, told himself they were simply echoes, the phantom symptoms that haunted him on occasion.

"It's been a long time, Lightfingers."

Leon stiffened, recognizing the voice. He still faced the

garden, faced the blood. He fought for calm and then twisted his head slowly, glancing into the kitchen where he noticed each of the knives had been removed from the sharpener.

"Marek?" The words tasted bitter in Leon's mouth.

The Polish Cleaver stepped into the kitchen from the shadows. Leon turned to him.

"You look…as *handsome* as ever," Marek said, reaching into his jacket. He brought out a cigarette, lit it, and took a long drag. The Pole smirked, his eyes cruel.

Leon straightened as best he could. "Where is she?"

Marek laughed. The Pole always looked like he knew something nobody else did, like he was the smartest man in the world.

"You stole from Jimmy. Not a good idea."

Leon didn't answer. Marek was older than him by ten years or so, but he was fit and strong and dangerous—maybe 6'4" and 17 stone—and most probably armed. Leon shrugged off the tension, and two tentacles left his chest to circle the Pole. Marek took another drag of his cigarette, oblivious as Leon searched his person. The spectral fingers found the gun first and then the machete, hidden beneath the Pole's long jacket in custom-made holsters. Leon gripped the cold metal of both but resisted the urge to turn them on Marek. He held them in case he needed to protect himself. Granted, it would be easier if he could control people as he could control the lock to a door or break the bulb in a light or move a pile of snow in the street. But it didn't work like that. Flesh and bone, anything with a will, was beyond him. God knows he tried on Willa enough times.

"Are you here to kill me?" Leon asked, testing his psychic ability as he talked. His will held firm.

I'm getting stronger. I'm ready.

"Jimmy would be here himself. You know that."

Marek's smile oozed contempt. Leon had seen that look a thousand times on a thousand faces—the look afforded to cripples. But never from Willa. She used to see past his scars, used to look at him like he was a man. Yet she still ended it. Maybe if she knew what he could do? Maybe if any of them knew?

"Jimmy wants to see you. He wants the money you took when you ran. £30 grand."

Leon shivered, wondered how much Marek knew. The words stuck in his throat at first.

"Willa…was pregnant…a boy."

Marek paused. Leon noticed the smirk falter albeit briefly.

"Jimmy won't care. He wants his money."

Jimmy wants to make an example of me more like, Leon thought darkly. There could be no chinks in Jimmy Delvita's armor. Too many scumbags out there to take advantage if he ever showed weakness. The Mouth of Truth, as he was known, never did. Jimmy was a veteran of the first Gulf War. A war was where a man like Jimmy belonged, atrocities and all.

Leon nodded to the broken door.

"It's messy. Someone might have seen."

Marek shrugged. "It don't matter. The Filth won't touch Jimmy. He owns half of the law. The rest are shit-feared of him."

"Where's Willa?" Leon asked, stubborn.

"She's at Jimmy's by now. Weasel Kep took her."

Leon's psychic arms disintegrated. He stared at Marek, horrified.

The Pole grinned. Kepner, thin-faced and ugly as a weasel, was a specific type of bastard, a rapist who didn't care what he stuck it in. Rape was one of Jimmy's favorite weapons. Man, woman, or child.

Marek finished his cigarette and threw the butt onto the wooden floor. He ground it with the spurred heel of his cowboy boot.

"We talk too much. You coming, or do I need to bring you?"

Leon nodded, limped forward. Fear coursed through him as he tried to center himself and conjure more tentacles. Nothing happened. All he could think of was Kepner's thin face, leering over Willa.

Marek seemed to recognize the change in him

"It's you Jimmy wants—perhaps he won't hurt her if you play ball."

Leon nodded weakly, not believing Marek for one second. He raised his hands, his left as high as it would go.

*** *** ***

"Sixteen years," Marek muttered. They were the first words spoken in almost an hour. "Sixteen years is a long time."

Leon stared out of the window into fluttering snowflakes.

"You didn't ask how I found you."

Leon shrugged.

Marek put his foot on the gas. They were in Manchester

now, and the roads were clearer than the hills of Sheffield where Leon had fled to.

"Somebody talked."

"Someone always does."

Marek smiled. "They didn't leave a name. Don't know why. Who cares if a cripple holds a grudge?"

Leon watched the snow. Jimmy would care soon enough. He trembled then, remembered how his concentration slipped when Marek told him of Willa. If he couldn't control his power, he was as good as dead. His stomach suddenly became a nest of vipers.

"Sixteen years with Jimmy––you were a kid when your father went down." Marek sighed. "You're not the only one to get a girl pregnant, y'know. But a father and son—that's special. You became Jimmy's son. And you threw it back in his face."

A father and son—that's special. Leon remembered the beating that fractured his skull and caused the stroke. He had no anger left for his old man. There were others ahead in that line. His father was just a drunk who died in prison. In some ways, he pitied his old man; in other ways, Leon owed him everything. It was during the six months in hospital when Leon felt the change, when he understood he could move things with his mind—when he realized his will could become tendrils snaking through the air that only he could see, that only he could control. On one hand, the thrombosis ruined him, but on the other, it was like the bleed unlocked something greater. He became more than his broken shell—more than man. Nobody ever knew. Not even Willa.

Leon scoffed aloud.

Marek gave him a curious look.

"I have a boy myself. Maybe I understand why you ran."

Leon shifted, where the pain felt fresh. He kept his eyes on the city streets. Men in hoodies, women with blueing legs in impossibly short skirts. Around here, the children of the night belonged to Jimmy.

"I ran…because…I couldn't protect him…from *himself*. I didn't want him to grow up near men like you."

"All men are like me," Marek laughed. "You would be too, Lightfingers, if that bleed in your brain hadn't made you half a man. You're a neutered dog. Look at the world. The difference between you and me is I still have my cock and bollocks. I can fuck whatever I please."

Leon stared at his distorted reflection in the wing mirror, his eyes wet and stinging.

Half a man.

Marek didn't speak for a long time. But suddenly, he did.

"There was no sign of any kids at your place."

There it was.

Leon blinked, felt tears hot on his cheeks.

"She told me afterwards—when I couldn't change her mind. By then, we'd already run."

Marek cursed beneath his breath.

Leon used to tell himself he understood. *She couldn't risk having to wipe two arses, mine and the kid's*, was what he used to think. *A callous deceit.*

"You were a boy when you had the stroke? Seventeen? Jimmy never cared. You think that bitch would've gotten rid

of your kid if you'd stayed with him? No chance. You were someone. You had *respect*."

Leon held his tongue. *Respect*. He remembered the highs, the sensation of feeling *alive* when he took from weaker people, but he never had respect. He was always the cripple.

The car skidded as they headed into the suburbs, and the snow clung to the wheels with more determination. Marek ignored the slippery surface, put his foot down.

"You were nobody when he found you. He made you somebody, took you from burgling houses to breaking bank vaults."

Leon sighed. The truth was somewhere in between. Once Leon understood what his stroke made him capable of, no lock or vault could keep him out. He could get inside any place, never needed tools. Back then, Jimmy made his money from smaller jobs, and Leon was always there to oblige. Over time, the Mouth of Truth used his earnings to suffocate the city. These days, the drugs, the whores, the protection rackets, they all belonged to Jimmy.

Marek cursed again, shook his head.

"And now…well, we both know how this ends."

Leon's hands shook. He had to get it together, or he was in big trouble. He witnessed Jimmy serve justice on a number of occasions. Leon was there when Jimmy tortured Price, when he cut bits off the copper's 4-year-old daughter, when Price wept and gagged as bits of severed flesh were forced down his throat. That was just one time. There were so many tales about Jimmy. They spread through the city like shivers along a spine.

The black saloon jerked as Marek brought them to a skidding halt outside two tall gates.

"Maybe…" Leon searched for his courage. "…maybe…I'll take *everything* from Jimmy this time."

The Pole stared at Leon like he was mad. "You fucking idiot," he muttered.

Leon couldn't speak.

*** *** ***

It was 4 am when the gates of Jimmy Delvita's estate opened. A security camera tracked them with a brilliant red eye as Marek drove inside the Mouth of Truth's stronghold.

Leon slipped as he climbed from the saloon. He grabbed the roof to keep his balance. Marek grinned when he saw Leon struggling to stand.

Half a man, Leon thought bitterly as he steadied himself.

His heart thumped as he surveyed the country house looming darkly before him. It had been a long time. Jimmy was in there somewhere, waiting. Some said the Mouth of Truth possessed supernatural powers, but Leon knew this was bullshit. Jimmy was grotesque, but there was nothing demonic about him. He was simply the worst of man.

Marek slowly led Leon into the house. A pair of narrow-eyed security guards watched them enter without a word. There would be more inside with more guns than a Hollywood action flick. Leon recognized the next hallway they came to, and his stomach fluttered. The banquet hall Jimmy called the Throne Room was at the end of it. They reached the two doors covered in ornate carvings of swooping dragons. A pair of goons stood

on either side. They nodded to Marek and opened the doors. Neither acknowledged Leon. It was like they couldn't see him, the cripple hardly worth their attention.

Jimmy Delvita sat on the jewel-encrusted, golden chair he bought from an antiques dealer in Norway. Moonlight fell on him from a great glass oval built into the largest wall. He was going for the regal look. "A seat fit for a Viking warlord," Jimmy once boasted to Leon.

Marek shoved Leon roughly into the room, and the memory fractured like a shattered mirror.

"Look what I found, boss."

Jimmy stared at Leon dispassionately. His head was hairless, a huge boulder, his face heavily boned and without the capacity for compassion. It looked small on the heaving mass of muscle that was Jimmy's body.

Leon didn't return the stare. He took in the Throne Room, assessing threats and opportunities. Blood thundered between his ears, and it was an effort for Leon to think clearly, but he somehow managed it. Jimmy sat maybe 80 feet away at the far end of the hall. Behind him were four glass cases of weaponry, a collection reflecting many a period and culture that Jimmy built up over the years. The sharp edges of bayonets and katanas and scimitars twinkled invitingly at Leon from beyond the glass. The room hadn't changed much in three years. Beside the cabinets was the door leading down to the soundproofed basements where the real fun took place. That copper Price might still be down there for all Leon knew. His eyes drifted to the painting of the Somme Offensive opposite the glass oval. It was of particular interest to Leon because of what was hidden behind it. He counted six bodyguards in the Throne Room. Maybe he would shoot them with their guns still holstered, through their chests, through their hearts—before they even knew he was a threat.

That left Jimmy.

The brute was exactly as Leon remembered him. Oversized, ugly, brutish. He wore army boots, khaki camouflage pants, and nothing else.

Jimmy stood, all 6'8" of him. Leon's eyes fell on the great scar on Jimmy's stomach, the Mouth of Truth itself. Jimmy laughed, a great, booming bellow. The scar wobbled, laughing too. It was grotesque, terrifying even, for Leon, who had seen the trick on many occasions. The scar stretched from the base of Jimmy's belly to the nape of his neck. Jimmy earned it when an exploding landmine killed four of his unit.

A normal man would've died, Jimmy told Leon one time. *But not me. It completed me.*

Leon's courage faltered. He shouldn't be here, couldn't hope to beat Jimmy. It was the scar, the grinning mouth Jimmy wore as a badge of honor. The fangs and the forked tongue were tattoos, as were the black lips and the dark, demonic eye sockets on each of his pectorals. Jimmy even had two eyes made of porcelain stitched into his chest. Over the years, he learned to use his body, to flex his muscles to form expressions. The Mouth of Truth could laugh. It could frown. It could roar.

My true face was how Jimmy often described it.

Leon steeled himself, wondered if the Mouth of Truth could weep.

Jimmy suddenly stopped laughing, and both faces fell still.

"Lightfingers, you return."

Leon met Jimmy's glare. He needed his mind clear, calm.

"It's like I never left," Leon breathed.

Jimmy tensed his abdominals, and the Mouth of Truth sneered.

"But you did. And now you're back. A thief in my house."

"Where is she?"

The vein in what little of Jimmy's neck was on view bulged furiously.

"Marek!"

The Pole, quick as a snake, slipped the pistol from his jacket and cracked it hard against the back of Leon's head. Leon cried out and collapsed to one knee, blood spilling from his mouth where he bit deep into his tongue. He eyeballed Jimmy and then glanced up at Marek. The gun was limp by his side. It was all he could do not to use his will to fire it through the Pole's knee.

Jimmy grinned and pushed out his stomach so the Mouth of Truth grinned too.

"Pick him up."

Marek grabbed Leon roughly by his right arm, the good one, and yanked him to his feet. The back of Leon's head screamed where the blow landed.

"Bring the bitch," Jimmy demanded. He flexed a pectoral to arch an eyebrow. "It might be time for her to bleed on my nice, clean floor."

Marek sniggered and pushed the gun into the side of Leon's head.

A tentacle snaked from inside Leon's skull. It reached out

and entwined itself around the trigger of Marek's pistol. The gun wouldn't fire until Leon needed it to. Another found the handle of the Pole's machete.

"You fucked me, Lightfingers. Took £30 grand. Maybe I fuck you tonight, eh? Or her?" Jimmy shook his head. "You know me. You know the truth…"

Leon sent more tentacles snaking out. They were strong, thick like the branches of a mighty oak. They swirled across the Throne Room and encircled each of the men in the room. One reared above Jimmy, poised like a snake about to strike. Leon shook with the effort of controlling so many, and beads of sweat trickled down his spine. He must keep his focus. Everything depended on it.

Jimmy continued. "…and the only truth in life…is death. You should have kept running."

A tear crept from Leon's left eye, and Jimmy grunted in satisfaction, mistaking exertion for fear.

Weasel Kep entered the room, dragging Willa behind him. Leon recognized the flowery dress she purchased for their anniversary the previous year. It was torn up to the crotch, dirty, bloodied. A purple swelling adorned her face beneath her right eye, and deep cuts and scratches covered her arms and legs. Kepner also carried a red fuel can, open for effect. Petrol splashed from it as he walked.

Leon lost control. Every inch of his will caved at once, and the tentacles smashed into nothing like waves crashing against a rock. He was doomed.

Willa saw him. Disbelief bled into her expression.

Jimmy smiled at Leon then looked to Willa. His second

mouth quivered hungrily. Willa stared only at Leon.

"Did you do this?"

Leon nodded numbly; anger, fear, and hate caused his head to spin.

"Dale is dead. I killed him as he slept," he managed.

Willa let out a wail, and Jimmy scrunched both his face and stomach into tandem frowns.

"Who the fuck is Dale?"

"You killed Dale…and…and now us. We're dead," Willa sobbed

"You maybe. Not me."

"What are you talking about?" Jimmy snapped.

Leon's anger took over. It hardened, locked into a cold focus. He smirked in a way Marek would have been proud of as a dozen snaking tentacles ripped from his chest.

"I made the call, Jimmy. I tipped you off."

Jimmy looked astonished then furious.

"Why the FUCK would you do that?"

Marek shifted beside Leon. If the Pole made a move, Leon would bury the machete deep in his belly.

"Because I wanted the two of you here together."

Jimmy gawped, still uncomprehending.

"Dale was Willa's *latest* lover. I guess not all men are broken like me. She told me about him, the night she ended things…"

Willa couldn't raise her head.

"So I killed him. Like any man would." Leon turned to Marek. "Even half a man like me."

"You think this is a game? You think I give a shit about

your limp-dick life?" Jimmy roared.

Leon shrugged. "I left you for *her* Jimmy. I left for *our* baby. I stole the money for *my* family."

Willa's tears became hysterical.

"Only… Willa told me something else the night she ended it, Jimmy. The baby was never mine. He was *yours*."

His words slapped Jimmy into silence. The vein in Jimmy's neck pulsed. He suddenly pushed Willa hard onto the floor, and she screamed as her head cracked against the wooden floorboards. Jimmy snorted like a bull about to stampede.

"It's okay; Willa never kept the baby." Leon smiled coldly.

Willa clutched her head, disoriented, tried to crawl. Jimmy snarled.

"So I fucked the cripple's whore a few times? Who gives a shit? *Marek!*"

The Pole froze, gasping in surprise as the machete slid from his holster to hover in the air. Jimmy watched in utter disbelief as Leon drove the blade into Marek. The Pole's mouth fell open in shock and he stared vacantly at the handle protruding from his gut. He clutched at it suddenly, and blood welled between his fingers. Leon twisted the blade, and Marek screamed, stumbling to his knees.

Jimmy's bodyguards looked on in astonishment. Leon turned on them. He cried out as his tentacles went to furious work, but his shouts were lost in the explosion of gunshots. The men fell, one after another. Blood and bone and smoke drifted to the floor like spitting rain. Leon shot Weasel Kep twice through his groin as the rapist made for the basement. He then gripped every door handle with a strength ten men

couldn't possess. They wouldn't be disturbed.

Jimmy was a statue, both mouths gaping.

"Leon…are you…*are you doing this?*" Willa's hair fell in straggles, framing the bruises on her face.

Leon's resolve faltered. The pistols clattered to the floor as he lost control.

Jimmy moved suddenly. He made a dart for the nearest gun.

Leon panicked, lashed out. The spectral arm exploded from him like a missile. Jimmy stooped, reached out a massive hand. But Leon was quicker. He flipped the pistol upright and shot Jimmy through the Mouth of Truth. The point-blank impact tore Jimmy from his feet, gore exploding from his back. Jimmy hit the floor hard and lay groaning in a pool of spreading blood; somehow, he pushed himself to a sitting position to stare murderously at Leon. Blood wept from him.

Leon limped toward Willa. "I wanted you dead, Willa—wanted Dale dead—and Jimmy too… I'm tired of being *weak*."

Willa sobbed, looked away.

"Gonna kill you…" Jimmy muttered, coughing up a mouthful of black blood.

Leon ripped the painting of the Somme from the wall with a flash of his mind to reveal the safe. The locking mechanism began to whir and click as if by itself.

"Nobody ever asked how someone who could barely walk could open so many locks. Houses, safes, bank vaults. You just sat back and took the money. Maybe you should have paid a little more attention? I'm taking everything from you, Jimmy."

"Fucking kill you…*freak*."

The safe door swung open with a satisfying click. Leon turned his attention to the can of petrol Weasel Kep had brought in. He lifted it in the air, and Willa screamed. She scrambled away from Jimmy and kept going.

Leon hoisted the can above Jimmy. The brute tried to stand but couldn't. More blood spilled from the hole blasted through his second mouth. Leon remembered the good luck charm he took from Dale's house. He smiled and took the solid silver cigarette lighter from his pocket.

Willa reached the ornate doors and hammered her fists against them when she realized she couldn't get out.

Leon ignored her. He approached Jimmy with the lighter. His blood thundered, but he was in no danger of losing control. There was excitement mixed in with his hate. It was intoxicating. Jimmy grunted and swiped a weak paw at Leon but missed. Leon regarded the mess on Jimmy's torso and gave a lopsided grin.

"I need a new good luck charm," he said, wrenching a porcelain eye from Jimmy's chest. The brute yelped in surprise. Leon let it hover beside the petrol can.

"Kill you," Jimmy breathed just as Leon tipped the petrol over him.

He flicked open Dale's lighter and brought a sniggering flame to life. Willa's cries became hysterical as Jimmy sputtered.

"Fuck you, Jimmy."

Leon tossed the lighter, and for the first time, Jimmy screamed.

The porcelain eye dropped neatly into Leon's good hand.

He held it up for a closer look, turned it, and then patted it safely into his jacket pocket. Fire blazed in his peripheral vision. Leon ignored the screams of agony.

Instead, he looked to Willa.

*** *** ***

Leon didn't need a bag. The contents of the safe floated behind him as he hobbled across the Throne Room, past the dying flames and the smell of charred flesh. His head ached, and the pain drifted into his shaking limbs. Still, he wasn't done yet.

One last push, he told himself, contemplating how much of the city Jimmy's money would buy him.

Willa sat beside the doors with her knees drawn up and her arms wrapped around her legs. She was half-crazed. He clicked the fingers on his right hand to divert her stare from the floating piles of money. She blinked, saw him.

"I love you," he told her. "But I hate you more. I'm tired of hiding. You tell them, Willa. When they come asking, you tell them everything. Tell them what Lightfingers did here."

Willa didn't answer. She stared past Leon into space, shuddering with the force of her tears.

Leon regarded the fire and the broken bodies. The safe door remained open.

Money is one thing, he thought, *but reputation has a higher value in some circles*.

He sent tentacles through the ornate doors and felt the men waiting in the corridor. He found their automatic weapons, entangled himself around the firing mechanisms.

Behind him, discarded guns bobbed beside the floating cash. They pointed wickedly ahead.

Maybe they'll stop calling me cripple.

A thought, and the handle depressed. The doors swung open into darkness.

FIXED

TRISHA J. WOOLDRIDGE

"VICTORIA, WOULD YOU MIND GETTING ANOTHER POT OF coffee? It's going to be a late night."

The woman gritted teeth behind her smile as she left the table of men. She would break into the notes later so she could stay updated on the new specs for the joint bearings. It was her personal mission to stay on top of this project despite Broderick's insistence upon treating her like an overpaid secretary.

She wasn't a day into this contract before realizing she was hired because she, alone, fulfilled three equal opportunity quotas: woman, Hispanic, and disabled.

Victoria flexed the fingers of the prosthetic hand that she'd been the lead engineer on. That project had lost funding almost two years ago, bankrupting the small company she'd worked for. She had at least ensured that she got the one working prototype. It had not been an entirely legal process, but it had worked.

The burnished steel coffee pot beeped. With a sigh, she carried the tray with her prosthetic hand into the board room. No one noticed how effortlessly she maneuvered the heavy tray with just one hand, placing it on the table without a drop spilled.

She fixed her attention on the presentation and frowned. "Wait, you think just a silicone coating will be enough for that projected usage?" She pointed to the list of stats on the corner. "Are you crazy?"

"The manufacturer specs—" Alan Garrison, Chief Mechanical Engineer, started to scoff.

"The manufacturer's specs are bullshit." She glared. "Read the fine print." Turning her gaze to Broderick, who appeared amused enough to lift his eyes to hers temporarily, she continued, "That coating assumes no weight bearing usage of the joint and only single-directional usage. Per the blueprints, this joint needs to lift or move up to a hundred pounds with full rotational capabilities. That coating will be worn down, and you'll have metal on metal in less than a year functioning at full capacity."

"And you know this from…tests you've run?" Garrison asked, waving a dismissive hand.

"Hijo de Diós," she muttered. "Yes, nearly seven years of testing and then almost two years of direct usage." Unbuttoning her right shirt cuff, she folded and shoved it nearly to her shoulder. Had no one read her work? The flesh around her prosthetic was a shade lighter than the rest of her body, but only that suggested it was not the limb she was born with. She rarely wore less than three-quarter sleeves, keeping the line of difference hidden. The men in the room glanced between each other and her in confusion except for Broderick, who stared steadily, perhaps the longest time on record without looking to her tits or ass.

Slipping her fingers under the flesh "glove," she unhooked the neural attachment that allowed almost perfect sensory simulation then proceeded to fold the glove until her elbow and half her forearm's mechanics were exposed. She managed to subdue most of a smirk upon the gasps then the murmurs of admiration.

Except Mason Broderick. Broderick gave a half nod and pulled a thick file folder from under his clipboard, proceeding to pass around packets of paper.

"You were the lead engineer on that project, weren't you, Ms. Chattham?"

"I was." Something in his tone chilled her, and she regretted her moment of indignant pride. She knew the smart thing to do was keep quiet about her arm no matter how thorough she'd been in doctoring the history and records so it "belonged" to her.

Leaving her arm exposed—it seemed the right thing to do—she reattached the sensory cable. It took a moment for the faux skin to get used to feeling folded upon itself, but it didn't hurt. She picked up the packet and leafed through it.

Or rather flipped through the first two pages before dropping it.

"Where did you get this, Mr. Broderick?" She tried to keep both the accusatory and panicked tone from her voice.

He gave her the slightest smile and flash of perfect white teeth below his sculpted moustache. "When the Medical Endeavors team lost their grant, I offered them an under-the-table buyout in return for all their information. It's how they could give all the laid off employees generous severance packets."

"Interesting," was all Victoria said. Scratch the "only hired for EEO purposes" theory; Broderick was a more manipulative bastard than she thought.

"As you know, I handpicked this entire team," he continued. "I wanted your particular expertise on these things."

With that, every other man in the room nodded approvingly at Victoria.

"Now, Ms. Chattham." Broderick grabbed the projection screen's remote, switching the view to his own tablet. "If you would kindly refresh us on your notes regarding bionic appendages and then give me feedback on how I applied it to our team project, that would move things along."

"Of course, Mr. Broderick." For the next hour and a half, Victoria jumped between excitement about her research, and terror regarding what other knowledge about her Broderick was hiding and how he would use it against her.

*** *** ***

"Another long day?" Bill placed a steaming cup of chamomile in front of his wife after she checked on the two sleeping boys.

She nodded, taking the warm cup with a murmured "thank

you" while trying to gauge her husband's mood and pain level.

He rubbed her shoulders. "A good day though?" He was testing her too. She couldn't blame him. She'd come home a right bitch more often than not lately.

"Mmmnn." Was it a good day? With one statement, her boss had elevated her from wait staff to new Chief Mechanical Engineer. It had been her work that was impressive. Then again, the tone of his voice, the baiting look in his eye whenever she looked at her notes…

"'Mmmmn' isn't very descriptive," Bill teased, tipping her chair back a few inches so he could kiss her on the nose.

"Ee!" She squealed, gripping his arms. "Don't do that!"

"Ow!"

Her chair banged back into place as he yanked his arms from her grip.

"Oh, God! I'm so sorry, Bill! I just…I don't like tipping… it feels like…" She bit her lip, fighting her mind from flashing back to the accident that had taken her arm—and nearly killed Bill.

"You don't know your own strength." He glared at her prosthetic arm. She stood, cradling it. Closing his eyes, he took a deep breath and leaned on the fridge. His lips silently counted, a trick their therapist taught him.

"I'm sorry." Her voice felt tiny. Despite the brain injury that had screwed with his temper, Bill had never, ever raised a hand to her or the children. He'd lost it once, just once, and smashed the family computers. She knew in her heart he'd never hurt them. Hell, the therapy had been his idea!

He stopped counting but still took deep breaths. He was

trying. Victoria put her left hand, her real one, on his chest, leaning her body on his and closing her eyes. After a few moments, he wrapped his arms around her. It felt good.

No need to worry him about what Broderick might know.

*** *** ***

Broderick was building a robotic suit.

Victoria sat back in her chair upon reviewing the full project stats sent to her internal email. Until now, she had only seen pieces. She knew that Broderick World Enterprises was the world leader in robotics and that half the parts on the Medical Enterprises project were sourced from them, but she'd never, no pun intended, put the pieces together.

It seemed too ridiculous. Too much…well, too much like a particular comic book series kept in her dad's pristine cardboard-backed sleeves. Victoria had been grounded, twice, for raiding his collection, but he'd eventually given in and started re-reading them with her when she was eleven. It had been her big Date with Daddy when she was thirteen to go see the movie.

Normal people, rich and über-smart as they may be—and Broderick was in the top tier of rich and über-smart—normal people did not try and build super human-robot fighting suits.

The specs didn't actually include weapons, but they were incomplete. There were various partially created plans for flight that spanned rocket-fuel to electromagnetism. It was kind of scary.

It was also pretty damned exciting.

By lunch, Broderick managed to get his hands on enough

supplies to let Victoria's team of mechanical engineers start mock-ups for the joints. The team listened to her. It was past dinnertime, again, when they had done enough testing to get optimal measurements for the software designers. After a catered evening meeting with Broderick, they had a timeline to begin simulations within six weeks.

For the first time in almost two years, Victoria drove home with a smile.

*** *** ***

"It's okay, honey." Victoria stood in a puddle of water amid the triangle of her red-faced husband, two tear-faced boys, and the still-trickling dishwasher, half-yanked from under the counter. "I can fix this. I can fix anything, remember?"

"I'm sorry, baby. I-I…" Bill cast a guilty glance to Mike and Petey. Neither of them had any injuries. Bill had a gash up his forearm that still seeped blood across a deeply purpling bruise.

"Shh… Sh-sh-sh." Victoria looked between them, soothing. She took a tentative step toward her husband then put a hand on his arm. No warmth, so no infection. "Just wash this out with antibacterial soap, and I'll take a look at it, okay, babe?"

He nodded. "Vic… I…" He glanced at the boys again. "I didn't."

She stood on her tip-toes and kissed his rough cheek. "I know, babe."

Leaning his head on hers for a moment, Bill sighed.

"I'm gonna tuck in the boys. Just wash that out and have a seat, okay?" She kissed him once again before heading toward

her sons.

When she returned to the kitchen, Bill was not resting in a chair but on his hands and knees, sweatpants soaked three quarters of the way up, mopping water and suds.

"I can get that—"

"You worked all day." His arm swept across the floor with the zeal of one slaying enemies with a dishtowel.

Victoria knew better than to argue; she knew the lines by heart. Taking a deep breath, she grabbed a chamois from under the sink. "Mikey really likes the manga you got him. He'll probably be exhausted tomorrow because he'll read through this one tonight."

Her husband sagged a little as she knelt beside him, and she almost melted from the gratitude in his eyes and the silent question of why she even put up with him. Picking up his towel and tossing it into the sink, where it landed with a sploosh, she edged closer and took his injured arm. Kissing his knuckles, she asked, "Can I see this now?"

Darkness touched his face again, though he relaxed his arm. "I know how to bandage a cut."

"I know you do. Doesn't stop that crazy mom instinct from wanting to check every little injury on my boys." He had, in fact, done a good job of layering sterile pads up his arm and neatly taping each overlap. Being the stay-at-home parent to two boys since even before the accident meant that Bill knew his way around the medical shelf in the linen closet. Victoria lightly kissed the bandage. "See, you couldn't do that yourself."

He smiled again, blue eyes hinting the playful spark she loved from the moment she met him. "No, you're right. That wouldn't work if I did it."

"All right, what I need is the area closest to the washer dry. Can you work on that while I get my toolbox and change real quick?"

He nodded. When she returned in her "dirty work" sweats and a so-worn-it-was-almost-see-through Batman T-shirt, heavy toolbox clutched in her prosthetic hand, cordless drill in her flesh hand, the area around the dishwasher was just about bone dry, and the rest of the kitchen floor had only sheens of leftover dampness. Bill grinned from the floor. "Good enough?"

"Perfect."

Victoria removed the front panel so she could access the internal motor. She really didn't need the tools or the drill. It wasn't a plumbing problem; a quick glance below the sink when she had grabbed the chamois informed her the pipes and hoses were intact despite Bill's hulkish moment. It wasn't electrical either, thank God. Not that she couldn't have fixed that just as easily—her talents actually seemed to have the most power over any current or charge issues—but that would be dangerous with all the water.

The motor for one of the blades was stuck. Victoria only needed to touch, caress even, the molded plastic above the motor to feel it, feel the life of the machine—which she knew sounded crazy, so she only thought this way to herself—and coax it to work. When she felt the mechanism was fixed, she reassembled the front panel and realigned it. Closing the dishwasher, she regarded the crack through the countertop that would have been outdated when she was a child.

She felt her husband's tense body behind her. Victoria

tried to mask her own deep breath. "If we just can edge it back in, it'll be fine," she said. "Then just epoxy the crack for now. My job is going good, so we'll be caught up on the bills, and we can start getting those renovations we planned."

He didn't say anything, but skinny as he was, he moved her out of the way with his body and muscled the washer back in place.

"We can just have the contractors start in the kitchen…" She continued her pep talk as if her husband wasn't doing exactly what his physical therapist had told him not to. If she pointed it out, he'd only push harder.

Bill grunted, not meeting her eyes. The red on his too-pale cheeks and the tight lines around his eyes confessed more pain than she knew he wanted to let on. Trying not to limp, he grabbed the epoxy from the broom closet and sealed the crack with the same precision as he'd bandaged his arm.

They finished cleaning up together before retiring to just an hour of television before Victoria had to go to bed for her next early morning.

*** *** ***

"Why is it that it seems only you can make the joints work correctly, Ms. Chattham?" Mason Broderick glanced between the armor on his arms and legs and the woman making minute adjustments.

Victoria pressed her lips into a tight smile, not missing the layer of acid concealed below his joking tone. "I've worked on joint mechanics longer than anyone else on the team, sir. And my day-to-day life kind of depends on it."

"I see."

Her stomach turned. She'd never planned on getting this close to her boss, but once he'd put on the armor, the joints seemed to have lost their fluidity. Proximity was only half of her discomfort. The mechanical team was stuck on this part when the prosthetics project lost its funding. Same problem. The joints only seemed to respond with proper sensitivity to Victoria.

She was basically puttering around Broderick at this point. In her mind, she was coaxing the machinery to respond to his body, pick up on nerve sensors they'd so carefully tuned to his physiology. There was some other signal she sensed wasn't coming from the armor. She couldn't pinpoint it, but not having encountered it in her prior projects, she dismissed it for the moment; she could investigate it later.

In a voice so low only she could hear, he said, "I never realized that just tightening and loosening the plating screws had so much effect."

"Amazing, isn't it." She allowed herself a moment of pride at how neutral she kept her voice. "Try moving now."

Mason Broderick proceeded through what looked like some martial arts kata. He didn't move quite like she'd seen in generic movie montages, but when he was done, he nodded.

"Better. But I think we can fine tune it a bit more. There's still a lag, and the hydraulics aren't compensating enough for the weight difference."

"It's also lacking the torso, which will smooth things out." Victoria folded her arms. Her phone vibrated for the fifth time that hour. Something must be wrong. Her lip twitched.

Bill could just be fretting over something silly like one of the boys misplacing something. She wished her voice didn't waver as she continued, "Weight has to be evenly distributed over the body. The arms and legs are designed to work with the strength enhancement of the torso to balance everything."

Broderick nodded and glanced at her glowing, buzzing hip. "Makes sense. Do you need to get that, Ms. Chattham?"

"Yes, please, excuse me." Ignoring her boss' amused yet disapproving face, mirrored by the rest of his all-but-clones, she casually retreated to the upstairs women's room and called her husband back.

"I rescheduled our session," came his icy voice. "They couldn't take us any earlier than four weeks out. If you think you can actually get out of work, of course."

Joder. Their couple's therapy had been today. She had missed one for the interview then missed another. This would be the third reschedule. "I'm sorry, baby. We started testing today, and I couldn't get out—"

"Couldn't even answer the phone for two hours?"

"No, I couldn't."

"What if it was an emergency?"

"I programmed Krissy's line into your phone for that. Under 'Emergency.'"

"What if I forgot?"

The question hung in the air.

"It wasn't though," she finally said. "And I said I was sorry. I'll be at the next meeting. I promise!"

"Yeah, whatever. Enjoy work." The sarcasm in his voice cut.

Victoria heard the click as he slid his phone shut, hard,

ending the call. Thank God she was gripping her phone in her flesh hand; her prosthetic one would have crushed the damned thing. With a conscious thought for each flexing muscle, like when she was learning to control the prosthetic, she moved her hand to her pocket and inserted the phone before she threw it across the bathroom and broke it.

*** *** ***

Only the kitchen lights were on when Victoria pulled into the driveway. Swallowing bitter bile, Victoria ascended the side porch stairs, each feeling higher than normal, and came into the warm kitchen. She picked up the faint smell of chamomile flowers even before she saw Bill at the stove, hand clenched around the tea kettle handle, squinting at the laminated yellow sheet on which the boys had drawn a steaming kettle (different from the steaming coffee-cup-adorned sheet by the coffee pot) in the corner to help Daddy keep track of different recipes and kitchen tasks.

What was there to say?

After he set the kettle down, counting five checks that it was on the burner that he'd ignited, Bill leaned on the handle of the oven.

Laying her head on his back, she wrapped her arms around him. "I'm sorry I missed our meeting today."

He didn't say anything, but he didn't push her away. When the kettle whistled, she let him pour into the two cups he'd prepared with tea bags. They sat in their usual seats at the table, kitty-corner from each other where each could face a kid or reach another kid.

"I miss you." Bill's comment shattered the tangible silence into slicing shards.

Victoria felt herself deflate. "It's testing. You know how my schedule is for testing. It's my job."

"I don't mean…" He stopped and scrunched his face. "Vic, is this what you want? This job I mean. Yes, the money's good…but are you happy?"

With her eyes closed, Victoria could hear unasked questions though she couldn't honestly say she wasn't hearing her own fears. Is this job more important than our marriage? Than our family?

There was also what she hadn't told Bill. She intended to, but every time she considered it, she was either afraid to ruin his good spirits or didn't want to further stress him when he was already stressed or in pain. Broderick knew something about her arm. And her abilities. With his lawyers, if he went to claim her arm, claim every penny of their savings, their house…she didn't know if she could stop him.

Was she happy? She loved the project, yes, but could she even quit now if she wasn't? Would Broderick come after her for whatever secrets he thought she knew to make her arm—and his suit—work? Would he go after her family?

"I don't want to leave my job," she said. At least that was truth. "I'll make things work. I won't miss our next session… I'll black it out on the calendar, set five different alarms on my phone, my email, everything. And I'll find a way to start cutting hours."

Bill stared at her for a long time. He had the most beautiful and intense blue eyes, and they could cut like diamonds. She didn't want to feel she had to hide pieces of her soul from his scrutiny.

She reached across the table and took his hand. "Baby, I just need you to trust me to fix things right now. Please? I need you to trust me."

He snatched his hand back. "Do you know what that sounds like?"

She cocked her head, not understanding what he thought it sounded like. "Huh?" Then it dawned on her. Late nights, grouchiness, missing family meetings, secrets… Shit! "Oh, God, babe, no-no! I…wouldn't even think!"

He snerked, clicking his cup down on the table and pressing his hand over his mouth, possibly holding in tea. After a swallow, he all but giggled. "Obviously not. I can't remember the last time I ever saw you that confused."

"Every guy I work with is an asshole!" was all she could sputter.

Bill raised his hands in surrender. "And you want to work there?"

"The project we're working on… Broderick bought out Medical Endeavors." She held up her right arm. "It's based on what I did with this… It means something to me."

"You never told me that."

"Non-disclosure agreement… Like fifty pages long. I shouldn't have even said this much." She begged him with her eyes to understand.

Taking and releasing a deep breath, Bill nodded and sipped his tea.

*** *** ***

Mason Broderick resembled a demon when he was not happy, but Victoria stared him down anyway.

"We are on schedule, and I cannot miss this appointment. I have had it marked on every calendar in this office for a month now."

"And we've had our testing schedule for two months. You helped put it together." His voice was a cold knife; he didn't even look up from shuffling papers.

"Nowhere in that schedule does it state that we would work eighteen hour days, every day, for all of testing with absolutely no personal time no matter how far ahead we schedule it." Victoria put her hands on her hips and glared harder, hoping to pry his eyes to hers through sheer will.

"It's your design that won't work when you're not around." He glanced at her then back at the papers, the few lines on his face hard as granite. "One might think you're trying to find a way to secure yourself on this project. Especially after I've dropped Miskal, Kerrigan, and Hendricks."

"They were dead weight, and Miskal was smoking pot in storage. We spent more time fixing their screw-ups, so no, I'm not trying to secure my way on this project. I know I'm better than anyone on this team, and so do you."

Now, he looked up. His eyes were coffee brown, like teddy-bear eyes if they weren't so damned cold, a sharp contrast to the fine, blond hair gelled perfectly atop his head and neatly groomed over his upper lip. Victoria refused to look away.

The desk phone vibrated Krissy's signature ring. Broderick clenched his jaw. When the phone buzzed again, he gave an almost-inhuman snarl.

"The torso attachments for the arms and legs better be perfect when I try it on tomorrow." He snatched the phone. "What is it?"

Not bothering to hide her smile—she'd take her victories where she could get them—Victoria exited Broderick's office. As she passed Krissy, she heard, "I'm sorry, Mr. Broderick, really. He said he was an attorney, and he swore it was important, and now the line's dead."

Victoria caught her eye and the slightest of winks.

She'd get those damned couplings to work when she got back from her appointment.

*** *** ***

It was nearly ten o'clock at night when Victoria admitted the damned couplings would not be perfect in the morning. Everyone else, even Broderick, had left for the night. It took twenty minutes of a frustrated pace, fighting tears, before a fix came to her. The fix would cost more, but it would work. And it was a reasonable issue—well, reasonable to humans with souls, something she was unsure applied to Broderick—so work could continue on the project without much of a blip. She just needed a certain material… She had better write a proper proposal while she was thinking of it.

Her cell buzzed on her desk. It was Bill. "R U ok?" She puzzled at the message before noticing the time.

Shit. Joder. Goddamnit! Hijo de Dios!

"Yes. Sorry. Leaving in 15."

She finished the proposal in exactly fifteen minutes and

promised herself she would go in early to double check it.

*** *** ***

Victoria did not go in early to double check her proposal. Mike woke up with a fever of 102, and Petey's ears hurt. They wanted Mommy.

She appreciated Bill's silence. He was holding back; she knew he wanted to say if she had been back last night, this wouldn't be a surprise for her. Then again, he'd walked in on her sobbing on the downstairs toilet.

"I'll call your sister. She can drive us to the ER." His voice was a mix of emotions she couldn't pick apart as he closed the door.

Broderick was going to fire her. No, worse, he was going to use whatever he knew about the fudged and "misplaced" forms around her prosthetic arm and sue the shit out of her because there was no way her family could afford any lawyer to go up against him. He'd own her.

She heard her sister's car arrive and leave the driveway with Bill and the boys. When she could no longer hear it, she lifted her head and let out a howl that ended in a stream of curses in three different languages that would be the pride or shame of anyone.

The goddamned mech suit wasn't going to work. It would never work. Like her arm, it only responded to her, to her talents, to her…power or whatever the hell it was. Victoria had pondered many times on the ability that had manifested in her teens. Her sister, Vivian, had her own gifts too…charming people, getting them to do things. Victoria could use that right now. Charm Broderick into…well, into not being a dick.

Still on the toilet, trousers and underwear around her ankles, Victoria blew her nose into sheets of toilet paper until she could finally breathe. Vivian had once said that she didn't use her power nearly as much as one would think; the trick was knowing what someone wanted and showing them how helping you got them there.

Broderick had handpicked their whole engineering team, signed them all to secrecy, placed them above every other employee at BWE in pay grade and attention—gave them offices in his personal building. She knew this. She also knew that everyone let go still got a ridiculous layoff payment. Every piece of this project had been funded from Mason Broderick's personal accounts, not the business accounts.

Hell, it was a super robot suit. Of course the man wanted it more than anything.

And she was the only one who could make it work.

Taking a deep breath, Victoria cleaned herself up, reapplied make-up, and drove into work.

*** *** ***

"So you decided to come in for testing after all?"

The men around Mason Broderick turned angry eyes on Victoria. Galliston, next in line for Chief Mechanical Engineer, harrumphed and turned back to the suit, trying to shove the right arm into the socket.

"It's not going to work with brute force. Or did we forget we're all Homo sapiens and can actually think?" Her voice was cool, and she stood straight as if she were taller than every

single one of them.

"Then why don't you demonstrate how you fixed the coupling problem last night? Or do I need to look deeper into your work with Medical Endeavors to see if I missed anything?" Broderick looked from her eyes to her arm, threat clear.

So this is it.

Victoria strode over to her boss. Eyes wide, as if looking at an oncoming tiger, Galliston moved from her path. She placed her hands on the arms of the suit then slid them onto the shoulders. It took a millisecond for her to coax the joints to attach to the torso. With her determination, she felt her power extending past what she touched. Even as she moved her hands from the suit, she could manipulate the energy.

This close, she could see the pulse jumping in his neck. Its pattern didn't match what she was picking up from the suit's readings. She frowned. The slight interference she'd picked up when he wore just the arm and leg armor felt stronger, more enhanced. It didn't make sense. The circuit was complete. Victoria knew every tiny part of this suit. There shouldn't be any signal she didn't recognize.

He was masking ragged breathing. She smelled cold sweat.

"Mr. Broderick…" Something was definitely wrong.

He stepped away from her. Surprise momentarily dissipated the fury and pain as he moved effortlessly.

"Now, show us all how you made this work," he said. "It needs to be replicated. I don't want to need you every time I want to use this suit."

Victoria lifted her chin in defiance. "No."

"What?"

"I have worked my ass off more than *any. One. Else.* On this team, including you, and you don't want to need me?"

He narrowed his eyes, but she noticed the day-bright overhead LEDs reflecting a sheen of sweat down his cheeks and neck.

"Have one of them get you out of that contraption." Victoria gestured dismissively at the suit. "And then tell me you don't want to need me. In the meantime, I have a proposal to rewrite so we can fix some of the problems the team will eventually find if they can work half as hard as I do." She turned on her heel, strode out of the testing area, and took the stairs back up to the offices.

Krissy was frowning on the phone, obviously on an intense personal call. Using the distraction to her advantage, Victoria walked past her own office, where her proposal lay in the middle of the desk.

She needed to know exactly what Mason Broderick had on her. How much was he bluffing, and how much of a case could he take against her and her arm?

With said arm, it didn't take much effort to break his lock.

She glanced around the sparse office. It was almost clinical, it was so clean. Five different sets of black file cabinets, unmarred by the least dust mote, shone in sunlight streaming through the wall of windows. Pursing her lips, she regarded his desk where a sloppy pile of mail, likely left by Krissy, rebelled against the pristine order.

One envelope was placed atop the others, and Victoria recognized the medical company's logo immediately.

They only made and patented one specific item: high-end pacemakers.

"The dude really is like Tony Stark." This certainly explained the unexpected feedback she'd sensed.

This changed everything.

Inhumanly heavy footfalls thundered from the stairs.

"Mason?!" she heard Krissy scream.

As she'd designed it, the suit moved faster than humanly possible. Broderick shoved the door open so hard it cracked against the wall, bouncing to slam shut behind him. Thoroughly drenched in sweat, face twisted in pain, he approached.

She ought to be terrified at the armored human before her. Even without weapons, the strength in the limbs alone could crush every bone in her body.

Victoria folded her arms and smiled.

"Get. This. Goddamned. Thing. Offa-me!" His voice betrayed the pain.

"You're experiencing myocardial infarction," she stated. "Brilliant as you are otherwise, you're an idiot. Did you think this huge magnetic machine set to your vitals wouldn't mess with your pacemaker?"

"I had…it…specially…made. It wasn't… Just. Take. This. Off!" His metal hand clutched his metal chest.

"See, I take it off, your heart stops. You don't want that, do you?" There was more than a twinge of guilt as she saw his suffering. But still. Things could not go back to how they were. She would not lose this contract. And she could not risk him destroying her family with his lawyers.

"You can. Restart it."

"Here's where I choose whether to play innocent and not know what you're talking about, or I can just cut to the chase because I was sick of these games when you started playing them." She paused for effect. "Yeah, I can restart it. And I can stop it again. And I can fix it so your mechanical ticker plays nice with your mechanical armor for the rest of your life."

"What. Do you. Want?"

"Glad you're with me on the done playing games part." She walked up to him and pressed her left hand to the armor chest. "I want…this arm." Victoria held up her right arm. "Mine. Period. No strings attached. And I want this contract." She tapped her forefinger on his chest. "Also mine, all mine. I'll even be nice and ask for the salary of only half the team combined. Saves you money for the improvements I can make on this." She tapped his metal suit again. "I can make this thing work, and I can keep it running, and I can keep your ticker issues secret…because that's the only reason I can see you being stupid enough not to let us know about it.

"Last, and not least, starting right now, my family comes first, and don't you ever forget that. You take care of them and let me enjoy my life with them; I'll return the favor. Go save the world, rule the world, I really don't care, but me and mine get taken care of. Am I clear?"

He paused. She wasn't sure if it was for effect, to maintain whatever dignity he felt he had left, or if it was the pain overcoming him. Finally, he nodded. "Clear. Deal."

"Good." Victoria pressed the flat of her left hand to his chest. With the help of her robotic hand, she eased him to the ground as the suit clanked to the floor around him, no

longer holding him up. He curled up as the rest of the armor released. She pressed her left hand to his chest, searching for the sub dermal bump of the pacemaker. He convulsed once, but she held him steady, sending the signal of her own pulse to reset the charges into his heart.

As soon as she felt it regulate, she stepped away from him. It did not escape her notice that she still felt the energy, like a slight buzz in the palm of her hand. One more step back made it weaken but not fade entirely.

He lay on the floor for several minutes, just breathing. As he sat up, he looked at her. The curiosity in his eyes tempered his threat. "I could have you arrested."

"You're not going to though."

He regarded her a few more minutes. Half-naked, covered in sweat, shorter and younger than Victoria, he didn't lose his imposing air. She didn't flinch.

"One addendum."

"Mmn?"

"You don't care if I'm saving the world or ruling it so long as your family is okay. Fine, then don't ask. No questions about where I'm going, what I'm doing, who I'm with. Nothing. No prying, peeking…or the deal's off. Am I clear?"

Victoria took her time considering. It didn't require the time, but she was getting the hang of the power of the pause. "Clear. And agreed."

"Good. Then, before you leave at five, I want a draft of the contract delivered to me personally along with your proposal for improvements based on today's test."

"I'll have both done by four, at which time I'm taking

a whole hour of the accumulated PTO from the past four months and going home."

"Past hours do not get figured into your new paid time off schedule."

Victoria tensed her mouth. She wasn't budging. Not this far into things.

"You can leave any time today once both the contract and proposal are in my hands. We start counting accumulated PTO tomorrow, when you'll still arrive at promptly 9:00 am."

She considered. It was a compromise but one she felt comfortable making. "All right. I will see you when I deliver the contract and the proposal and again at 9:00 am."

At his nod, she turned to leave then paused. The connection to his pacemaker, she could identify it now, barely tingled her palm. Turning once more, she smiled. "Also, so you don't think your lawyers can work me over later…" She closed the fist of her flesh hand and watched him clutch his chest. "From anywhere. Good day, Mr. Broderick." Opening her hand, she turned to go, leaving him sitting amid a mess of robot armor parts. He didn't have to know that she was just discovering her range.

Tonight, she would cook Bill dinner and make him tea, definitely tuck in her boys. And maybe break out her dad's old comic collection.

ACQUAINTED WITH THE NIGHT

CAT RAMBO

RAIN SLEETS DOWN LIKE MULTICOLORED, METAL NEEDLES to splatter against the chill, neon-lit street's surface. The light gutters across the wet surface of his black, plastic rain poncho, picking out abstract tattoos.

Somewhere in the night, he knows there is darkness brewing.

The mask fits loosely on his face under the rain poncho's shroud. Some people look at him as they go past in the rain, but their eyes skitter away, seeing him faceless in the dark.

At one point, the mask was crimson, and golden wind vortexes, bright as daylight, rode his face on either side, framing his power, his strength.

Far away, he hears a shout. He pauses to listen, but it does not come again, and he is not sure of the direction. Cars hiss past in a spray of sparkling, heavy, wet mist and touch the surface of his jacket with beaded jewels.

He tugs at his dark gray face covering, pulling it into place. Rain has seeped in through the eyeholes and walks along his face like the memory of tears.

Is he crying, or is it the rain? The question seems overwrought, and he feels himself slipping into one of those dark, cinematic moods where he sees everything from the outside. It's starting again, the loop of film that is his life.

*** *** ***

Part 1: The Origin

He was an ordinary boy in an extraordinary place, he tells himself. Working in Miracle Labs, he was a go-fer, fetching coffee and sandwiches for the scientists in their bright white lab coats. Everyone was so pleasant, so marvelously cheerful! He whistled on his way to work every morning.

As time passed though, he became aware of undercurrents. Doctor Octo hated Doctor Sept, and they both vied for the attention of receptionist Wye, who was worth vying for, he admitted to himself, but he knew that he—pimple-faced and adolescent gangly—wouldn't have a chance with her. Most of the scientific in-fighting, though, had to do with who published what where. Most of them worked hard at publishing and conducted their research with scrupulous but eager abandon.

It was easy for someone like himself to pick up some extra cash acting as a guinea pig. It paid well, and his mother's birthday was coming up. Sept was working on a military

project—augmented strength, while Octo was working on a similar project—increased speed.

Tuesdays and Thursdays, he sat in Sept's lab squeezing grip-meters, while on Mondays and Wednesdays, he used a mouse to click colored shapes on a computer screen. He swore to both of them that no one else was interfering with his physical structure, and they both were horrified but intrigued when their experiments collided, geometrically increasing both strength and speed as though cross-multiplying.

Military types swarmed the labs, smoking jovial cigars while the scientists ran him through test after test with suppressed jubilation, which faded into pretense as every other test subject underwent both treatments to find themselves no stronger or faster than before.

He was their golden boy at first, and even Wye unbent in his direction, admitting she wouldn't mind a cup of coffee, which led to one thing, then another, then him offering in-home demos of what it was like to bang a genuine superhuman. But more test subjects came and went in failed succession. The doctors became less fond of him as the military soured.

He lost his job at the laboratory although no one ever really gave him a straight answer as to why.

So he became a superhero, which seemed like a viable option at the time.

*** *** ***

Part 2: The Career

He got an agent who he'd seen on early morning TV, representative to a group known as the Weather Team. He

took the name Captain Hurricane, super speed and strength qualifying him, he figured.

It was never clear how many superheroes Alan Mix had in his stable. Although his Variety piece when Captain Hurricane joined him said seven, two of those, Ebon Lightning and el Invierno, were sometimes there, sometimes not due to other gigs with the world of superhero wrestling.

They offered to cut their fellow heroes in on the deal.

"Sweet money and not that hard," Ebon Lighting urged three of the others, Sunshine Princess, Tsu-nami, and Captain Hurricane. Sunshine Princess did try it, as he recalled, but did not do well in a match against the Hunktress.

Women liked him. What's not to like about strength and charisma? They liked his gee-whillikers good looks.

He was a little bit in love with Sunshine Princess at one point when he was depressed, but the woman that he would go to his grave loving was another of the Weather Team: Waterlily Elegance, an enormous-haired alien, cerulean-eyed with pumpkin-colored skin from beyond Betelgeuse.

She did not return the affection though. The mate waiting for her, after she had spent a year in their world, was an enormous purple flower, forever stationary, who floated on a lake of violet emulsion on her home planet.

When she returned home to engage in the mating ritual that would lead to her explosion in a rain of seeds, he spent three nights running in a bar with Sunshine Princess. Each night, they staggered home to his apartment and made clumsy love in his unwashed bed. On the third morning, he woke up to find her making eggs and coffee in the tiny kitchen.

He drank the coffee in a sullen silence that ate away like acid at her happiness, making it more and more brittle as she moved around cleaning the small space, wiping at the counters with a lemon-colored sponge.

"Sit down, for the love of God," he finally snarled, and she sat, pouring herself coffee and sweetening it with lavish spoonfuls.

"Is everything okay, babydoll?" she cooed, and he could tell she was latching on, sinking in the hooks that would drag him into married life and an eternity of lemon sponges.

"I'm not your babydoll," he told her startled face. "Not your gumdrop, not your honeybunch, not anything. You were convenient; that's all, Eleanor."

She went white as she stood, swaying, and then stiffened herself and marched out to collect her things. She wrapped the yellow cape around herself, sodden still from the previous night's rain and clinging in damp folds to her skin. He caught a glimpse of her eyes, which were enormous and bruised dark.

That night, he patrolled Central Park and beat three muggers so savagely that they could not walk.

*** *** ***

Part 3: The Announcement

Three months later, when she came to see him about the pregnancy, he already had felt it in his heart. He pushed money into her hand and then pushed her away, physically, a hard shove that sent her sprawling. He turned his back and walked away.

He'd gotten a photogram that morning from Waterlily

Elegance. She stood by the shore of the violet lake, one slender hand cupped around her swelling body, ripe with the offspring that would kill her. He wondered what it would look like. Would the seeds explode outward, scattering her flesh, leaving scraps of squash color to dry and brittle on the ground? He asked around, asked Silver Spring, the other alien on the Weather Team, but Spring ignored him in a way that screamed impoliteness. Realizing he was violating some taboo, he dropped the subject with reluctant haste.

*** *** ***

Part 4: The Arrival

He met his daughter first when she was four, hair like cotton-candy floss, colored with pale light. She had inherited powers from both of them although he could sense she would never be as strong, as fast, as him. From her mother, she had taken the trick of fostering light beneath her skin, letting it go in pulsations of brightness. He called her his Firefly.

He took her every Saturday: to the zoo, to the harbor, to the botanical gardens, to the sculpture garden, to the playground, to the grocery store, to the laundromat.

They had a year of such meetings before she vanished.

Someone took her out the window, the thirteenth story window that she looked out of each night, her small, luminous moon face pressed up against the clear surface. They melted through the glass as though it was water and abducted her in silence.

He nearly died when the police showed him the film,

which they said was selling well in underground circles. Although she wore a mask, he recognized the flashes of light that trembled on her naked skin. The men with her wore masks too. They said it was a snuff film and would not show him more than the moment he needed to identify her. The corpse was never found.

He never found the men either though he has spent a decade looking. Princess Sunshine committed suicide, and most of the Weather Team was gone. He had to leave it after three years and the fourth scandal of a criminal killed in the course of apprehension. In another decade, one of Waterlily Elegance's children might come back to this planet and perhaps join a new superhero group. He knew that twenty-two had survived her death. Their names blended together for him: Casual Horizon, Immaculate Bliss, Serenity of Spite…

Sometimes, he wrote to her mate and received in return graceful thought-grams, blended nuances of mental energy and sensation that conveyed regret and well wishes and never spoke of her.

*** *** ***

And now, the loop complete for another hour, he steps forward again into the darkness. The mask he wears is a duplicate of one from the film. He has no wish to explore why he chose it.

But every night, it's the same, his mask looming down over the fallen form of the mugger, the purse snatcher, the rapist, the suspected harasser, the suspicious stranger out late at night

as he kicks and slaps at them, superhuman strength making bruises bloom like light flashes on their skin. Tonight, jewels of light will glitter on their unturned, blank face, and he will feel the blood hot within himself, boiling hot and mammal, unlike the rain's cool and vegetative touch.

GONE ROGUE

THE FIRST TIME IT HAPPENED, WE WERE ON OUR WAY TO knock the stink off of The Midshipman. Lame name, I know. He was a lame villain, the kind nobody cared to read about. He surrounded himself with a team of henchmen, the Able-bodied Seamen, Oddjob-types with bow ties that shot at you like spinning ship propellers. Once you were past them, The Midshipman was a pushover with an armored face mask, extendible limbs, and a riding tractor.

Zooster and I blasted our way down Clark Street in our Zoo-cycle, him in the driver's seat, me in the side-car like an old lady or runaway junior high-school girl. We passed the Midshipman off Ohio Street. He sat in the tractor, excavating the sinkhole leading down to the "top secret" terrorist holding cell beneath the old Water Tower, where Cabin Girl was rumored to be held. His henchmen were nowhere to be seen.

"Could be a trap," I said.

"How many fallen cops did you see?" Zooster said.

I gave him a look, and he thumped me upside the cowl.

"We've been topside since Randolph. This stretch is cop central. How many have you seen?"

Embarrassed, I said nothing. I hadn't noticed.

"None. No cops. That's the point. Dammit, Z-pack. Pay as much attention to the missing details," he said. "Those are clues too."

"What do you mean?" I said, still running the calculus in my head.

"The cops are somewhere else," he said. "Which means the Able-bodied Seamen are creating a diversion."

"So The Midshipman is all alone."

"He may have one or two Able-bodied Seamen on standby. Keep your eyes open. We go now," Zooster said, crossing over to Superior Street to swing around for the attack.

As we moved eastward, Zooster got a call on his helmet cell. I tapped in to the RF waves to listen in.

"Zoo, we've got new problems. Admiral Soju is at the surface and sending an assault team down to the Tub. He's got something big with him." It was Guppy, calling from the command station inside our submerged hideout about a quarter mile off Navy Pier. The Tub had enough armor to withstand depth charges and torpedoes, but knowing Soju, he had something else in mind. Something that would get him inside. An airlock and diamond auger bit, for example. He wanted to occupy, not destroy.

"Got it," Zooster said, also clearly concerned about Soju. "I'll be right there. Don't answer the door."

As he hung up mid-chuckle, he switched back to our cowl-to-cowl comms, not knowing I'd already been listening in. I expected him to abort The Midshipman job and divert us to Soju.

Instead, he said, "Can you handle this one alone?"

I fingered the concussion tubes hooked to my belt, counting them as I went. "Sure, I got it," I said, trying to sound more confident than I felt. Then I extended and retracted the wrist-mounted Taser. The Midshipman was one of his weakest rogues, but I had never gone in on my own before. Jesus, I was just a kid, a high school student. I could barely pass physics. Who would send me to fight a grown man with a riding tractor?

"First time for everything," Zooster said, leaning into the turn.

"Piece of cake," I said.

"Hit fast, hit hard. If he gains an edge, however small, disengage and wait for me," he said. I think he was truly concerned. I wanted to give him a hug.

"I will," I said. Seconds later, half a block from Ohio, Zooster jammed on the brakes and hopped off. I took the driver's seat and watched as he yanked a manhole cover up, revealing a Zooster personal missile silo for his return flight to the Tub. He saluted and closed the hatch. I heard it lock, and then everything was burnt fuel and fire as he launched into the Chicago sky, leaving me alone.

*** *** ***

Word got around the hero community quickly and around the sidekick community even faster. I was on the couch, watching a movie with Morning Myst in the Tub's break room the following morning. Her hand played with my utility belt, and she occasionally dug her elbow into my bruised thigh. I reached down to unbuckle the belt for her when she said, out of nowhere, "Do you think he'll be the one?"

"Who?" I said, sitting up.

She wouldn't meet my eyes, and I thought she meant Zooster.

"No, he's not the one," I said. "I like girls. Girls my age. You, for…"

"I mean Midshipman," she said, now looking at me squarely. "Is he yours?"

"My what?" I said.

"Your arch-nemesis."

I adjusted my codpiece to buy more room and stood up. "He's a fifty-year-old man in a pair of topsiders."

Myst grabbed my hand and pulled me back to the couch. "I'm just jealous; you know that. We're all wondering."

She popped open my belt and pulled it out from behind my back. As she worked, I said, "Zooster always tells me that a hero is only as good as his rogues' gallery. And the rogues' gallery is only as good as the arch-nemesis—the one who never dies even after falling into the vat of acid or the fresh concrete for the bridge abutment. When that happens, that's when you know you've found the one."

Myst leaned forward to kiss me and said, "You're going

to have an awesome arch-nemesis. I just know it."

*** *** ***

Before I met Zooster, I was a tough bruiser of a kid with decent grades and an unmistakable ability to hack cell phones. Zooster was a hero who posted his email address on his homepage for a couple hours. And the fact that he didn't want the pics of his hairy ass abutting five members of the Sterling, Virginia high school cheerleading squad made public didn't hurt my campaign to work for him.

Truth be told, he needed the help. There were conventions nearly every weekend somewhere in the country, bi-weekly Association of Super Soldiers meetings, and new products to test and review for his tech blog. Zooster's ability to run his hero-dom as a one-man show had been surpassed long before I stumbled along.

It sounds like I blackmailed him, but he was happy to put me on the payroll. Zooster and I started out with the typical hero-sidekick relationship. He taught me to fight, and I covered his back when we went up against the big boys.

Admiral Soju and the Bulgogis.

Hemingway's Ghost.

Kitty Twister.

Churro.

And against the smaller fries, I still offered some assistance, particularly with RF comms disruption. But I never had to take the lead. At least not until that day with The Midshipman. Somehow, it became habit after that. So long as the call was to stop one of the minor characters, Zooster always had

something else he'd rather be doing.

*** *** ***

The second time it happened, it wasn't nearly as dramatic as the first time. Zooster had something else on his calendar. A cosplay convention or a bi-weekly Association of Super Soldiers meeting. He was in the Tub, getting ready. He had his dress cowl and chest armor on, which worked together to pull his skin tight against his jawline. It give him the chiseled movie star look he was known for. This told me he would be spending time with Mama Athena at some point before dawn. Guppy and I sat at the stainless steel dining table, working a crappy hand of Gin.

Zooster got the call from Captain O'Malley. This time, I didn't need to tap into the waves. I just listened to Zooster's side of the conversation. It was The Arborist and his army of Saplings down at the State of Illinois Building.

Zooster's face looked like a man not believing what he was saying. "I'm tracking Soju as we speak. He's on the move, buying up antique furniture. I don't know exactly. Something about the finish lacquer. No, I'm pretty tied up with this. No time. But you know… Z-pack is available. I can send him."

Guppy folded her hand and opened the cabinet to our selection of flame throwers, "Better get ready."

When Zooster ended his call, I said, "Tracking Soju?"

"It's just The Arborist," he said, shrugging. "Guy's got a glass jaw and a wooden leg. Call if you have trouble."

"If I can't get through to you?"

"Leave a message." He smacked his cheeks with aftershave

 **GONE ROGUE**

and flicked his fingers at me as he headed out.

*** *** ***

The third time was because Zooster had a date with Mama Athena again. A new guy was climbing the Sears Tower with suction cups on his hands, threatening to rain down bags of pennies from the fiftieth floor. Zooster showed up late and brought coffee to the cops down on the street. They sipped and slurped while waiting for me to deliver the Arid Arachnid with grappling hooks and steel cable. Afterwards, you could see Zooster's hickey sprouting on his neck in the Daily News' cover shot. I didn't make the paper.

The fourth time was because Zooster had another date with Mama Athena—a double date along with the Cardboard Cowboy and Dame Mayday—but the fifth time, he was out with both Mama and Auntie Athena, dealing justice two sisters at a time. I was left dealing with prison breaks in Joliet both times and both within a week of each other. I put Frisco Filly down on my own, once in Manteno and once in Orland Park outside the Home Depot. Zooster gave the victory interview from outside The Pump Room in Chicago even though Frisco came nowhere near the city limits. Nobody asked about me, and once again, Zooster didn't offer.

By the time I trounced Whoopie Pete, Zooster had stopped sparring with me. He also stopped answering O'Malley's calls all together. I'd get a call forwarded to my cell during dinner at Gino's East or while at Comisky Park, and it would be O'Malley himself. "Where's Zooster?" he'd say, and I wouldn't know how to answer. When you're the side-kick,

your job is to know, to hand the phone over to the hero. But Zooster was out there, somewhere, probably savoring his time away with another lady friend or giving an interview, leaving me to hold the keys to the family station wagon.

So I got accustomed to covering. I'd say, "I'm ready, Captain. Where do you need me?"

Twenty-four hours later, it was always Zooster in the papers, Zooster in the news, Zooster invited to New York for the early morning interview shows.

That was the worst, when Zooster was out of town. The idiots came out of the woodwork. New guys or guys who had been bounced from smaller cities and wanted to make names for themselves in Chicago. But Zooster never bothered to ask Sergeant Squid to slide over from Green Bay to cover the city while Zooster traveled. He expected me to cover, and it came with a cost. That's how I failed trig.

*** *** ***

That July, the astronaut wing of the Museum of Science and Industry announced a temporary exhibit starring an actual Apollo space capsule. Earlier in the year, a New York villain known as Swinging Richard had tried to swipe the same capsule from the Bronx Academy of Science, and Star-blazer had stained the mortar on the Brooklyn Bridge red with Dick's guts. Rumor had it that cosmic residue on the capsule could be used to manufacture a low-grade dirty bomb, and it was arriving in Chicago for a short stay. But Zooster had a costume-design conference in Minneapolis and left the city to me as the exhibit opened.

When O'Malley called in the robbery attempt, by Kitty Twister and Hemingway's Ghost this time, I swore I'd get Zooster's help.

"Kitty and the Ghost," I said to the conference vid-screen.

Zooster's nostrils flared widely. He had his back to the table in Frostline's conference room up in St. Paul. His wrist-camera picked up the Athena sisters in their bras and panties behind him, cycling through wardrobe racks, hunting for outfits.

"You can handle this one, Z. I'm confident."

"What if I can't? It's two of them this time. Biggies."

One of the Athena sisters giggled. Zooster checked behind his back then brought the camera in closer to his face.

"You don't have to beat them. You just have to stop them. Look for the missing details. I'll be there as soon as I can."

*** *** ***

Outside the museum, I hid behind the U-505 sub's command tower. Ghost and Kitty had a big flatbed parked on the lawn, ready to drive the capsule out of town. Kitty's helicopter hovered above, waiting to lift the capsule out through the museum roof. The Ghost's henchmen, the well-armed Ex-pats, circled the flatbed and museum entrance. I had no prayer of taking them head-on or even sneaking past, so instead, I mucked with the comms between the Ghost and Kitty's helicopter pilot. When Ghost ordered it left, I sent the helo right. When he called for the helo to climb, I had it descend. Finally, when he shouted for it to "hold still, don't move, we're getting hung up on the building framework," I gave the helo

pilot a clear order.

"Full power, now. Climb, climb, climb!"

Something broke loose inside the museum, sending century-old stonework downward in a great plume of dust and debris. The capsule suddenly popped free, and I saw a bend in the steel cables like slack in a fly fisherman's line for just an instant. Then it fell, and the cables snapped, sending the capsule flying toward the flatbed and the Ex-pats. It struck at least two, pounding them into the grass like nails in soft pine, and then it smacked the flatbed's cab sideways. Free now, the chopper pulled away. I ordered it back to land and come help out those inside, but the pilot either didn't hear me or didn't obey.

The body count was steep. Two Ex-pats dead outside, seven more inside the museum when a 1970s retrofit steel beam buckled sideways then collapsed. Ghost and Kitty were also presumed dead, but in typical arch-nemesis fashion, no bodies were recovered.

Zooster arrived in time to talk to the press. Cameras focused upward, on his face. I stood behind him and to the left, off-camera. If anyone else noticed that his codpiece was on backwards, they didn't mention it.

"When did you lose control of the situation?" asked one reporter.

The question caught Zooster off-guard. "Nobody lost control of anything. I stopped two extremely dangerous criminals from taking possession of the Apollo capsule."

A tough reporter from the evening news leaned in. She said, "Captain O'Malley is investigating whether criminal

charges should be brought against you. How do you respond to that?"

Zooster swallowed hard then looked my way. Before I knew it, he had me by the shoulder and was dragging me into the shot. I scratched at a pimple on my lip, trying to hide it. At least my codpiece was on straight.

"Some of you may recognize my side-kick, Z-pack. Truth be told, Z handled this operation himself tonight. And he handled it admirably. Not many kids could step up and protect the city like…"

The woman from the evening news interrupted. "And where were you, Zooster, while Z-pack was out committing these murderous acts?"

Zooster looked down for just an instant, like he was trying to get his story straight. "I was traveling back from a secret assignment when Captain O'Malley's report came through. My instructions to Z-pack were to survey the scene, monitor the culprits, and stand by until I arrived. If he did more, it was against my orders."

I turned to him and started to speak, but Zooster pushed me out of the shot. The woman was already asking the next question. I caught something about "negligence" mentioned between them. By then, a cluster of reporters had broken off and encircled me. Above the din of their clattering, I thought I heard Zooster describe my actions as "rogue activity."

*** *** ***

"I want to change my name," I said. We were back in the Tub.

"Leave it. It's a good name," Zooster said. He sat shirtless

at his computer station, receiving a back massage from the allegedly reformed Cabin Girl. One monitor's tuner scanned constantly through static for network videos about him. When it found a station, the static faded only to be replaced by newscaster reports of Zooster sightings, Zooster's love life rumors, Zooster's Holiday Must-Have Gift List of 2003. Zooster refused to mute it, so I did for him.

"It was always your name for me," I said. "I don't like it. Z-pack makes me sound like antibiotics."

"So you have the power to heal," Zooster said. He paced his words slowly, fitting them in between Girl's massage kneading action. "That's good."

"It's not good," I said. I laid out cards to play solitaire on the steel table, trying to fill a few minutes before the next call. "Nothing's good anymore. I'm doing all the work. You just sit here, or hang out with the Athena sisters, or give interviews. You aren't a hero. You're a public relations man, and that's it. No substance."

At that statement, Zooster was out of his chair. As he walked toward me, he flexed his pectoral muscles one at a time. They flip-flopped like a juggled pair of tennis balls. "This is Zooster's city, not Z-pack's. You might remember that."

Zooster stepped right up to me and thumped his fingers into my chest. He was still strong from weights, but weights weren't everything. On the second thump, I smacked his arm away with one hand while my other hand shot up toward that chiseled jawline of his. He tried to stop me, but his reactions were so slow, I could have hit him twice.

He went down flat on his back, and I didn't give him time

 GONE ROGUE

to breathe. I pressed my boot into his neck and leaned. He tried to throw me off, but I wrapped up his hands until he started turning blue. "I always look for the missing details," I said. "Lately, the only missing detail is you."

At that, I lifted my boot. He sat up, hacking and coughing and holding his throat. The pinch of my boot treads on his loose neck skin reminded me nicely of the hickey he'd gotten from Mama Athena those weeks ago.

"Get out of here, murderer," he said with a voice that sounded like it came from a broom's splayed bristles. "Get out before I remember that I don't kill."

So I went. But Cabin Girl went with me.

*** *** ***

Anybody who wants to be anybody always asks me how to find an arch-nemesis. I used to smile and shrug at that question. Now, I rinse the fresh concrete from my hair or neutralize the acid with a strong base compound stolen from the chemical supply company warehouse that sits above my underground lair and say, "It all depends on the company you keep."

I should know. My name is Rogue Agent. My arch-nemesis is Zooster. He's a real dick.

MAX AND ROSE
ANDREW BOURELLE

ROSE LOOKS TIRED. I NOTICE THIS AS OUR LIMOUSINE PULLS up in front of the hotel. She is reclined on the leather seat, her eyes sleepily gazing out at the city. I can't read her mind like I can other people's. She's developed a resistance to me; I guess it's because she's been around since all this started. But it occurs to me that maybe she's not happy. Maybe she doesn't like this new life of ours. It's ridiculous. But maybe.

The driver opens the door. We get out. She takes my arm. We walk up the stairs to the lobby, which is beautiful and filled with rich, smiling people, the kind of people we could never be among before. The lobby is vast and spectacular with more green vegetation than a city park, more shining marble than an ancient Greek palace. Both the employees and the guests turn to look at us. I could read their minds, but I don't have to. They sense me, what I am, that I am not like them. They know they are in the presence of greatness.

"Wow," Rose says, looking upward.

I look up too. The inside of the hotel is hollow, with the rooms only along the outer shell, and rows and rows of parallel balconies running up the inside. A cluster of glass elevators glide up and down a large pillar. At the center of the ground floor is the restaurant, accessible from a series of walkways spanning large pools of water and spraying fountains on the basement level.

"I told you it would be nice," I say.

She nods.

We cross a catwalk toward the restaurant. The maître d' stands where the catwalk meets the restaurant, like a guard just inside a castle gate, waiting as we cross the draw bridge.

"What's the name?" he says, smiling, beaming at me.

"We don't have a reservation," I say.

"Uh, sir." He's flabbergasted. He wants to let us through, but his sense of duty prevents him. "I'm sorry, sir, but you have to have—"

I look away from him and walk forward, pulling Rose. He puts out his hand and touches my shoulder. I grab it and squeeze. He gasps. Bones crack. I let go then extend my arm, palm out, like I'm opening a door. The push sends him off the balcony like he was hit by a car. He holds his scream in, trying to please me in at least this way. He splashes into a pool below.

"Max," Rose says, her tone shocked.

I turn to her and smile. I take her arm and lead her into the restaurant. No one tries to stop us.

"You could have just *made* him let us in," she says.

"The old Jedi mind trick? I know. But that was more fun."

She shakes her head.

"How about this table?" I say.

"Sure."

I pull out her chair then sit across from her. Her dark hair is done up nicely with long, curling locks hanging around her shoulders. Her blue dress hugs her body, showing off her nice figure. The new necklace I gave her hangs around her neck, pretty next to her golden skin. She is the sexiest woman I've ever been with; I've always thought so and even now, when I could have any woman I want. But she looks so very, very tired. Puffy bags hang under her eyes. Her face is slack.

"Are you okay, honey?"

"Mmm-hmmm."

A waiter comes, carrying two menus. He is excited and eagerly lists the night's specials. We order wine, the most expensive bottle on the menu. Who cares? They're not going to make us pay. And the waiter leaves. Seconds later, he returns with the bottle, filling our glasses and taking our order. I have steak; Rose has a salad.

"You think they'll call the cops?" Rose says, referring to the host down in the fountain.

"No. They're not even going to call an ambulance. They're making a busboy drive him to the hospital."

"You *know* this?"

"Yes. They're so fucking excited right now. They don't even see that as a bad thing."

"Neither do you," she says.

I smirk, giving her the look I sometimes give her, trying to tell her not to be a bitch without actually saying it aloud.

"That host wasn't too excited about you," she says.

"He was. He was just confused."

"Maybe," she says, taking a drink of her wine. "And maybe some of these other people around here can think for themselves too."

"I'm not *making* them be excited about me," I say.

"Are you sure?"

This stops me. I never thought of that before. Since this began, I assumed people treated me this way voluntarily, sensing something about me, my superiority, but not based on anything I did. Like I secrete a pheromone that pulls people to me, making them desire to be around me. The idea that I could turn this off hadn't occurred to me.

"I'm not sure," I say, reaching for my glass. "I'm still figuring all this out."

The waiter brings bread, and we sit silently as he delivers it. When he leaves, I say, "And I'm sure it hasn't stopped yet."

"Stopped?"

"You know," I say, "my development."

"Your super powers?" she says.

"I don't like to call them that, but yes."

"It's not enough for you?" she says, reaching for the bread.

"I didn't ask for this," I say.

"But you're sure enjoying it." She puts a piece on her plate, but then, she doesn't touch it. She peers at me.

I shrug. "Yeah. So?"

She shakes her head sideways, as if I'm supposed to know

what that means. I take a piece of bread and grab my knife to butter it.

"You think you'll be able to get all stretchy like that guy from that comic book *The Fantastic Four*?" She smirks. "Or maybe you'll turn into that rock guy."

"I don't think so," I say, giving her the look. "Although I would like to be able to fly." I grin as I say this; I can't help myself.

"Have you tried flying, Superman?" she says sarcastically.

"No. But I didn't try to read minds or become stronger either. Those just happened."

"What happens if your powers just fade away?"

"That's not going to happen," I say. "They're only going to grow."

"How do you know?"

"I just do. I can feel it."

She tears off a small piece of bread and pops it into her mouth. She shakes her head, looks away from me. I follow her gaze. The restaurant is abuzz with excitement. The people love having me here. They don't know who I am. Or what I am. But they can sense something is special. It's like a drug is floating in the air, and they're all inhaling it, high on my presence.

"What makes you so special?" she says.

"Excuse me?"

"What makes you so God-damn special? Why do you get to have this happen?"

"I don't know, hon. Are you jealous?"

"No," she snaps then stares at me.

"I don't know, baby. Maybe I'm just lucky." I say this, but I don't believe it. "You're the scientist; you tell me."

"I studied biology in college before dropping out. I'm no scientist."

"You're scientific," I say.

She's quiet.

"Do you wish I didn't have this?" I say, thinking again if it might be possible to just turn my abilities off, turn my aura off so no one around us would sense what I am. The idea of this hurts me a little. I wouldn't want to do that, but I say it to Rose anyway. "Maybe I can just learn to shut it off. Not *be* this person all the time."

Rose looks at me, staring silently. I find myself wishing I could read her mind. The waiter comes, setting down our plates. He's enthusiastic, wanting to please. But he senses that we don't want to talk, and he walks away quickly.

Rose picks at her salad, hardly eating. I devour the steak.

"Isn't this nice?" I say. "We could never eat in a place like this before."

Rose shrugs.

"Honey," I say, "you're happy, aren't you?"

She looks at me sadly.

"I was happier then."

I drop my knife onto the table. "What?"

She nods, confirming this.

"Living in that shithole? No money to eat? No money to do anything?"

She keeps nodding.

"We were so unhappy."

"It's all relative."

"I can walk into any store in the city, and they'll give me a suit. Give. That necklace you're wearing. That dress. All free. All because of who I am."

"It's all taking," she says. "It's all stealing."

"*That*," I say, "is all relative."

She gives me a look like the ones I was giving her earlier: Don't be an asshole.

"Only once since this has started has anyone *really* tried to deny me anything," I stress the word "really" to make her know I'm not talking about the dumb-ass maître d' of the restaurant.

"Yeah," she says, "and you put two cops in the hospital."

"So," I say. I lean forward. "They're not going to come after me. I'm untouchable. Why is that a bad thing?"

"Why is that a good thing?" she says.

I lean back in my chair, frustrated. I wad my napkin up and toss it onto my plate. I pour myself more wine. Rose's glass is still nearly full.

She shakes her head. "What if someone comes along, someone who's developing like you, just in a different way? What if that person can keep you from doing whatever you want?"

"I'm not worried."

"You're not invincible," she says. "Not yet. Probably not ever. Every super hero has a kryptonite."

"Hon," I say. "This is the real world. I can't fly to the moon, and I can't survive a nuclear explosion. I'm not saying I'm God. But I am godlike. And I'm getting better and better every day."

"What if you got shot? You know, with a bullet?"

"I don't know. But I'll probably be able to survive that soon if not already."

"Could you survive a fall from up there?" she says, pointing to the top balcony some fifty stories up.

"Not yet, I don't think. Soon maybe."

"Do you think you'll be immortal?"

"Maybe."

"Do you think you'll go and find another woman, one who's better looking than me and doesn't ask all these questions?"

I smile. So that's what this is all about.

"Honey," I say. "I want only you."

It's true. I could take and fuck any woman in this restaurant. In this city. But I love Rose. The two times I've messed around on her since all this began were emotionless conquests, like games, just to see if I could. But the games were too easy. By the second one, there was no challenge. And there was certainly no feeling, no love.

I take Rose's hand and wish I could will her to look at me like I could anyone else.

"Baby," I say. "I don't want things to be like they used to. But I want *us* to be like we used to be. I want to lay on the couch all day and watch TV. I want to have kids, raise a family. I want—"

"I have to go to the restroom," Rose says, standing quickly. She takes her purse and walks away.

"Jesus Christ," I say.

I want to punch the table, but I might split it in half. The waiter approaches.

Get the fuck away! I say with my mind. He stops and does an about-face. I take a deep breath, exhale. I feel better. I stand.

"How y'all doing?" I say to the next table.

There are two couples. Young. Good looking.

"Great," they say, almost in unison. "How are you?"

"Good," I say, smiling.

I am not controlling their minds. But they love me. I walk through the restaurant. I say hi. The people are exuberant. They want to talk. They want to love me. I am a celebrity, a star athlete, a super hero. And this is all just me. I'm not forcing their minds to think a certain way. I'm not twisting their arms behind their backs. I could do both. But I don't have to.

I approach a table where a waitress is taking a couple's order.

"Hi," she says, smiling.

She is pretty.

"I think this nice couple would like you to dance for them," I say.

"What?" she says, confused.

Dance, I think toward her.

"Oh," she says, and begins jumping around, moving her hips and her arms. There is no music, but she dances as if there is.

The couple laugh.

Do a handstand, I order the woman.

She tries, balancing for just a moment, her skirt falling down, showing a glimpse of black underwear, before she falls. She hops up off the floor. She's ready to try again, ready to

please me, but I release her. The couple applaud and thank her. The waitress keeps smiling, unaware that anything is unusual about what she just did.

I walk to the bar. I hop easily onto it and start walking down its length, my shoes clicking on the marble top. The people seated grin at me, lift their drinks to toast me. The bartender applauds. I say hi. I wave. I see our table, Rose's and mine, about thirty feet away. I bend my legs and jump. I rise into the air, soaring forward and up, enjoying a feeling of weightlessness. I go as high as the second-floor balcony and then start to descend. I land right next to the table, sticking my landing like a gymnast. The table shakes. The restaurant applauds. I raise my wine glass and hold it up to them. I'll be able to fly soon. I smile. I read their minds. One man thinks that was the greatest thing he's ever seen. Another wants to send over a bottle of champagne, but he's nervous that I wouldn't be moved by the gesture. A blond woman at the bar is imagining herself getting fucked by me.

I see Rose walking back from the restroom, her purse slung over her shoulder.

"Rosebud," I say, using my old nickname for her. "Let's not fight anymore." I kiss her cheek. I inhale her scent; I've always loved how she smells.

She sits. "Max," she says. "Let me just ask you one thing."

"One thing and then we'll stop fighting?"

"Yes."

I can tell by her manner that she has been practicing this in her head.

"Okay," I say, but I know that we won't stop fighting.

Whatever she wants to ask is going to cause us to keep arguing.

She takes a deep breath.

"It sounds silly to use these words," she says, "but I'm going to. Are you…" She stops, apparently nervous. "Do you realize that you aren't behaving like a super hero? You're more like a super villain?"

"Honey!" I say. "That's a mean thing to say."

"Well, you're not out stopping criminals and pulling people out of burning buildings."

"If I see something happening, I'll help out," I say. "Just because I haven't signed up with the police force to get a junior G-man badge doesn't mean I'm a bad guy."

I hold my arms up, trying to say, *Come on. Cut me some slack here.*

She just stares at me.

"I admit I've been a little selfish," I say. "But I'm still just learning about this stuff. I'm still developing. Besides, I think we're entitled to have some good things happen to us for a change."

She nods, but it seems reluctant.

"I don't know what's going to happen next, honey, but it isn't like I'm Dr. Doom out to take over the world."

She nods, smiles.

"Okay," she says, holding her hand across the table for me to take it. "Let's not fight."

I can't read her mind, but I think she's up to something. It has nothing to do with my abilities. It's that she's been with me for so long; I know her. I reach across the table and take her hand.

"I'm sorry we were fighting," she says. "I love you."

"I love you t—"

As fast as she can, she brings her other hand up from beneath the table. It's holding a syringe. She tries to stab me in the wrist, but I'm too quick. I let go of her other hand and easily grab her wrist as it comes down in a stabbing motion. I could squeeze until her hand comes off, but I don't. I hold it just firmly enough that she can't stab me and she can't get away.

"What the hell are you doing?" I say.

She says nothing, just releases the syringe. It falls into her salad plate.

"Is that tranquilizer or poison?" I say.

"Does it matter?" she says. "Would either have worked on you?"

"Probably not," I say and release her wrist.

She collapses back into her seat, looking exhausted.

I want to take our table and throw it across the room. I want to take that blond woman and make her fuck me. I want to take our waiter's head and crush it between my hands.

"Why?" I say.

She shakes her head, saying nothing. Tears rise in her eyes. She looks up, blinking, trying to keep them from falling down her cheeks.

"Rose, I really do love you," I whisper. "I would never try to hurt you."

"You love yourself," she hisses.

"How can I prove to you that I love you?"

"I shouldn't have to tell you."

"Rose, you—"

"I want to go up there," she says, gesturing to the upper levels of the hotel. She wipes her eyes with her napkin. "I assume I'm going to be returning to our old lifestyle after tonight. I'd like to look down from up there. Like I'm rich and famous and can afford to stay in the top floor of a big hotel."

I look at her, saying nothing. It's over. My relationship is over. All my powers, and I can't save this.

"Okay?" she says.

"Okay."

She stands, taking the syringe and putting it in her purse.

"Don't want anyone to pick this up," she says.

I let her. I know she won't try to stab me with it again. I rise.

She takes my arm as we walk, leans into me. She is loving in her tenderness. It's genuine. She loves me still, somewhere inside of her. I wish I could reach in, find the part of her that still loves me, and enhance it, give it power just the way something has given me power. I feel sad about this. Yet somewhere, somewhere deep inside of me, I'm relieved. I'm ready to get on with my new life. It's like I've been running with a weight belt—what will Rose think?—and here's a chance to go forward, free of that load.

The people smile as we walk by. Rose clings to me. She puts her hand in mine, wraps her fingers in my fingers. I wish I could know what she's thinking.

The elevator comes, and we step inside. We face the glass bubble wall. Rose turns to me and smiles, then the elevator lifts off like a rocket ship. My organs seem to move inside me. Rose clings tighter to me. We're flying up and fast, and

through the glass, the world around us changes. The restaurant gets smaller. The people shrink. My heartbeat quickens. The balconies zoom by rapidly.

"So you'll be able to do this on your own?" Rose says. "Fly like this?"

"I hope so," I say. "I think so."

"It will be pretty."

"You could be there to share it with me, you know?" I say it, and part of me means it.

At the top, the elevator stops, and we step out. Rose still holds me. We walk to the edge of the balcony and look down. The drop is frightening. The people below are just specks, the restaurant tables no more than black dots. Soon, not only could I fly up here without the elevator, but I could leap from up here and land just like I landed earlier jumping in the restaurant. Soon.

"I never expected something inside to be so pretty," Rose says, putting her hands on the balcony, looking down. "Something human-made."

"It is pretty," I say, looking down at the inside of the hotel, its architecture like something out of a science fiction movie.

"I guess," she says, staring down, ignoring what I said, "when you look at anything from a new perspective, it can be pretty."

She turns toward me. Her eyes look more awake than they've seemed all night. Her face has a red flush. She really looks beautiful in this moment, and I feel like I'm making the wrong choice. I should be doing whatever I can to keep Rose, to retain what we have. Give up my powers. Never use them. Whatever it takes.

"I'm sorry I can't see you from a better perspective," she says.

"Rose," I say, "I'm still the same person I always was. I'm the same person you wanted to have a family with, the same person you wanted to spend the rest of your life with."

"I know," she says, taking a few steps away from me. "You really haven't changed at all. That's part of the problem."

"I don't understand."

She smiles. "Well, Superman doesn't know it all, does he?"

"Rose," I say, not knowing what else to say.

"I love you, Max," she says. She looks at me as she says it, then she turns and looks back down below. She steps farther away, leaning on the railing as she walks. "I always will. I can't help myself."

"Rose," I say.

She looks at me, still taking slow steps away, leaning on the railing, gliding it.

"I love you, and I don't want to be apart," I say. "I mean it."

"You mean it?" she says.

"Yes."

"Then prove it."

With that, she kicks off her shoes and, with surprising dexterity, climbs up onto the railing. In her bare feet, she balances on the six-inch beam like an acrobat.

"Rose!" I say, and then she opens up her mind to me.

I see her sadness and her hatred of me, and I see her hatred of herself. She was excited about my powers in the beginning, happy to partake in whatever I did; then her conscience grew

as well as her guilt for her complicity. She suspects everything I've done, even what I kept hidden from her. I saw none of this until now. And I see her plan, clear and simple. She will jump and either fall to her death alone, or I will jump after her, thinking I can save her, and I will die along with her. If the latter happens, she will have saved the world from me. If the former happens, she won't have to see what I will become. She doesn't want to live either way.

She smiles at me, looking strangely peaceful. And then she jumps forward into the air, into nothingness, turning as she goes so she can look back at me. I want to fly after her, but I stop myself, hands gripping the railing, watching her go. She falls quickly, growing smaller and smaller. I reach out to her with my mind and I see through her perspective, looking upward, seeing me, mouth open, at the top level. I grow smaller and smaller. The emotions she feels are unlike any I've ever felt in a person before. Such exhilaration. Such fear. Such happiness and relief mixed with regret. She loves me, and she hates me. I hate myself. I pull away from her before she hits, too afraid to stay with her at the end.

I see her, from the top of the building, just a speck on the floor. Screams come from below, so far away they're hardly audible. A pain is in my chest, hard and sharp, like claws opening me up. I haven't felt pain in a long time. It's crippling. Like part of her was in me, and that part is now dead. I'm dizzy, and I step away from the balcony. I need to get out of the hotel; I need to run. I look around, to orient myself. My head clears a little. Rose's shoes are lying on the tile by where she jumped. Her purse is there too. I think of the syringe

inside. It's poison; I'm sure now. Poison as potent and deadly to me as my love was to Rose.

I run over to the elevator and press the button to go down. I hate this. I want to be able to jump from up here, to survive the fall. I want to be able to fly. I want to be able to pick Rose up off the floor down below and *make* her live. Just make her. But I can't. The elevator begins to descend, my stomach tightens, and the view of the world changes again. The levels of the hotel whir by. The ground floor grows. I can see Rose's body clearer and clearer, lying facing up as if she's sleeping. I want to be able to control my thoughts right now, take hold of my emotions and keep myself from feeling guilt and self-loathing and relief. Yes, it's there: relief. And I can't stop it, just like I can't stop the pool of black-red blood growing around Rose.

KRIS ASHTON

Kris Ashton is an Australian author best known for his tales of horror and dark speculative fiction. He has published three novels and more than 20 short stories. His third book, *Invasion at Bald Eagle*, was released in January 2015. Kris is also a noted journalist and has worked as a film critic, travel writer, and book reviewer. He lives in Sydney with his wife, daughter, and a slightly mad boxer dog. Find his blog and other ramblings at kris-ashton.wix.com/spec-fic.

ANDREW BOURELLE

Andrew Bourelle's fiction has appeared recently in *Jabberwock Review*, *Red Rock Review*, and *Rosebud*.

PETER CLINES

Peter Clines grew up in the Stephen King fallout zone of Maine and—fuelled by a love of comic books, Star Wars, and Saturday morning cartoons—started writing science fiction and fantasy stories at the age of eight with his first "epic novel" *Lizard Men from the Center of the Earth*. He is the author of *The Fold*, the bestselling Ex-Heroes series, the acclaimed *--14--*, *The Junkie Quatrain*, the mash-up novel *The Eerie Adventures of the Lycanthrope Robinson Crusoe (with Daniel Defoe and H.P. Lovecraft)*, numerous short stories, and countless articles about the film and television industry. He currently lives and writes somewhere in southern California.

MALON EDWARDS

Malon Edwards was born and raised on the South Side of Chicago, but now lives in the Greater Toronto Area, where he was lured by his beautiful Canadian wife. Many of his short stories are set in an alternate Chicago. Currently, he serves as Managing Director and Grants Administrator for the Speculative Literature Foundation, which provides a number of grants for writers of speculative literature.

EDWARD M. ERDELAC

Edward Erdelac is the author of seven novels (including the acclaimed weird western series Merkabah Rider) and dozens of short stories. He is an independent filmmaker, award winning screenwriter, and sometime Star Wars contributor. Born in Indiana, educated in Chicago, he resides in the Los Angeles area with his wife and a bona fide slew of children and cats. He blogs at emerdelac.wordpress.com.

KARINA L. FABIAN

In addition to psychics whose powers drive them insane, Karina Fabian writes about a dragon detective, zombie exterminators, and nuns in space. The award winning author lives in Utah with her family, where she writes product reviews for Top Ten Reviews. Her final novel in the Mind Over trilogy, *Mind Over All*, comes out summer 2015. Explore her many worlds at fabianspace.com.

ANI FOX

Ani Fox has previously published science fiction and horror short fiction through BAEN and Ragnarok Publications but has never before submitted a novel. Fox pursued a PhD in Indigenous World History from the Australian National University, an academic interest which flavors his work with complex systems, indigenous culture, and a stridently gender-equal view of people. Fox has lived in the continental U.S., Hawaii, Australia, and currently resides in Luxembourg where he works in technology strategy and consulting. His work in tech security means he recruits signals, intelligence operatives, and spooks for commercial security, as well as interacts with various members of organized crime. Crime, espionage, and technological advances play heavily in his written work.

WAYNE HELGE

A native of Chicago's south suburbs, Wayne Helge served in the Coast Guard for a dozen years before wading ashore, and now works and writes in Virginia. He wrote his first piece of fiction about a murdering dentist while in high school, and sometimes wonders if things have been going downhill ever since.

JEREMY HEPLER

Jeremy Hepler's a stay-at-home dad who lives in the Texas Panhandle. His work has appeared in various magazines and anthologies over the past seven years. Most recently, he placed second in the Panhandle Professional Writer's Short Story Competition and just completed his first novel. Follow him on Twitter (@jeremyhepler), his blog (jeremyhepler.wordpress.com), or contact him via email (jeremyhepler@hotmail.com).

KAREN H. KOELER / WARREN STOCKHOLM

Warren Stockholm is the pulp pseudonym of K. H. Koehler, who is the author of various novels and novellas in the genres of horror, SF, dark fantasy, steampunk, and young and new adult. She is the owner of K.H. Koehler Books, and her books are widely available at all major online distributors. Her covers have appeared on numerous books in many different genres, and her short work has been featured on *Horror World, Literary Mayhem, Fossil Lake Anthologies*, and in the Bram Stoker Award-winning anthology *Demons*, edited by John Skipp. Her novel series include *The Kaiju Hunter, The Mrs. McGillicuddy Mysteries, Anti-Heroes, Planet of Dinosaurs*, the Nick Englebrecht Mysteries, and the forthcoming prehistoric pulp series The Archeologists from Severed Press. She lives in the beautiful wilds of Northeast Pennsylvania with two very large and opinionated Rottweilers. Visit her website at khkoehlerbooks.wordpress.com.

ANTHONY LAFFAN

Anthony Laffan works in IT in New England. When not at work, reading, or writing he enjoys game design and writing about the theory behind different kinds of storytelling. More from him can be found at www.realityrefracted.com. "Sabre" is his first published work.

WAYNE LIGON

Wayne Ligon was born in Montgomery, Alabama. Fascinated by comics at an early age, he quickly branched out into science fiction, fantasy and horror literature while still retaining a strong love of the superheroic.

MALCOLM McCLINTON

Just a guy making a living from his art and imagination, Malcolm has found a nice little niche for himself that satisfies his anti- authoritarianism, reclusive nature, and need for adulation all at once. You can visit him online and find links to his galleries at hangedmanstudio.blogspot.com.

JOE McKINNEY

Joe McKinney is the author of several horror, crime and science fiction novels, including the four-part Dead World series, made up of *Dead City, Apocalypse of the Dead, Flesh Eaters* and *The Zombie King*; the science fiction disaster tale, *Quarantined*, which was nominated for the Horror Writers Association's Bram Stoker Award for superior achievement in a novel, 2009; and the crime novel, *Dodging Bullets*. Upcoming releases include the horror novels *Lost Girl of the Lake, The Red Empire, The Charge* and *St. Rage*. Joe has also worked as an editor, along with Michelle McCrary, on the zombie-themed anthology *Dead Set*, and with Mark Onspaugh on the

abandoned building-themed anthology *The Forsaken*.

In his day job, Joe McKinney is a sergeant with the San Antonio Police Department, where he helps run the city's 911 Dispatch Center. He has also worked as a homicide detective and a disaster mitigation specialist. Many of his stories, regardless of genre, feature a strong police procedural element based on his fifteen years of law enforcement experience.

TIM MARQUITZ

Tim Marquitz is the author of the Demon Squad series, the Blood War Trilogy, co-author of the Dead West series, as well as several standalone books, and numerous anthology appearances including *Triumph Over Tragedy*, *Corrupts Absolutely?*, *Demonic Dolls*, *Neverland's Library*, *At Hell's Gates*, *That Hoodoo, Voodoo That You Do*, and *Blackguards*. Tim has compiled and edited anthologies such as *Fading Light: An Anthology of the Monstrous* and *Manifesto: UF*, as well as Ragnarok Publications' *Kaiju Rising: Age of Monsters*.

LEE MATHER

Lee Mather writes dark fiction. Hailing from Manchester, England, he lives with his wife, Jen, and his daughter, Isabelle. At the time of writing, Lee is expecting his second child. Lee's standalone work includes *The Green Man* and *First Kiss, Last Breath* as well as contributions to anthologies such as *Fading Light* and *Bloody Parchment* volumes two and three.

WESTON OCHSE

Weston Ochse is the author of twenty books, most recently

SEAL Team 666 and its sequel *Age of Blood*, which the *New York Post* called "required reading" and *USA Today* placed on their "New and Notable Lists." He is a veteran with 30 years of military service.

CAT RAMBO

Cat Rambo lives, writes, and teaches by the shores of an eagle-haunted lake in the Pacific Northwest. Her 150+ fiction publications include stories in *Asimov's, Clarkesworld Magazine*, and Tor.com. Her short story, "Five Ways to Fall in Love on Planet Porcelain," from her story collection *Near + Far* (Hydra House Books), was a 2012 Nebula nominee. Her editorship of *Fantasy Magazine* earned her a World Fantasy Award nomination in 2012. For more about her, as well as links to her fiction, see www.kittywumpus.net.

WILLIAM TODD ROSE

Named by *The Google+ Insider's Guide* as one of their top 32 authors to follow, William Todd Rose is a speculative fiction author whose short work has appeared in various magazines and anthologies, as well as several podcasts. In 2009, his debut novella *Shadow of the Woodpile* was released as the flagship publication for Fetid Press. This was followed by the apocalyptic novel *Cry Havoc* in 2010, as well as *The 7 Habits of Highly Infective People: A Novel of Contagion, Drugs, Time Travel, The Living Dead*, the grindhouse inspired e-book *Shut The F*%k Up And Die!*, his short story collection *Sex in the Time of Zombies* and *The Dead and Dying*. The *7 Habits* was recently re-released by Permuted Press. While Mr. Rose has

been known to delve into the worlds of Sci-Fi and cyberpunk, his main affinity is for dark fiction with a particularly special place in his heart for zombie lit.

A.D. SPENCER

A.D. Spencer lives in Alabama with her Chihuahua sidekick. Her short stories have appeared in several anthologies, including *Fish* from Dagan Books and *Menial: Skilled Labor in Science Fiction*, published by Crossed Genres. "Oily" is her first tale to feature Cat's Eye. For more information, visit her blog at busyprocrastinator.blogspot.com.

JEFF STRAND

Author of a bunch of demented books, including *Pressure, Dweller, A Bad Day for Voodoo, Wolf Hunt, Single White Psychopath Seeks Same, Benjamin's Parasite, Fangboy, The Sinister Mr. Corpse*, and lots of others. Three-time Bram Stoker Award finalist. Three-time Bram Stoker Award loser. Four-time Bram Stoker Award Master of Ceremonies.

JASON M. TUCKER

Born and raised in the wilds of upstate New York, Jason M. Tucker now resides in the mystical land of California where he works as a full time writer. It's a place where the sun always shines and the only things rising faster than the cost of living are all the damned zombies. He's the author of *Meat City, Wetwork, Lou vs. the Zombies*, and more. Recently, he sold a short film (*Greenies*, based on his short "Coventry Greens") and a feature film called *Deadwater Devil* to Breaking Fate Entertainment.

TRISHA J. WOOLDRIDGE

Trisha J. Wooldridge is the current president of Broad Universe and a senior editor for Spencer Hill Press. Under her full name, she writes grown-up horror short stories that occasionally win awards, like the EPIC 2008, 2009 for anthologies *Bad-Ass Faeries 2: Just Plain Bad* and *Bad-Ass Faeries 3: In All Their Glory* and a Stoker nomination for the anthologies *Epitaphs* and *Wicked Seasons*. You can also find her in *Holiday Magick, Once Upon An Apocalypse,* and *Demonic Visions 5*. She has co-produced the Spencer Hill Press anthologies *Unconventional* and *Doorways to Extra Time*. In her child-friendly persona of T.J. Wooldridge, she's published three novels: *The Kelpie, The Earl's Childe,* and *Silent Starsong*. As if she weren't busy enough, Trish is also the writing partner for the webcomic *Aurelio* at www.thevampireaurelio.com. Find out more at www.anovelfriend.com.